The Mango Season

Also by Amulya Malladi

A BREATH OF FRESH AIR

The Mango
Season

Amulya Malladi

Ballantine Books ❋ New York

A Ballantine Book
Published by The Random House Ballantine Publishing Group

Copyright © 2003 by Amulya Malladi

The Mango Season is a work of fiction. Names, characters,
places, and incidents either are a product of the author's
imagination or are used fictitiously.

www.ballantinebooks.com

Book design by Julie Schroeder

The Library of Congress Cataloging-in-Publication Data
for this title is available from the publisher.

ISBN 0-345-45030-2

Manufactured in the United States of America

First Edition: June 2003

10   9   8   7   6   5   4   3   2   1

For Søren and Tobias,
for all that I am and all that I hope to be

Acknowledgments

My deepest thanks to Søren for being my first reader and listener, Tobias for taking naps, my wonderful in-laws, Ruth and Ejgil, for giving us refuge and me a place to write, and to all my family in Denmark for their warm welcome, love and generosity.

I am truly grateful to Allison Dickens, Wonderful Editor, for making this book better than it was when it left my hard drive and for helping me out during a difficult time; and to Nancy Miller for her continuing support and confidence in me. I will always be indebted to Heather Smith, Amazing Publicist, for patiently putting up with all my hysterical phone calls and email.

A very special thanks to Jody Pryor, Alaskan, friend and fellow writer, for reading a draft of this book through a night and giving me some brilliant advice because I needed her to; special thanks also to Matt Bailer, Kelly Lynch, Milly Marmur, Susan Orbuch, and Priya Raghupathi for enriching this book with their advice and insight.

I took advantage of Steven Deutsch's sense of humor in coming up with the first sentence of this book; of Radhika Kasichainula's memory in remembering where everything in Hyderabad was; and of Shanthi Nambakkam's hospitality when I was last in the United States—I thank them for their generosity.

And lastly, a big thanks to Arjun Karavadi for his critique, honesty and friendship, and for being available to me regardless of the time difference between Chicago and Denmark.

Contents

Prologue

Happiness Is a Mango

Don't kill yourself if you get pregnant, was my mother's advice to me when I was fifteen years old and a classmate of mine was rumored to have committed suicide because she was with child.

Along with the firm advice that I shouldn't commit suicide was the advice—or rather the order—that I shouldn't have sex until I was married and that I should marry the man of her choice, not mine.

Even though I was raised in a society where arranged marriage was the norm, I always thought it was barbaric to expect a girl of maybe twenty-one years to marry a man she knew even less than the milkman who, for the past decade, had been mixing water with the milk he sold her family.

I had escaped arranged marriage by coming to the United States to do a master's in Computer Sciences at Texas A&M, by conveniently finding a job in Silicon Valley, and then by inventing several excuses to not go to India.

Now, seven years later, I had run out of excuses.

"What are you looking forward to the most?" Nick asked, as we were parked on the 101-South carpool lane on our way to the San Francisco International Airport.

"HAPPINESS," I said without hesitation.

Summer, while I was growing up, was all about mangoes. Ripe, sweet mangoes that dripped juices down your throat, down your neck. The smell of a ripe mango would still evoke my taste buds, my memories, and for a while I would be a child again and it would be a hot summer day in India.

There was more to a mango than taste. My brother Natarajan, whom we all called Nate because it was faster to pronounce, and I, would always fight over the sticky stone at the center of the mango. If Ma was planning to chop one mango for lunch, the battle for the stone would begin at breakfast. Sucking on the sticky stone while holding it with bare hands was the most pleasurable thing one could do with a mango. Nate and I called the mango stone HAPPINESS.

HAPPINESS was a concept. A feeling. Triumph over a sibling. I had forgotten all about HAPPINESS until Nick's rather pertinent question.

"It's like drinking a pint of Guinness in the office after tax season," I said in explanation when he didn't seem to grasp the fundamentals of HAPPINESS.

Nick the accountant nodded his head in total understanding. "But there isn't going to be much HAPPINESS in your trip once you tell the family about the handsome *and* humble American you're involved with."

When I first came to the United States, if anyone had told me I would be dating, living with, engaged to an American, I would have scoffed. Seven years later, I wore a pretty little diamond on my ring finger and carried in my heart the security only a good relationship could provide.

When Nick dropped me off at the international terminal he made sure I had my papers and passport. Careful, caring Accountant Nick!

"Off you go," he said with a broad smile. "And call me once you get there."

He wanted to come with me to India. "To meet your family, see your country," he had said, and I gave him a look reserved for the retarded. He must be joking, I thought. How could he be serious? Hadn't I told him time and again that my family was as conservative as his was liberal and that he would be lynched and I would be burned alive for bringing him, a foreigner, my lover, to my parents' home?

"Off I go," I said reluctantly, and leaned against him, my black leather bag's strap sagging against my shoulder. "I'll check email from Nate's computer. If I can't call, I'll write."

I didn't want to go. I had to go.

I didn't want to go. I had to go.

The twin realities were tearing me apart.

I didn't want to go because as soon as I got there, my family would descend on me like vultures on a fresh carcass, demanding explanations, reasons, and trying to force me into marital harmony with some "nice Indian boy."

I had to go because I had to tell them that I was marrying a "nice American man."

All Indian parents who see their children off to the Western world have a few fears and the following orders:

Do not eat beef. (The sacred cow is your mother!)

Do not get too friendly with foreign people; you cannot trust them. Remember what the English did to us.

Cook at home; there is no reason to eat out and waste money. Save money.

Save money.

Save money.

DO NOT FIND YOURSELF SOME FOREIGN MAN/ WOMAN TO MARRY.

Even though the "do not marry a foreigner" order would usually be last on the list, it was the most important one on the list. Any of the other sins the parents could live with; a foreign daughter- or son-in-law was blasphemous.

"If they try to get you married to some nice Indian boy, remember that there's no such thing and you're engaged to a nice American man who dotes on you," Nick joked.

"According to them you're just another corrupt Westerner and I'd be better off with a nice Indian boy," I countered.

"I'm sure you'll convince them otherwise," Nick said, and then hugged me. "You'll be fine. They'll yell and scream for a while and then . . . What can they do? You're a grown woman."

"Maybe my plane will crash and I won't have to tell them at all," I said forlornly, and he kissed me, laughing.

Nick waved when I looked back at him after I crossed security and entered the international terminal.

I waved back, the brave soldier that I was, and walked toward the plane that was going to take me home to India, mangoes, and hopefully HAPPINESS.

Part One

Raw Mangoes

Avakai (South Indian Mango Pickle)

5 cups sour mango pieces (medium sized)
1 cup mustard seed powder
1 cup red chili powder
1 cup salt
a pinch of turmeric powder
1 teaspoon fenugreek seed powder
3 cups peanut oil

Mix the mango and dry ingredients and add three cups of peanut oil to the mixture. Let the pickle marinate for four weeks before serving with hot white rice and melted *ghee* (clarified butter).

Use Your Senses

I t was overpowering, the smell of mangoes—some fresh, some old, some rotten. With a large empty coconut straw basket, I followed my mother as she stopped at every stall in the massive mango bazaar. They had to taste a certain way; they had to be sour and they had to be mangoes that would not turn sweet when ripened. The mangoes that went into making mango pickle were special mangoes. It was important to use your senses to pick the right batch. You tasted one mango and you relied upon that one mango to tell you what the other mangoes from the same tree tasted like.

"No, no." My mother shook her head at the man sitting in a dirty white *dhoti* and *kurta*. His skin was leathery around his mouth and there were deep crevices around his eyes. His face spoke volumes about his life, the hardships, the endless days under the relentless sun selling his wares, sometimes mangoes, sometimes something else, whatever was in season. He was chewing

betel leaves, which he spat out at regular intervals in the area between his stall and the one next to him.

"*Amma*," the man said with finality, as he licked his cracked
lips with a tongue reddened by betel leaves. "Ten rupees a k-g, *enh*,
take it or leave it."

My mother shrugged. "I can get them for seven a kilo in
Abids."

The man smiled crookedly. "This is Monda Market, *Amma*.
The price here is the lowest. And *all* these, *enh*"—he spread his
hand over the coconut straw baskets that held hundreds of mangoes—"taste the same."

That had to be a stretch, but I didn't say anything, didn't want
to get embroiled in this particular discussion. I stood mute next to
my mother, patiently waiting for the ordeal to be over. My light
pink *salwar kameez* was dirty and I was sweating as if I had never
been through an Indian summer before. But I had been through
twenty Indian summers, and now seven years later, I was having
trouble acclimating to my homeland.

I pushed damp sweaty hair off my forehead and tried to tuck
it inside my short ponytail. I had cut my hair a few years ago and
stuck to the shoulder length hairdo. My mother had been appalled
when I sent her pictures and had bemoaned the loss of my waist-
length black hair.

"You go to America and you want to look like those Christian
girls. Why, what is wrong with our way? Doesn't a girl look nice
with long, oiled hair with flowers in it? Even when you were here,
you didn't want the nice *mallipulu*, fresh jasmine, I would string.
Always wanted to look like those . . . Short hair and nonsense,"
she complained on the phone before thrusting it in my father's
hands.

I would have preferred to wear a pair of shorts to ward off the
tremendous heat but Ma instantly rebelled at the idea. "Wearing
shorts in Monda Market? Are you trying to be an exhibitionist?
We don't do that here."

Since I had arrived three days ago I had heard that many times. "We don't do that here." As if I didn't know what *we* did or did not do. I *was* "we."

My mother picked up a mango and asked the mango seller to cut a slice. She handed the slice to me. "Here, taste," she instructed, and I looked, horrified, at the slimy piece of raw fruit thrust under my nose.

Was she out of her mind? Did she expect me to eat that?

"Here," she prodded again, and shoved it closer to my mouth and the strong smell of mango and its juices sank in. And memories associated with that distinct smell trickled in like a slow stream flowing over gently weathered stone.

I remembered stealing mangoes from the neighbor's tree and biting into them with the relish of a theft well done. I remembered sneaking into the kitchen at night to eat the mangoes Ma was saving for something or other. I remembered sitting with Nate and eating raw mangoes with salt and chili powder, our lips burning and our tongues smacking because of the tartness. Now, I couldn't imagine putting that piece of white and green fruit inside my mouth. It was not about taste, it was about hygiene, and suddenly everything everybody had warned me about India came true.

My Indian friends who visited India after living in the United States said: "Everything will look dirtier than it did before." I never thought myself to be so Americanized that I would cringe from eating a piece of mango that had languished in that man's basket where he had touched it with his hands and . . .

I shook my head when the man scratched his hair and used the same hand to find a piece of food between yellow teeth, while he waited for judgment to be passed on his mangoes.

Ma sighed elaborately and popped the piece of mango into her mouth. From her eyes I could see she was excited. From the myriad mangoes she had tasted all morning, this was the one that would be perfect for her pickle. But she was not going to let the mango seller know it. It was Haggling 101.

"They are okay," she said with a total lack of enthusiasm.

"Okay, *enh*?" The man frowned and slapped his thigh with his hand in disapproval. "*Amma*, these are the best *pachadi* mangoes in all of Monda Market. And"—he paused and smiled at me—"I will give them to you for nine rupees a kilo, *enh*?"

Ma waved a hand negligently, and memories of my mother bartering over everything came rushing back like a tidal wave. The worst of all incidents was when we were on vacation in Kullu Manali in Himachal Pradesh. It was a popular vacation spot in the Himalayas before Kashmir had become such an issue with Pakistan. In a bazaar in Manali, Ma was trying to buy a shawl; it was not just any shawl, this was an in-fashion and in-high-demand woolen shawl, which had different colors on each side. This was a blue and black shawl and Ma was haggling like she had never haggled before.

The bargaining had stopped over one single rupee. The man said fifty and Ma said forty-nine and they went on for ten minutes after which Ma just walked out of the store. I was about thirteen years old and unhappy that we had just spent half an hour haggling over something she was not going to buy. I didn't know that she was using another haggling tactic of walking out of the store and then being called in by the vendor who would then believe that she was serious about one rupee.

As I was dragged by the hand out of the shawl shop I cried out, "It is just one rupee, Ma, why do you have to be such a *kanjoos*?"

As soon as the word was out, I knew it was a mistake. Ma slapped me across the face in the center of the market and took me weeping and wailing back to our hotel.

She never forgave me for letting the entire marketplace know that she was haggling over one rupee or for the loss of the blue and black in-fashion and in-high-demand shawl. The vacation went to hell after that as Ma kept telling me how she was not a *kanjoos*, not a scrooge, and she was only trying to save money for our future,

Nate's and mine. When I reminded her that she was buying the shawl for *herself*, I was awarded another sound slap. I sulked for the rest of the vacation and for a couple of weeks even after we got back home to Hyderabad.

Thanks to happy memories like that I never, ever, bargained. It was a relief that in the United States I didn't have to do it for groceries and clothes; everything came with a fixed price tag. And even when I went and bought my car, I didn't barter or bargain. The nice Volkswagen dealer gave me the price; I agreed and signed on the dotted line even as Nick insisted that I was being conned.

"You could get it for two thousand dollars less, at least," he told me when I was signing the loan papers.

"I like the car, I'm not going to fuss over it," I told him firmly, and Accountant Nick's eyes went snap-snap open in shock.

And that was that. Nick told me that from now on, when I wanted a new car, I should tell him what I wanted and he would buy it. "Getting conned while buying tomatoes in India is one thing, but when you buy a car it's criminal to not negotiate," he said.

But to haggle equated being like my mother and I was *never*, ever, going to be like my mother.

The mango seller picked out two more mangoes and set them in front of Ma. "Try more. See, they are all the same," he challenged eagerly, in an attempt to convince her.

Ma ignored the mangoes he chose and pulled out one at random from the basket in question. The man cut a slice off with his knife. Ma tasted the piece of mango and instead of swallowing it, spit it out in the general direction of the ground.

"Eight rupees," she said, as she wiped her mouth with the edge of her dark blue cotton sari.

"Eight-fifty," he countered.

"Eight," she prodded and the man made a "since-you-twist-my-arm" face, giving in to her bargaining skills.

"Okay," he sighed, then looked at me. "She drives a hard bargain, *enh*? I am not going to make any money on this sale."

I made an "I-have-no-say-in-this" face and put the straw basket I was holding in front of him.

"How many kilos?" he asked, and I gasped when my mother said twenty.

How on earth were we, two women with no muscles to speak of, going to carry twenty kilos of mangoes all by ourselves?

I found out soon enough.

It was excruciating. Ma pulled the edge of her sari around her waist and heaved to lift one side of the basket, while I lifted the other. We looked like Laurel and Hardy, tilting the basket, almost losing the goods inside as we paraded down the narrow crowded aisles of Monda Market.

We reached the main road and set the basket down on the dusty pavement. My mother looked at me and shook her head in distaste. "We will have to go home and you will have to change before we go to *Ammamma's*. I can't take you looking like this and we have to take clothes for tomorrow anyway."

We were all meeting at my grandmother's house to make mango pickle. It was a yearly ritual and everyone was pleased that I had come to India at the right time. I regretted my decision dearly. If I had to pick a month, it should have been anything but blistering July. I was glad that Nick wasn't there with me because he would have melted to nothingness in this heat.

I wiped my neck with a handkerchief and stuck it inside my purse. I probably smelled like a dead rat because I felt like one. My body was limp and the sun blazed down at eight in the morning as if in its zenith.

A whole day at my grandmother's house scared me. The potential for disaster was immense. I had no idea how I was going to tiptoe around the numerous land mines that were most certainly laid out for the family gathering, as always. When I was young it hadn't mattered much. I used to find a way to block out the bickering and the noise. But now I was an adult and I was expected to join in the bickering and contribute to the noise. I was hardly prepared for either. In addition, I had to break my not-so-good news to one and all—land mines would multiply.

It had just been three days, but I was already tired of being in India, at *home*, and especially tired of my mother. My father and I got along well, but when it came to taking sides between his children and his wife, *Nanna* knew which side his *idli* was smeared with *ghee*. According to him, Ma was always right.

When Nate and I were younger and fought with Ma, *Nanna* would always support her. His logic was quite simple: "You will leave someday," he would say. "She is all I have got and I don't want to eat at some cheap Udupi restaurant for the rest of my life. She is right and you are wrong—always, end of discussion."

Calling my mother a nag was not a stretch—she was a super nag. She could nag the hell out of anyone and do it with appalling innocence.

"No autos," Ma complained airily, and looked at me as if I was somehow to blame for the lack of auto rickshaws. "Why don't you try and get one," she ordered, as we stood on the roadside, unhappy in the skin-burning heat, a large basket of mangoes standing slightly lopsided between us on the uneven footpath.

I waved for a while without success. Finally, a yellow and black three-wheeler stopped in front of us, missing by inches my toes that were sticking out of my Kohlapuri slippers.

With her usual panache Ma haggled over the fare with the auto rickshaw driver. They finally decided on twenty-five rupees and we drove home holding the mango basket between us, making sure none of the precious green fruits rolled away.

The road was bumpy and the auto rickshaw moved in mysterious ways. I realized then that I couldn't drive in India. I would be dead in about five minutes flat. There were no rules; there never had been. You could make a U-turn anywhere, anytime you felt like it. Crossing a red light was not a crime. If a policeman caught you without your driver's license and registration papers, twenty to fifty rupees would solve your problem.

Everything that had seemed natural just seven years ago seemed unnatural and chaotic compared to what I had been living in and with in the United States.

The breeze was pleasant while the auto rickshaw moved, but the heat and the smell of the mangoes became intolerable when the auto rickshaw stopped at a red signal or for some other reason. There were many "other" reasons: stray cattle on the roads, frequent traffic jams, a couple of Maruti cars parked against each other in the middle of the road as the drivers passionately argued over whose mistake the accident was.

"If *Ammamma* had only given us mangoes like she did Lata, we wouldn't have this problem, now would we?" my mother said as the auto rickshaw leaped and jerked over a piece of missing road.

I had heard nothing but this complaint since I got back. My grandmother had given mangoes from the ancestral orchard only to my aunt Lata. This year the harvest had not been good and there weren't enough mangoes for everyone. My mother was still seething and would probably continue to seethe for the next fifteen years. After all, she was still angry that her wedding sari had cost less than the sari her parents had given their daughter-in-law, Lata, for her wedding.

The battle between Lata and Ma was fought with jibes and remarks. My mother held her head high because my father was the managing director of an electronics company and we lived rather luxuriously compared to Lata. My uncle Jayant was an engineer at BHEL, Bharath Heavy Electronics Limited, a public company where everyone got paid like government officials. Lata and Jayant had a small one-bedroom apartment where they lived with their two young daughters. Ma never ceased to mention how crowded it must be.

My parents had built a large house. They hoped that once my

brother and I got married and had children, there would be plenty of room when we came to visit them. But now that I was going to marry an American, I could imagine Ma and *Nanna* would not want us to visit because then they would be able to avoid the pointed question from neighbors and other family members, "How could you allow this to happen?"

Nate of course could not be counted on to spend much time in my parents' house once he left for good. Even when I was living in my parents' house, he was rarely found there. He was now in engineering school in Madras and lived in the university dorm. He came home for the summer but usually found something to do with friends that prevented him from staying at my parents' house for more than three days in a row.

"The fourth day, there is always hell to pay," he told me. "First three days she pampers, fourth day she wants to take me to *Ammamma's* house and there is Lata there and Anand and his illicit wife. . . . And from then on things start going from bad to worse to really rotten real fast."

Nate had spent three days with me and had escaped on a hiking trip in the Aruku caves with his friends the day before our pickle-making ritual.

"But I planned this six months ago," he lied easily when Ma threw a tantrum. "I can't back out now."

Nate and I had a good relationship. We communicated regularly via email and he and I spoke on the phone if my mother was out of earshot on his end. There was no sibling rivalry between us. Nate was ten years younger than I, and we believed that he was too young and I was too old to feel any rivalry. Because of the age difference, there was no race for the attention of my parents. We were family and we fought over HAPPINESS and other assorted food items and philosophies, but we acknowledged the fact that we both had spent time in the same womb, and accepted each other, flaws and all.

My father had sneaked off to work this morning in the car

despite Ma's nagging and she lamented about that as well. "Couldn't he have taken the day off?" she said when the auto rickshaw stopped in front of my parents' house. "Now we will have to take an auto rickshaw to *Ammamma's* house, too."

"He's taking tomorrow off," I said as I helped her haul the large basket of mangoes inside the veranda, after she paid the auto rickshaw driver with the grace of a *kanjoos*, *makhi-choos*, scrooge, scrooge, who would suck the fly that fell in her tea.

"Now go change; wear something nice," she ordered as she collapsed on a sofa.

The electricity was out. For six hours every day in the summer, the electricity was cut off to conserve it. The cut-off times changed randomly but were usually around the times when it was most hot. Today seemed to be an exception, because instead of cutting off the electricity from eleven to one in the afternoon, they had taken it out at eight-thirty in the morning.

I sat down on an ornate and uncomfortable wooden chair across from my mother who was resting her feet on the large, ostentatious coffee table centered in the drawing room.

"What should I wear?" I asked. I was here for two weeks and had promised myself I'd do exactly what my mother wanted me to do. Maybe that, I thought, would help ease the blow when I landed one right there where her heart was.

"The yellow *salwar kameez*." Ma's eyes gleamed. She probably thought I had changed. Never as a teenager had I asked her what I should wear when we went to visit relatives.

"Which yellow one?" I asked, slightly annoyed because it felt like surrender.

"The one with the gold embroidery." She picked up a newspaper to fan herself.

I gaped at her. The yellow one with the gold embroidery was made of thick silk. Was the woman off her rocker?

"It's too hot, Ma," I argued lightly. "Why don't I wear a cotton one?"

She agreed, but grudgingly. This was her chance to show her American-returned daughter off. But she couldn't *really* show off. I was unmarried, I was twenty-seven, and sometime soon she was going to find out I was living in sin with the foreigner I intended to marry. Life would have been easier if I had fallen in love with a nice Indian Brahmin boy—even better if I hadn't fallen in love at all and was ready to marry some nice Indian Brahmin boy my parents could pick out like they would shoes from a catalog.

I hadn't planned on falling in love with Nick. We met at a friend's house. Sean was a colleague and a friend and his sister was Nick's ex-girlfriend and now "just a good friend." As soon as Nick said, "Hello," I knew he was trouble. I had never before found an American attractive—well, besides a young Paul Newman and Sean Connery, and Denzel Washington—but no one in real life. I think most Indian women are trained to find only Indian men attractive; maybe it has something to do with centuries of brainwashing.

I was of course flattered that Nick was attracted to me as well, but I didn't expect him to pursue a relationship. And I really didn't expect that I, even in my wildest flights of fantasy, would be amenable to dating him. But he was, and I was.

Before I knew how it happened, and before I could think of all the reasons why it was a really bad idea we were dating, we were having dinner together. As if things were not bad enough, we started to have sex and soon we moved in together and after that everything really went to the dogs because we decided to get married. And now I was sweating in my parents' home, dreading having to tell them about Nick.

To remove the sweat and the two layers of dust that had deposited on my skin after my trip to Monda Market, I took a quick bath, dipping a plastic mug in an aluminum bucket filled with lukewarm water, heated by the sun in the overhead tank. My mother still had not installed showers in the bathrooms. "Save water," she said.

I put on a yellow cotton *salwar kameez* to appease Ma and looked at myself in the mirror. My skin had turned dark almost as soon as the Indian sun had kissed me and I knew no amount of sunscreen was going to stop my melanin from coming together to give me the ultra-ultra-tanned look. My hair had also become stringy. It was all the extra chlorine in the water. And my . . .

I winced; I was doing that complaining-about-India thing that all of us America-returned Indians did. I had lived here for twenty years, yet seven years later, the place was a hellhole. Guilt had an ugly taste in my mouth. This is my country, I told myself firmly, and I love my country.

✳ ✳ ✳

To: Priya Rao <Priya_Rao@yyyy.com>
From: Nicholas Collins <Nick_Collins@xxxx.com>
Subject: Good trip?

Hope you had a good flight. So sorry I missed your call. I was in a meeting and I turned off the cell phone. And so sorry that your mother is giving you a hard time about being single. I don't know what to say except that you are NOT single.

I miss you. The house feels empty without you. I slept on your side of the bed last night. I think I'm getting sappy in my old age.

Call me again, this time I'll keep the cell phone turned on, hail or snow. Jim and Cindy invited us to go camping at Mt. Shasta. What do you think? And there was a message from Sudhir for you on the answering machine. He wanted to wish you bon voyage.

Take care, sweetheart.
Nick

✳ ✳ ✳

To: Nicholas Collins <Nick_Collins@xxxx.com>
From: Priya Rao <Priya_Rao@yyyy.com>
Subject: Re: Good trip?

I just wish they knew I wasn't single—without my telling them. Anyway, we're going to go mango pickle making at *Ammamma*'s house and I think I could tell them then. I wish you were here. No, that isn't true, I wish I wasn't here.

It's strange to be in Hyderabad again. I look at my mother and I think about all my aunts and my grandma and I have to wonder how they stay at home all day, every day, with no life besides family. Sudhir always said that Indian women (his mom especially, I think) are demented because they stay home doing nothing but raising their kids. I don't agree with the dementia part but I must say that life sounds extremely claustrophobic.

Regardless, I'm here. Looking for approval. Some kind of okay sign for my marriage plans. I need them to say, "Yes, it's all right for you to marry the man you're in love with." Which is ridiculous! Who else should I marry but the man I love?

At least they haven't thrown any "suitable boys" my way . . . yet. They haven't even hinted, which makes me very suspicious. Coming here made me

REALIZE THAT I MISSED INDIA, MY FAMILY, EVEN MA. AND I MISSED NATE. HE HAS GROWN UP. HE'S A MAN NOW AND IT SEEMS SO STRANGE TO SEE HIM ACT LIKE ONE.

I MISS YOU. I MISS YOU VERY MUCH.

AND YES, TELL JIM AND CINDY THAT WE'D LOVE TO GO CAMPING. I GUESS ONCE I'M BACK I'LL BE READY FOR A VACATION.

I'LL TRY AND CALL AGAIN, BUT IT COULD BE TRICKY. I CAN CERTAINLY SEND EMAIL. MA DOESN'T UNDERSTAND COMPUTERS SO SHE'LL NOT SNOOP AROUND NATE'S COMPUTER AND HE'LL DEFINITELY CHEW HER OUT IF SHE TRIES.

I LOVE YOU,
PRIYA

✳ ✳ ✳

I went downstairs and found my mother lying haphazardly on the couch, snoring harshly. Her thin hair, which had been through repeated bad dye jobs, lay lifelessly against the maroon fabric of the sofa. Her lumpy stomach went up and down and I could see the flesh at her midriff spill each time she breathed out. I never understood why Indian women wore saris in this day and age when alternatives like *salwar kameez* would not be frowned upon. A sari was uncomfortable, and the midriff—the area where most of the battles of the bulge were fought and lost—stood exposed like an unraveled guilty secret.

I looked at my wristwatch and frowned. She had made me hurry up but had fallen asleep herself.

"Ma," I called out. She stirred a little, so I called out again and this time her eyes opened. They were bloodshot and she looked at me, slightly disoriented. Her gaze then fell on the clock. She sat up groggily.

"Go and get an auto," she told me, then stood up yawning and stretching. "And not one *paisa* more than fifteen rupees. Tell the auto *rickshawwallah* that and if he does any *kitch-kitch*, I will deal with him."

I slipped on my sunglasses, took my purse, and went through rows of houses to reach the main road. A buffalo strolled on the newly laid asphalt street and I tiptoed around it in fear. I was always afraid of stray animals on the road. The fear of buffaloes was deep-rooted, probably embossed onto my consciousness because of a "bad childhood experience" as the shrinks in all the movies say about serial killers. According to my father (my mother tells a slightly different version of the same story), when I was just seven months old we went to visit some relatives in Kavali, a small town in the same state as Hyderabad. My mother left me in the open veranda on a straw mat, while she went inside the house for something or the other. All of a sudden a buffalo came charging through the street, inside the gate, and onto the veranda. By the time my mother called out and my father came rushing outside, the buffalo was towering over me, sharp horns pointed toward me, a leaky snout dropping mucus close to where I lay unaware of the perilous situation I was in.

"God knows why, but the bull went away, though for a while we thought it would hurt you," my father said.

My mother's version of the story was mostly the same as my father's, only in her story it was *my father* who had left me on the veranda, not she. "I never left any of my children anywhere without supervision. It is your father . . . always wants this and that and leaves children where they are without any thought," she explained.

I reached the main road and found an auto rickshaw. The driver was smoking a *bidi*, lounging on the vinyl-covered seat of his three-wheeler, while a small radio at his feet was playing the latest hit song from a Telugu film. "Come and take me in your arms, come and take me and make me yours. You are gone I know but I wait you know, for you to come and make me yours," a female voice sang to an oft-used melody.

"*Himayatnagar*," I said loudly to be heard over the song, and the auto rickshaw guy nodded and turned the radio off just as a woman's heartbroken voice begged her lover yet again not to leave.

"*Chalis rupya*," he said, and I shook my head. I hated to barter, but even I knew forty rupees was too much.

"*Thees*," I countered, holding up three fingers, and he agreed without any resistance, which underscored the point that forty rupees was too much and probably even thirty was excessive, but I didn't have the stomach to go on.

I pulled out fifteen rupees from my purse and gave it to him. "I will give this to you now and my mother will give you another fifteen," I told him and he looked at me quizzically. I got into the rickshaw and asked him to drive to my parents' house. "And don't tell my mother that the price is thirty, just fifteen. *Accha?*"

The auto rickshaw driver winked at me. "Take it easy, *Amma, apun* can keep secret," he said as he hitched his pants up to his knees and started the scooter of the auto. "*Vroom-vroom* . . . to your castle, *hain?*"

I gave the man directions and he drove, chuckling to himself. When we reached the gate of my parents' house, I asked him to wait while I went to get my mother. The *rickshawwallah* didn't listen to me and even before I had set foot on the road, he honked three times, loudly enough to wake up the dead.

Ma came out of the house hurriedly, responding to the honks, wearing a red and yellow cotton sari, and my eyes took time to adjust to the bright colors. I didn't like knowing that I had to adjust to India—it was absurd. I *was* Indian, yet everything seemed only vaguely familiar. I couldn't remember how I used to feel when my mother wore a sari that made her look like a large Tequila Sunrise.

With the help of the auto rickshaw driver we put the twenty kilos of raw mangoes in the auto rickshaw. Ma and I squeezed on the slightly torn brown vinyl seat with difficulty, our legs hanging limply on the side of the large straw basket. I put a cotton bag with a change of clothes between us, along with a bag of gifts I brought for the family, and got ready for a bumpy and uncomfortable ride.

"Now, if *Ammamma* wants to give you something, just take it, okay? " Ma told me. "But if she gives you something very expensive, like jewelry, then,"—she paused and shrugged—"ask me if you can take it."

"And what'll you say?"

"I will ask you to take it," Ma told me irritably. "But that doesn't mean you have to take it right away. Nothing wrong in showing some reluctance."

Familial politics always made me want to be without family. I never understood the intricacies. It was like facing a complex math problem that had numerous ways to solve it and you didn't know which one was the right way because the answer to the problem changed randomly. When was it right to look reluctant and when was it right to look eager? I didn't have a clue seven years ago and I was not any wiser now.

"And if anyone asks you about marriage, just ask them to talk to me," she further instructed.

My marriage, but she wants to talk to them, whoever they were—typical Ma. "And what will *you* tell them?" I asked patiently.

"If they have a good U.S. boy in mind and he is in India on leave like you, we can probably arrange something," she explained. "If it works out, you will be married and happy. It will be a load off my chest. An unmarried daughter . . . What must the neighbors think?"

I glared at my mother. She was holding tightly to an iron handle on her side of the auto rickshaw and her naked potbelly heaved through her sari's *pallu* as the auto rickshaw went through bad roads and worse roads.

There was this misconception my mother refused to discard. According to her, a woman was happy only if she was married. She had not once asked me if I was happy *now*. The question was moot; how could I be happy if I wasn't married?

I wanted to lash out, tell her that I was getting married very soon, but I knew now was hardly the time. Maybe at dinner, I told myself nervously. Dinner would be a good time. Everyone would be there and we would be spending the night at my grandma's house. There would be safety in numbers.

"If anyone tells you that you are too old to be unmarried"—my mother paused dramatically—"it is your fault."

If I expected Ma to be compassionate, I was living in a fool's paradise. And I was anything but a fool.

"That nice boy in Cheee-cah-go," she continued, "he was perfect. But you didn't want him. You don't want anyone, all *nakhras* you have."

Here we go!

"Ma, the nice *boy* in Chicago had a girlfriend, an American girlfriend. He didn't want to get married and was only agreeing to talk to girls to get *his* parents off his back." I repeated what I had told her three years ago when the same matter had come up.

Ma shook her head. "All boys wander a little and I am not saying that being with one of those Christian girls is good, but he would have said yes."

"I wouldn't want him to," I exploded. "He was *living* with this woman. They had a relationship going on for *three years*. I wasn't going to marry a man who was in love with another woman."

"Love, it seems, is very important," Ma said sarcastically. "He was making eighty thousand dollars a year. Do you know how much that is in rupees?"

"I make eighty-five; do you know how much that is in rupees?" I countered.

"You didn't three years ago," she shot back. "He must be making so much more now. All that money . . ." She clicked her tongue and started giving directions to the driver instead.

I leaned back and closed my eyes. Another week and a half, just another eleven days, and I'll be out of here. I repeated it to myself like a mantra.

✳   ✳   ✳

My grandmother's house had always been a home away from home, a place where my mother couldn't always dominate and coerce. A home where I was spoiled often and where not all of Ma's rules applied. I had played in this house since I was born, and as we got close to it, I immediately recognized the smells emanating from the streets and the surroundings. It was a blow to my olfactory senses that even after seven years I still knew how this place smelled and how the air tasted.

The house stood on a large premium plot of land in the center of the city. Coconut trees grew around it and there was a well that had been used for years in the old-fashioned way to draw water. The well now had a motor pump that extracted water from the ground and filled the overhead tanks, but evidence of the old ways hung on the well in the form of a piece of old frayed coconut rope dragged over a rusty metal pulley.

When I was twelve years old it had been a rite of passage for me to be allowed by my grandfather to bring up a bucket of water from the well. Ma had been scared that I wouldn't be able to pull the heavy bucket and that it would pull me inside the well instead. She wanted me to have help, but *Thatha* had been adamant that I do it all by myself. I had rope burns on my soft palms but I strutted around like a proud peacock for days after that.

There was a small two-room house for the servants in one far corner of the plot and on another corner there was a large house that my grandparents rented. They had even constructed a second floor to their house. It was a modern three-bedroom apartment, which my grandparents rented out, too. They lived downstairs with my aunt Sowmya. Sowmya was three years older than I, and like me was not married, but unlike me had always wanted very much to be.

Ma paid off the auto rickshaw driver who winked at me as he told my mother with a straight face that the fare was only *pandrah rupiya*. We carried the basketful of mangoes to the house gate. Ma opened the gate and yelled for my grandparents' servant.

Badri was my grandparents' new servant. He and his wife Parvati had taken residence in the servant quarters just a year ago. Badri did all the gardenwork and cleaned the yard, while Parvati did the dishes and swept and mopped the floors in the house.

The old maidservant I grew up with, Rajni, was as much a part of my childhood as my grandparents' house. She had left a year after I went to the United States, to go back to her village to live with her son.

Rajni was not a Brahmin and so she was not allowed inside the kitchen, but my grandparents had given her access to pretty much everything else. Sowmya cooked and left the dishes outside where Rajni cleaned them. Sowmya would take the clean dishes back inside the kitchen to put them in their rightful places. I used to think Rajni was a slacker because she didn't do that part.

It had been a rainy day when my grandmother explained to me that Rajni was from a lower caste and we were from the highest caste. She couldn't enter our kitchens; in fact, in the good old days, lower caste people wouldn't even be allowed inside the house and Rajni would be untouchable, in every sense of the word. Things were apparently better now, *Ammamma* had said. "We Brahmins have become more tolerant, what with the days being so *mordern* and everything." She hadn't sounded too happy about the modern days.

I picked up our bags and helped Badri put the basket of mangoes on his head. My mother walked into the house like a queen as Badri and I followed like servile courtiers.

I smiled when I entered the grilled veranda on which a huge wooden swing swayed, covering it almost entirely—an obvious hazard for children. The swing had always been on the veranda. I probably wouldn't recognize the veranda without it.

I removed my sandals and peeped inside. The living room was empty, but I could hear sounds coming from the womb of the house, resonating with my memories as if a tuning fork had been put into motion.

One could see to the other end of the house from the front door. All the rooms lay on opposite sides of my line of vision and I saw a smiling Sowmya step outside the dining area next to the kitchen.

She ran to me and we hugged.

The Politics of Giving
and Receiving Gifts

My grandmother hugged me so hard that I almost cracked a rib. *Ammamma* had this strange notion that the harder the hug, the more the love. Despite the discomfort, the subtle smell of betel leaves and cloves that clung to her body pervaded my senses and I soaked the smells in. This was familiar territory and at that instant it didn't seem so bad to be back.

I knew that today or tomorrow, literally, I would have to tell them all about my plans for the future, and about the man in my life of whom they would wholeheartedly disapprove. But for now *Ammamma* was hugging me the way she always did and it was enough.

My aunt gave me a perfunctory hug. Lata and I never got along, to a great extent because of the cold war between Ma and her. I didn't have any feelings toward her, good or bad—I just thought of her as my very beautiful aunt about whom I didn't feel one way or the other. I remember, when I was around fourteen years old, my uncle Jayant got married and I had showed off to all my friends that I was getting a very beautiful aunt.

I was not wrong; Lata was beautiful. She was tall and walked like a "graceful deer"—so everyone said—and she was fair. Unlike me, she was very fair. Fair somehow always meant beautiful and having darker skin was a flaw. I got my father's dark color, my mother always said, clicking her tongue disapprovingly, and Nate got her fairer skin. According to Ma, that was my bad karma. A boy could get a good wife irrespective of how he looked if he was financially viable; for a woman, however, physical appearance was important. My dark skin color, Ma felt, could pose a problem when the time came to find me a suitable husband.

Nick was heartily amused when I told him how my own mother had discriminated against me because I was dark. He couldn't see the subtle differences between the various shades of Indian dark, which made the situation even more preposterous to him.

"All Indians are dark," Nick pointed out. "Compared to say a Scandinavian . . . what chance does your mother have of being called fair?"

But my mother was fair, fairer than most, and everyone including her talked about how beautiful she had been when she was young. Just like a marble doll, they would tell Nate and me. Then they would look at me, make sad sounds, and sympathize with Ma: "Too bad your daughter didn't get your looks." I was raised under the limelight of a mother whose beauty was long gone, but hardly forgotten. Today my mother could not be called beautiful. Her face, along with the rest of her body, had puffed up and any remnants of beauty were submerged by obesity.

Ma blamed her weight problem on birth control pills. They did the damage, she would accuse, as if eating mountains of white rice with lots of fat smeared on it was not responsible for the abundance of fat tissue in her body. She also blamed the doctor who had prescribed the criminal birth control pills to her almost twenty-seven years ago.

"That quack, gave me these awful pills and look . . . When you get married, Priya, no birth control pills, just have those babies and then . . . ask your husband to have a vasectomy, " she advised.

Unlike most Indian men, *Nanna* didn't care that Ma wanted him to get a vasectomy; he had never been that much of a chauvinist but what rankled and even amused him was Ma's reason.

"In case I die and he marries again, I want to make sure his new wife doesn't have any kids, so that you both are taken care of and not neglected for the new wife's children," she reasoned.

Ma had a twisted mind, Nate and I deduced, but we agreed that her motives were noble. *Nanna* I am sure felt insulted for being told that he didn't love his kids and that if Ma wasn't alive he would discard us as easily as he would marry another woman. "Radha, you just don't have enough faith in the universe," he would always say to Ma when she went on her pessimistic rants.

Seeing the family again after seven years was like being slammed in the solar plexus. My center of gravity had shifted and I worried about losing my balance, both physically and emotionally.

It was difficult coming home and facing my parents and now the rest of the family. Especially when I knew that they would not be happy, to understate their feelings, when they found out about Nick.

"Tell them I'm a Brahmin from Tennessee," Nick had joked when I told him that my family would most probably perform death ceremony rituals for me if we were to get married.

Sometimes I imagined they would accept Nick. Why shouldn't they? He was well educated, came from a good family, made good money—if my parents were to arrange my marriage it would be to someone like him, only he would be Indian and a Telugu Brahmin.

Marriage was on my parents' minds as well. I had spent my first night in India crushed in a one-sided conversation with my mother regarding my inability to appreciate the ominous situation I was in by being single at my age; while my father and brother watched a late-night cricket broadcast from England. India versus England, and India was most probably on the way to being thoroughly clobbered as Sachin Tendulkar had just got out on a duck score.

"Has she gone from bad to worse, or what?" I asked Nate when I cornered him alone in the kitchen. He was pouring himself a glass of water during a tea break in the cricket match.

"She *has* gone from bad to worse," Nate agreed as he patted my shoulder with little sympathy. "Now if you had a boyfriend . . ." He paused when he saw the look on my face and then shook his head. "American?"

"Yes," I said glumly, not surprised that Nate should be the one with the golden insight.

"You're so a dead woman, " Nate said cheerfully. "When do you plan to tell them?"

"I was thinking at *Ammamma's* this Friday when we go to make mango pickle," I said. "You know, tell the old and the older people all at the same time and get it done with."

"I'm not sorry I won't be there for the massacre," he said grimly. "You know, don't you, that there will be bloodshed?"

"I know, " I muttered.

"I mean *Thatha* will probably try to kill you," Nate added.

"I know. "

"Well, good luck. This should make things infinitely easier for me," Nate said as he gulped down all the water in the glass he was holding. "My girlfriend is from Delhi, north Indian; she is going to look *so* good in front of your American boyfriend."

"You're all heart, Nate," I said in sibling disgust and walked back into the living room where my mother sat in judgment of my life and me.

* * *

Ammamma's living room, the hall, was large. It could, during festivals and other celebratory occasions, hold at least sixty seated people for a meal, and it had, several times.

The floor was stone, polished and weathered by time. It glistened beautifully when Parvati mopped it and it was cool to touch, which was a blessing during the hot summer days.

At home Nick and I had hardwood floors and carpet and I could never walk barefoot on either since neither was as cold as stone. It was just one of those things I had brought along with me to the United States, like my inability to eat beef, no matter how many times I told myself that the cow in America was probably not sacred.

I sat down on the floor next to mounds of mangoes. Sowmya sat next to me, while *Ammamma* was settled comfortably on a new sofa, which was a step up from the old one that had springs coming out from the fabric and needed to be covered with thick towels to prevent bottoms from being pierced. Lata sat on a chair and immediately Ma demanded a chair for herself and Sowmya got one for her from the dining room.

I had no idea how to break the ice with people I had known for a good part of my life. The saving grace was my grandmother. *Ammamma* could talk anyone under the table and she almost always did. She usually launched into vitriolic tirades about something or the other. This time the spotlight was on my younger uncle and his "elopement." Anand, to everyone's surprise, had a love marriage. He fell in love with a colleague, Neelima, at the company he worked for. Neelima was a Maharashtrian and they got married in secret without telling anyone about it until after the three knots of the *mangala sutra* had been tied.

Their marriage had been the subject of numerous phone

conversations between my parents, grandparents, and me for the past year. The conversations always ended with someone warning me against a love marriage. It was because of how Anand's secret marriage had broken everyone's heart that I decided to tell my family before doing the deed, though it was very tempting to take the easy way out and tell them after the fact.

My grandparents and most of my family members did not have high hopes for Anand's marriage and they all were convinced that Neelima was not the right woman for him. They also believed that Neelima was actually a witch who had brewed a nasty potion to ensnare their poor little innocent son into her web.

"She is fair-skinned . . . but . . ."—*Ammamma* shrugged and tied the edge of her sari around her potbelly—"not like our Lata." She smiled at her daughter-in-law, who returned the smile.

Something was going on, I noted suspiciously. Lata and *Ammamma* had never really gotten along. *Ammamma* and *Thatha* had expected Jayant to follow the archaic joint family system and live with them after his marriage.

It didn't work out that way.

Six months after the wedding, Lata didn't say anything to anyone, just packed her bags and Jayant's, found a flat, and left. The family went into total cerebral shock. *Thatha* argued, begged, and pleaded for her to come back, but Lata stood her ground. She told him she was tired of living with people to whom she was merely a cook and a maid. (Who could really blame her for that?) She also said that she wanted her own home, where she was the mistress. Jayant quietly followed his wife and broke my grandparents' hearts. But now *Ammamma* was being nice to the traitorous daughter-in-law. It was more than enough to bring out the Sherlock Holmes in me.

"Don't listen to them, Priya, Neelima is a nice girl," Sowmya interjected. "And she is a Brahmin," she added for good measure.

"But not our type," *Ammamma* argued. "She is a Maharashtrian Brahmin, not Telugu."

And being Telugu was very, very essential. Telugu was the official language of my state, Andhra Pradesh, and we were called Telugu or Telugu people. Being of the same caste was not enough to sanctify a marriage. To marry someone, that someone had to also be from the same state. It was very simple: "they" were somehow lower because "they" were not Telugu.

At least "they" were Indian, I thought unhappily; my "they" was American and an un-devout Christian to boot.

"Neelima is a very good person," Sowmya pointed out. "And her family has lived in Hyderabad for generations. She speaks Telugu fluently and cooks our food."

Food was also very, very essential. But not as essential as the caste.

"But she brought no dowry," Lata said calmly as she looked over the pile of mangoes my mother and I had bought today at Monda market. "Where will the money for your dowry come from?" she taunted softly, her eyes downcast as she arranged the pleats in her sari, and I saw all fight abandon Sowmya.

"I better get the knives and the chopping boards," Sowmya said hastily, and disappeared into the kitchen.

Everyone squirmed a little after that. The subjects of dowry and marriage were a soft spot for Sowmya. She had been twenty-seven years old for the past three years and those "three years" made her feel a little less like an old maid. It also made a difference to the suitors *Thatha* managed to find for her. After all, a girl in her late twenties had a chance at making a better match than one who was thirty.

Objectively speaking, Sowmya would be considered plump; she wore thick glasses and had dark skin—even darker than mine. Her hair was curly and thin and she was not a beauty by anyone's standards. But what no one saw was that Sowmya's heart was as big as the pot she used to make *payasam* in during festivals.

Arranged marriage is not just a crapshoot, as many believe it to be. It is a planned and business-like approach to marriage. A man's parents want certain qualities in their daughter-in-law, and a woman's parents want certain qualities in their son-in-law. What the children want usually does not figure in the equation. The parents try to find the perfect match and hope for the best.

Women like Sowmya get caught in no-man's-land. They have no qualities that anyone is looking for, which means that they have to settle for someone who is in the exact same position, someone who has been rejected by numerous suitors for being less qualified. It's like finding a job. The job you get is equivalent to your qualifications and what you want does not really matter.

Despite having a bachelor's in Telugu literature, Sowmya had never held a job in her life. Working, my illustrious and narrow-minded *Thatha* said, was not for women of our class. And what job could she get anyway? With her education, at best, she could be a secretary or a clerk. Unacceptable to *Thatha*. Those were careers and jobs for people with a lower socioeconomic status than his.

In the food chain of the Indian academic world, doctors and engineers took the top spots. Ma had been pleased when I got through the entrance exam to get into an engineering school. After all, that ensured a good marriage match for me. It also meant that I could get a job that would not embarrass my parents and would be appropriate for a woman of my social station.

However, Sowmya could not get a job equivalent to her social status because she was not academically qualified, just as she couldn't get the life partner she fantasized about because she was not physically qualified.

The sad part of it was that Sowmya accepted it as her fate and did nothing to change any part of it and write her own destiny. She probably didn't fantasize anymore, didn't even dream about a husband and family anymore. She had sat through many ceremonies during which the prospective groom and his family visited my grandparents' house to see the prospective bride. Earlier, Sowmya had kept count, but now, almost ten years since the whole drama had begun, she had stopped. My mother, however, hadn't.

"Sixty-four matches and not one worked out," she told me during my current visit.

In the beginning, *Thatha* had refused to budge from his goal of getting a good-looking doctor or engineer for Sowmya. Even when it became evident that the matches he was finding were not going to pan out, he continued. It was when Sowmya turned twenty-five that *Thatha* started to realize he may have been aiming too high. He started looking at bank managers and the like, but again nothing worked out because he wanted a young man for Sowmya, but men who were twenty-seven years old were looking at girls who were twenty-one, not twenty-five. Now *Thatha* was looking at lecturers and older men. While *Thatha* looked for a suitable boy, Sowmya sat through bride-seeing ceremonies and rejections.

"God knows when she will get married," Ma complained bitterly. "An unmarried daughter, Priya, is like a noose around the neck that is slowly tightening with every passing day."

I sometimes imagined how it would be to live with my parents and be constantly reminded of how lacking I was. I would slit my wrists in no time and I was amazed that Sowmya hadn't. She was still the same person I had grown up with; the bitterness that no one would blame her for having seemed to have never touched her.

"Maybe you shouldn't say things like that," I said to Lata, wanting to defend my nonconfrontational aunt against the harsh dowry remark. "It isn't fair to turn this on Sowmya because she likes Anand's wife."

Lata quirked an eyebrow. "You are back, what, half an hour, and already you are taking sides?"

My mother held up her hand to silence me before I could

respond, her posture clearly saying that she would take care of this one for me, with pleasure. "Lata, my daughter is not taking sides, just trying to be considerate of other people's feelings."

The only way to prevent World War III, now that I had spilled pearls of wisdom unwisely, was to change the topic. So I pulled my gift bag close to me—it was time to play Santa Claus.

"I have gifts for everyone," I said cheerfully, before Lata could tell my mother what she thought about my being considerate of other people's feelings.

❊   ❊   ❊

Sowmya blushed when she saw the makeup kit I got for her. She touched the plastic-covered blush and eye shadow and picked up the lipstick and unrolled it to see what color it was. She closed it and put the cap on and shrugged. "What am I going to do with this, Priya?" she asked, I think just to sound reluctant.

"Wear it," Lata suggested lightly, but with just enough dabs of sarcasm, and I wondered again. Usually *Ammamma* protected Sowmya from barbs like that, but the dynamics seemed to have changed. Lata was ruling the roost. First it was the mangoes and now this.

"*Ammamma.*" I put a blue and white cashmere shawl on her lap and she touched it with curious fingers. She hugged me once again, this time a little lightly, and kissed me on the forehead. "You shouldn't have. You are here and that is all we care about."

I agreed with that notion, but I also knew the ritual. Oh yes, there was a ritual: the homecoming ritual. The cardinal law was that "you cannot come home without a substantial amount of gifts, irrespective of your financial predicament."

The gifts also cannot be bought and dispensed of without drama. Every gift will be analyzed. For example, I cannot give *Ammamma* a less expensive gift than the one I would give to Neelima. That would offend *Ammamma* because she was senior to Neelima.

Similarly, I cannot buy Lata something more expensive than what I would get for my mother. I also cannot buy something so cheap that Lata would be offended.

With all the opposing and contradicting rules, buying a gift for Lata had been a grueling task.

"Just pick out something womanly," Nick suggested. "Works for my aunt who hates my mother's guts. I just buy her perfume every year for Christmas and she's happy."

I explained to him that it was not quite that simple. I was buying my mother a bottle of perfume along with other assorted gifts. Ma had specifically asked me to get her some perfume and that was why I couldn't buy Lata perfume, too. I had to buy her something that I hadn't given my mother but it also should be something that my mother would not want.

"This doesn't sound like buying gifts but more like a diplomatic mission to the Mideast. I'm very confused," Nick confessed, and I agreed wholeheartedly with him.

I handed a gift-wrapped box to Lata. "For you."

She looked at the box and took it with a negligent shrug. "You didn't have to bring me anything," she remarked. "My brother who lives in Los Angeles gets me whatever I want."

My mother's jaw tightened and she glared at Lata. "If you don't like it, Priya can take it back," she retorted smoothly.

I gave Ma a warning look and put on my most winsome smile for Lata. "I couldn't not buy you something. I spent a lot of time looking for the right thing. . . . Now if you don't open it, I will feel bad."

Lata opened the box and I could see surprise and pleasure glimmer in her eyes. She pulled out shimmering silk—a delicately embroidered shawl of Navajo design. "It is beautiful," she murmured.

Ma seemed to agree but wasn't too happy about it. "It is just like the one she sent me last year," she said peevishly.

I didn't argue and moved on to the next batch of goodies.

"I also got something for Apoorva and Shalini," I told Lata, and gave her two gift-wrapped boxes for her daughters. "I got them identical things—don't want them to fight over whose is better."

"What did you bring for them?" Ma asked nosily.

"Just some stuff, " I said, not wanting to give the surprise away. "I think they'll like it."

"Thanks, " Lata said, beaming now. "This is so nice of you, Priya."

I was relieved. The gifts had been given without a hitch. I had some more gifts for my grandfather and uncles and one for my new aunt. I suspected the family was treating Neelima like used bath water and I wanted to welcome her—Anand would definitely want that.

"Is Neelima going to come?" I asked as flatly as I could, and *Ammamma* instantly recoiled at the question.

"Why, did you bring *her* something?" she questioned.

"Yes," I said in a tone that did not broach further argument. But who was I kidding? No one in my family had ever paid attention to that tone.

"Why? She isn't *really* family," *Ammamma* said harshly. "She stole my little boy."

Yeah, and the "little" boy was completely innocent. I couldn't believe the hypocrisy. Anand was a grown man and I couldn't imagine any woman conning him into matrimony.

"She didn't force him to marry her," Ma said. "He married her with his eyes open. What can we do when someone takes your trust and throws it away?"

Direct hit!

What can we do when someone takes your trust and throws it away?

Oh, this was going to get unpleasant and I wondered if maybe it would be better to not say anything. But I knew that if I didn't, I wouldn't be able to face Nick when I got back. He was not some dirty little secret that should be tucked away. I loved him and I was proud of him and I wanted my parents and my family to know about him. I wanted to tell them what a wonderful person he was, but I knew they wouldn't be able to see beyond the color of his skin and the fact that he was a foreigner. It wouldn't matter if he was the kindest, richest, and most good-looking man to ever walk the earth—his nationality and race had already disqualified him as a potential groom for me.

"Neelima will be here soon," Sowmya said, and looked at the mangoes spread out in small piles on the cold stone floor of the hall. "We should wait for her before we start cutting the mangoes. Does anyone want coffee in the meantime?"

There was a round of nods and Sowmya slithered away from the living room into the kitchen once again. I followed her this time and sat down on a granite counter as she puttered around.

"Have you learned to cook yet?" she asked, and I grinned sheepishly.

"Some," I said. "But not Indian food. It takes too long and it's too spicy to eat every day. And if I really feel like it, I just go to a restaurant; they do a better job than I ever can."

"You should learn to cook," Sowmya admonished. "What are you going to do when you get married? Make your husband eat outside food?"

Outside food versus homemade food! In India there was no contest. The food cooked at home by the wife was the best food. No restaurant could compare to that and in any case why would you spend money going to a restaurant when you could get home-made food?

"I will teach you how to cook," Sowmya suggested, and I shook my head, laughing.

The idea of learning how to cook to feed Nick was amusing. Once in the matrimonial section of a Silicon Valley Indian magazine there was a girl's profile that had made quite an impact on Nick.

23-year-old, beautiful, BA-pass Telugu Reddy girl looking for handsome and financially settled Telugu Reddy boy in the U.S. Girl is 5′4″, fair, and is domestically trained. If interested, please apply with photograph.

After that Nick started complaining that I was not "domestically trained." It was a joke between us, but a woman not knowing how to cook was unacceptable to Sowmya.

"I'll just find a husband who can cook," I said to her, and changed the topic to matters that were raising my curiosity. "What's going on with Lata?"

"Don't mind Lata, she . . . is just . . ." Sowmya poured milk into a steel saucepan and added an equal amount of water and set the saucepan on the gas stove.

I got up to pull out the steel coffee glasses from the cabinet next to the sink; they were exactly where they had always been. Shining, washed, and thoroughly dried by Parvati.

"No, we use cups now; steel glasses are only for morning coffee," Sowmya said, and I put the glasses away surprised.

Everyone at *Ammamma's* house used to drink coffee only in the steel glasses. The hot coffee was poured into the glasses, which would be put in small steel bowls. Then the hot coffee was poured in small amounts into the bowl to cool, and was drunk from there. It was an interesting South Indian ritual that I had almost forgotten. It appeared some things had changed here as well. They used coffee cups now.

The coffee cups were actually teacups, white with a golden lining around the rim of the cup and saucer. I set the cups on the saucers and placed a teaspoon alongside each one of them.

Sowmya leaned against the wall next to the Venkateshwara Swami temple in the kitchen and looked at me with obvious relief. "I am so glad you are here," she said. "At least now they can concentrate on you for being unmarried and leave me alone."

"Thanks," I retorted in good humor and then I quieted. "Has it been very bad?"

"Terrible," Sowmya sighed. "It was getting better, but then . . . Now *Nanna* doesn't even bother to ask me if *I* like the boy; he just says if the boy likes me, that is it."

My grandfather was getting up there in the age department and I knew he was worried that Sowmya would be unmarried for the rest of her life. Who would take care of her after he died?

"You know that's not how he means it. He'd never ask you to marry someone you didn't want," I tried to reason.

"I know," Sowmya said, and shrugged.

"How did they react to Anand's marriage?" I asked, changing the direction of the conversation.

Sowmya rolled her eyes. "It was a nightmare. They went on and on, and when he brought Neelima home the first time, *Amma* actually asked her to leave. Then *Amma* and *Nanna* went to Anand's flat three days later and asked them to come back. They even paid for their wedding reception, but I don't think she has forgiven them for throwing her out of the house the first time Anand brought her here."

"Can't blame her for that."

Sowmya straightened, pulled out a bottle of instant coffee from the open cabinet next to the gas stove. She opened the bottle and poured one teaspoon of coffee into each of the cups I had lined up by the stove. "But she comes back; Neelima keeps coming back. I think Anand makes her because he wants her to get along with *Amma* and *Nanna*. I don't think anything is going to get better until . . . maybe they have a child."

"Are they planning to have children?" I asked the natural question.

Anand and Neelima had been married for over a year now and by all Indian standards they should at least be pregnant. It always boggled me, the lack of contraception and planned parenthood. Most of the married couples I knew from India had a child within a year of their wedding, which meant that they never thought about contraception. Most Indian couples wouldn't dream of having sex without the benefit of a nice, five-day marriage celebration. Some of my Indian friends were adamantly staying childless, but the pressure from their families was pushing them into having unprotected sex with their spouse.

Sowmya held the steel saucepan in which the milk had been boiling with a pair of steel tongs. The milk looked frothy and I wrinkled my nose at the familiar smell of slightly burned milk. As the milk sizzled into the cups, Sowmya clicked her tongue sadly. "Neelima says that they have been trying, but no baby yet."

"It's just been a year," I said. "You like her."

"She is nice to me," Sowmya replied casually. "She is a good girl. She helps me whenever she comes home. *Amma* never cooks and *Nanna* . . . well, he doesn't like to cook . . . and why should he when I am here?"

My grandmother was a strange creature. She came from a generation where women were treated like doormats, yet she had managed to stay out of the kitchen for most of her life. Earlier in her marriage her mother-in-law did all the cooking, and by the time she passed away my mother had been old enough to do the cooking. During the times my mother couldn't cook, my grandfather wielded the spatula.

There was a ritual in most Brahmin families, even now in some, during which women who are having their period had to "sit out." "Sitting out" literally means they are relegated to one room at the end of the house—the room next to the veranda in my grandparents' house—and are not allowed to touch anyone or anything during their "contaminated" period. When I was young I would always want to touch the women who were sitting out. I didn't know what "sitting out" meant and I would try to get away with touching the women. Once it was my grandmother and I ended up being doused with a bucketful of water from the well to cleanse me. Needless to say, after that I never had the desire to touch any woman who sat out.

When the women sit out, the men have to cook, and that was how my grandfather and most Brahmin men learned how to cook.

Now, when Sowmya has her period, my mother comes and cooks or Lata does it. After all, it was not right for the man of the house to spend any time in the kitchen when he had grown daughters.

I wondered if *Ammamma* knew how to cook—she must, I rationalized. Her parents would never have permitted her not to learn. I wondered why Ma never encouraged me to cook. She was always trying to get me out of the kitchen: "You will mess everything up and then I will have to clean it. Just stay out of here and let me deal with my headache. . . . I don't need any help."

I learned to cook a few dishes but all in all there was no way I could cook a meal for several people the way Sowmya or Ma could.

When I used to complain to *Nanna* that Ma would not let me cook, he would say that I was going to be a "career woman" and didn't need to learn how to cook. "You will make lots of money and you can just hire a cook. No chopping and dicing for my little princess."

To Ma cleanliness *was* next to godliness and there was no way in this big wide earth that she would let anyone besides herself cook in her kitchen. After a while my enthusiasm also waned and I just never got around to learning the most important art of all for a woman, cooking.

I heard the rumble of the metal gate being opened and I twisted my head to look out the kitchen window.

"That must be Neelima," Sowmya said, as she loaded the cups on a tray. "You take this out and I will make sure they don't kill her with the mango knives."

* * *

Neelima looked exactly like the kind of person I thought Anand would marry. She was tiny, five feet no inches, and she was very pretty and perky with her shoulder-length hair swishing around her face whenever she talked. She smiled sweetly and looked like a doll in her beautiful red sari.

She was genuinely pleased with my gift. I had seen a picture of her in which her hair had been tied in a French knot, so I got her ivory combs.

Lata immediately leaned over to look carefully at the combs and I could hear the calculator hum inside her head. She was probably thinking how the shawl, even though expensive, was probably not as expensive as the combs . . . or was it? My mother was torn between anger and pride. She was upset that I had spent all this money and she was also pleased that I was giving away such expensive-looking gifts. My giving expensive gifts guaranteed that when the situation arose (like my wedding), I would get expensive gifts in return.

"You are late," was all my grandmother said to Neelima once the introductions were made and the gift given.

"I had to stop by at the doctor's clinic," Neelima said shyly. "I am ten weeks pregnant," she announced.

Sowmya and I hugged her and rambled on about little babies and how wonderful it was. The contrast was painful. *Ammamma* asked us to spread the mangoes, Ma just glowered, while Lata started talking about how the first trimester was the time when most miscarriages took place. I was appalled. Who were these people? And why were they behaving like women from a B-grade Telugu movie?

I dropped a basket of mangoes between Neelima and me and sat down cross-legged. "Here." I handed her a large knife and put a cutting board in front of her as I did in front of me as well.

"Wait," my grandmother said. "Don't mix the mangoes." She pointed to the ones between Neelima and me. "Those are ours. Sowmya, you take care of them. Let us chop our own mangoes. That way the good and bad mangoes won't get mixed."

There were different piles of mangoes in the hall. The mangoes Ma and I had purchased that morning, the mangoes Lata had been given from the ancestral orchard, the ones that belonged to *Ammamma*, and those that were Neelima's, which had been bought under *Ammamma*'s supervision the day before. It was easy to know whose mangoes *Ammamma* didn't want her mangoes mixed up with.

"Are you saying my mangoes are bad?" Ma asked instantly, her eyes blazing, a knife held firmly in her hand. Warrior Pickle Woman was ready to defend her mangoes.

Ammamma leaned down and picked up a mango from "our" basket and sniffed. She dropped it instantly, her nose wrinkled. "Radha, you were never good at picking mangoes. You should have taken Lata with you."

"I always pick good mangoes," Ma said, and yanked a mango out of the basket. "Cut and give me a piece," she ordered Neelima, who put the mango on the wooden cutting board and hammered the knife through it. The knife cut the mango, stone and all. She cut out a smaller piece with a paring knife and gave it to Ma.

"Taste," she instructed my grandmother, who moved her head away.

"I don't have to taste; I know that they are not very good by the smell. Priya, you have to use your senses ... your sense of smell to buy mangoes. I will teach you; if you learn from your mother, you will pick mangoes like these," *Ammamma* said, looking at the mangoes Ma had just purchased with distaste.

"Maybe if you had given me some mangoes instead of giving them all to Lata, I wouldn't have made this *big* mistake," Ma said sarcastically.

"The harvest was not very good, there were only a few mangoes," *Ammamma* protested. "We had to take some and the rest we gave to Lata."

"Why give the rest to her? I am your flesh and blood," Ma said sourly. "Maybe I should just take Priya home and—"

"Ma," I interrupted calmly before my mother could finish threatening my grandmother into submission. "*Ammamma*, why don't you taste the mango and see? I helped Ma pick them out, you know," I said, putting on my best granddaughter face.

My being the oldest and most doted on grandchild and the fact that I was there for only another week and a half propelled my grandmother to do as I asked.

Ammamma swallowed the piece of mango and smacked her lips. "They will do," she said and my mother raised an eyebrow. "They are not bad," my grandmother added grudgingly. "Now let us cut these mangoes before lunch," she ordered.

❋　❋　❋

To: Priya Rao <Priya_Rao@yyyy.com>
From: Nicholas Collins <Nick_Collins@xxxx.com>
Subject: Re: Re: Good trip?

At 11:05 PM, Friday, Priya Rao wrote:

>At least they haven't thrown any "suitable boys" my way . . . yet.

I have no idea why you continue to call them "boys" when they're actually grown, adult, ready-to-marry men. Very perplexing, I must say.

I'm glad your parents are not throwing eligible men your way. I have to admit a part of me is/was afraid that your family will/would convince you to marry a nice Indian boy. Rationally, I know you're coming home to me but there is this irrational part of my brain that's convinced your family can manipulate you.

I MISS YOU. THIS TRIP FEELS LONGER THAN YOUR NORMAL BUSINESS TRIPS. USUALLY, YOU'RE GONE TWO-THREE DAYS OR MAXIMUM A WEEK AND IT'S IN THE U.S. THIS FEELS DIFFERENT. I FEEL THAT I CAN'T REACH YOU.

NICK

✳ ✳ ✳

Chopping Mangoes and Egos

Cutting mangoes for making pickle is a skill that is honed over years of practice, under the critical eye of one's mother or mother-in-law, aunt, or some other anal older female relative. In the olden days when joint families were the norm and women didn't work out of the home, wives and daughters were trained in cutting mangoes as they were in everything else that pertained to keeping order in the household.

There is a certain precision to cutting pickle mangoes, a certain methodology, and I was sorely lacking in both.

A sharp and rather heavy knife is used to cut mangoes so that the blade easily sinks into and then past the mango stone. Since the knife is sharp and heavy it's not prudent to hold the mango in place with one hand—unless you are an expert—and slam the sharp object with the other; a small miscalculation and you may be missing a few fingers.

With this in mind, I stationed the mango on the wooden

cutting board, a board on which generations of my mother's family had chopped mangoes in the pickle season, and took aim. The mango flew and struck me on the forehead before falling into my lap.

My mother made a disgruntled sound and looked at the now half-squished mango lying unceremoniously on my yellow *salwar kameez.*

"You have to hold the mango, Priya, " my mother said, and proceeded to demonstrate with expertise how a mango should be cut. I narrowed my eyes in frustration, but she didn't seem to notice. She was busy cutting me into size along with the mango.

The first slash of the knife split the mango in two halves. Then Ma used a paring knife and removed the stone, but let its hard casing stay stuck to the flesh of the mango.

"Now you have to cut it again," she told me and did so. Four pieces of the mango lay in front of her, their proportions hideously the same. They were mocking me, just as my mother had wanted them to. "If the mango is small"—she picked up an example—"then only one-half is enough."

Lata snickered softly and muttered something about modern girls. My shoulders slumped. I didn't want to get defensive, but I would like to see any of these women manipulate databases the way I could. So, they could cut some measly mangoes. So what?

Being competitive by nature and having the need to prove to the world around me that I was not only a good database programmer but also a good mango chopper, I wielded the knife one more time. This time I cut the mango, not in two clean halves but two squishy portions. After the fourth mango had gone to waste, my grandmother asked me to come and sit next to her and watch and learn. I didn't want to watch and learn, but the writing was on *Ammamma's* polished floor. It was pathetic to admit defeat to a lousy piece of fruit but I did it as gracefully as I could.

Between the sound of knives coming down on wooden

boards and paring knives scraping against the hard coating of the mango stone, the house seemed like a mango pickle sweatshop. They were good at what they did and they all did it with ease. Their eyes focused on green fleshy fruit and the knives in their hands gleamed with juice while their mouths gossiped.

"When is the boy coming to see Sowmya?" Lata asked conversationally.

This would be boy number 65 according to Ma's scoreboard.

"Tomorrow evening," *Ammamma* said, as she opened her brass betel-leaves box.

That box had fascinated me since I was a little girl. I liked *paan*, when it was sweet, but my grandmother liked it bitter. She was an expert at making it and I watched in childlike fascination all over again as she put together a *paan*. She opened a green betel leaf that was slightly darker on the edges because of sitting in an uncomfortable position in the box. Then she opened a small box of light pink paste and applied it on the betel leaf with her leathery fingers.

"So, he is some lecturer at some college?" Lata asked mockingly. I couldn't understand why Lata was being so antagonistic toward Sowmya. Granted Lata and Sowmya were not good friends, but Lata usually didn't go off quite like this. What was really shocking was how my grandmother was not supporting Sowmya anymore.

Had they given up? When Anand got married it had been a blow, not only because he had married a woman from another state, but because he had married before his younger sister had. The rules were clear about this, too. The brother closest in age to a sister has to wait to marry until his sister does. If that doesn't happen, the chances of the sister getting married are pretty slim. In the olden days when girls were married before they hit puberty this rule was put into place so that the brothers would not spend all the dowry money set aside for their sisters.

"Not at some college, at CBIT," Sowmya blurted out. "And he has already seen my picture," she added.

"So did that homeopathy doctor," Lata countered.

"Hush," my mother said. "Just because you are pretty and married doesn't mean you have to talk like this. She will get married when it is time. God has it all planned."

Yeah, right! Poor Sowmya, caught in a society where she couldn't step out of the house and couldn't stay in.

A crackling sound dragged my attention back to my grandmother who was crushing betel nuts with a small brass nutcracker. She spread the nuts on the betel leaf, wrapped it up, and popped it inside her mouth.

"Want one?" she asked me, her mouth dripping with red saliva.

I nodded gleefully and ignored the look Ma gave me. When I was a child there was no way she would have allowed me to eat *paan*, but now I was twenty-seven years old and I could have betel nuts and more.

"My older sister didn't get married until she was thirty-one," Neelima offered in support.

"In our family we don't let our daughters chase and marry men from other castes," *Ammamma* said as she chewed noisily on the *paan*. "Here." She gave me a *paan* that I stuck inside my mouth with the hope that I would not speak up against the injustice.

"She had an arranged marriage," Neelima countered, and let her knife drop on the wooden cutting board. I saw the tears in her eyes and once again forced myself not to say anything. I was here for just a few days and I didn't want to get into any unnecessary fights. In any case once they heard about Nick, Neelima would start looking really good to the family. At least she was Indian and I knew that counted for something.

A friend of mine, who had now been relegated to being only

an acquaintance, had been appalled when I told him about Nick. His instant reaction was "How can you, Priya? He's not even Indian" as if that made him a cat or a dog.

"If your sister had an arranged marriage, why didn't you?" Lata asked Neelima. "You married Anand in a great hurry. Did you think what would happen to Sowmya here? Who will marry her now? The brother got married and the sister is still sitting at home."

"She hasn't gotten married for ten years," Neelima cried out. "How long were we supposed to wait? We waited two years but she was not getting a match. That isn't my fault." She stood up and rushed outside to the veranda.

Sowmya used the edge of her sari to wipe her face of sweat and probably tears. The heat in the room was increasing by the minute and the fact that all the windows and doors were left open was not helping. Added to that, the slow creaky fan on the ceiling was barely moving the air around.

I stood up nervously and went to check on my new aunt. She was sitting on the steps that led to the well from the veranda, her face buried in her hands.

I sat down beside her and put a hand on her shoulder tentatively. "Are you okay?" I asked, as I swallowed the *paan*.

She reared her head up. "I hate them all," she said passionately. "Anand married me. *He* asked me to marry him; *he* pursued me. And now they are blaming *me* for Sowmya?"

"There's no one to blame," I told her. "But I think what you said really hurt Sowmya."

If anyone could understand what Sowmya was going through it would be Neelima. After all, Sowmya was alienated by her own family for being unmarried and she had nowhere to go. All through my life I had heard people say things to put her down. First, it had been because she was overweight and then because her hair was falling out, which made my grandparents nervous that she would soon go bald. She took care of *Ammamma* and *Thatha*, ran their house for them, and they treated her as if she were a burden. Forget gratitude, *Ammamma* and *Thatha* made her feel like she was a load they couldn't wait to dump on some unsuspecting "boy." I wondered how they would survive once Sowmya did get married. Who would cook and clean? Who would make sure the maid came and did her work properly?

"I didn't mean to hurt Sowmya," Neelima apologized. "But I am going to have a baby and no happiness from their side. Why?"

"If you have a son, you will have them kissing the floor you walk on—they will have their heir then," I joked but I also knew it was true. My grandfather was obsessed with perpetuating the line of Somayajulas. He wanted a son's son and that was why Nate, the only grandson, was not qualified to be heir.

Neelima wept some more at my joke. "They told Anand that our son would *never* be the rightful heir because of me. I am not the right woman to bear their heir," she sighed sadly. "That is why Lata is pregnant again."

"What?" It was preposterous. How could Lata be pregnant again?

"They are hoping she will have a son and he will be the grandchild to carry on the family name."

For an instant I wanted to tell her that she was mistaken, that *Thatha* was not such a chauvinist, or so old-fashioned, and then I remembered that he was all those things, that he was capable of asking his "pure-blooded" daughter-in-law to bear another child, to bear a son. Burgeoning hope crushed, I realized that he would never accept Nick; he would never accept even the idea of Nick and me. What was I going to do?

"So she's pregnant . . . like, now?" I asked, wanting to be absolutely certain.

Neelima's head bobbed. "Almost four months gone and they want to do a test soon to find out the sex of the baby. Have you seen the way she treats your grandparents? She doesn't even let her children come here to see them. But now"—she took a deep breath—"now they are all best friends. And my baby has no right to be born. She says that I might have a miscarriage."

I patted her shoulder in a weak attempt to assuage her. It was an impossible situation, a pointless one. What difference would it make to my seventy-plus-year-old grandfather if he had a grandson or not?

But the Indian in me understood him. You were measured in heaven by the blood of your heirs and *Thatha* didn't want to fall short. At his age, where life was not ahead of him but behind him, it was more important than ever that the Somayajula family name be carried on.

I loved my grandfather dearly despite his anachronistic ways. *Thatha* was a man from an era long gone. A white burly moustache on his creased face made him look distinguished and his eyes were bright as if he couldn't wait for the next day. Unlike *Ammamma*, *Thatha* was always ready with a quick joke, some smart repartee, and mischief. He was also one manipulating son of a bitch and I was now old enough to see it, but it didn't change how I felt about him. I had seen *Thatha* twist and turn people around to suit his needs; I still adored him.

My father disliked my grandfather and disliked him immensely. *Nanna* always had a tough time fitting into my mother's family, but he tried and I commended him for that. My father didn't have a large family and his parents were always traveling— my paternal grandfather worked in the Indian Foreign Services— and *Nanna's* only sister, a doctor, was single and lived in Australia; we hardly ever saw her.

Thatha didn't like my father either. He would always say, but never to *Nanna's* face, "Radha liked him and we said yes, but children make mistakes sometimes."

And maybe it was a mistake. My mother and father were unsuited in so many ways, yet they had managed to stay married for over twenty-eight years. In some sense of the word, they were probably even "happy." But happiness is such a relative term that it sometimes loses definition.

When my father turned twenty-five his family pressured him to get married and four years later he relented. His first arranged proposal was with my mother and he agreed to the match immediately. I think it was because he didn't want to go through any more bride-seeing ceremonies. My father had probably not anticipated the problems that came of living close to his wife's family. Many a fight ended with Ma bringing Nate and me to my grandparents' house. Then *Nanna* would come to get us and there would be a drama of theatrical proportions. All through that drama, *Thatha* would play the villain, at least in *Nanna's* eyes.

During the elaborate fights, Nate and I would pretend that we were on just another trip to *Ammamma's* house. We wouldn't talk about how we felt, but it was there, a lurking fear that Ma would not take us back home and we would never see *Nanna* again.

My parents fought; they always had. But there would be special fights when the argument would escalate to the point where Ma would yell and scream and drag us out of the house. She would be either carrying Nate or dragging him along on one side and on the other she would have my hand in hers in a firm grasp. There would be no running back to Evil *Nanna*.

✳   ✳   ✳

The gate crackled open and I lifted my eyes. *Thatha* was home from the construction site where he was building a new house that he could rent out. When he had told me that they were building yet another house, I had joked he was becoming a regular slumlord. But for *Thatha*, building houses on the land he had purchased years ago was an investment, a future for his heirs, the ones yet to be born.

He stepped inside his plot of land and opened his arms wide.

I raced into them and felt like a little girl again, little Priya with her big old grandfather.

"I was not here to welcome you," he apologized. His eyes wandered to Neelima who had stood up and his sharp gaze I'm sure didn't miss the tears on her cheeks. "What is with her?" he asked me, and nodded at Neelima who scurried inside the house.

"Everyone is being perfectly mean to her," I told him, and inhaled the smell of tobacco and cement that hung on him. *Thatha* chewed tobacco, a nasty habit in any man but him. He made it look dignified; or maybe I was just biased.

"She is imagining it," *Thatha* said, putting his arm around me. We walked inside the veranda and he groaned comically at the voices coming from the hall. "They are *all* here?"

"Mango *pachadi*," I supplied laughing. It was good to see the old man and it was good to be this comfortable with him even after seven years.

He looked around mischievously and then winked at me. "The pomegranate tree has some red, red fruit; let's go," he whispered, and we both sneaked out holding hands.

The pomegranate tree and a few mango trees were scattered in the area between my grandparents' house and the house they gave up for rent. As a child I was not allowed to wander around the fruit trees because more than once I had fallen sick eating too many not so ripe pomegranate seeds.

It was a ritual. We would come for a visit and *Thatha* would sneak me away to eat the forbidden fruit. We would usually get caught because I would end up with some fruit stains on my clothes. My mother would never let it slide. She would kick up a fuss and *Thatha* would apologize and the next time we came for a visit, he would take me to the pomegranate tree again. We were partners in crime. We were pals.

"Here." *Thatha* peeled a pomegranate fruit with his pocketknife, broke it open, and handed me a piece of the fruit. We sat down on the stairs that led to the apartment upstairs and watched the traffic go past the metal gate of his house.

"So how is my American-returned granddaughter?" he asked amicably.

"Doing well. But things here don't seem that . . . well," I said, slurping over juicy pomegranate seeds.

He sighed. "Anand . . ." He paused thoughtfully, then continued, "made a mistake. . . . But what do they say in English? To err is human?"

I shook my head. "He married the woman he loves; that's a blessing, not a mistake."

Thatha's eyes twinkled. "Love isn't all that it is cracked up to be, Priya. Marriage needs a lot more than love."

"But love is essential," I argued.

"You fall in love later," he said with a patriarchal wave of his hand, "*after* you get married and have children "

I wanted to argue the point with him, even though I knew it was futile. He was set in his ways and I in mine. We lived by a different set of philosophies. In his rulebook, duty was high on the list, and in mine, personal happiness was a priority.

"What if you *never* fall in love with your wife . . . or husband?" I questioned.

Thatha gave me another piece of fruit embedded with bright shiny pomegranate seeds. I took it from him and started peeling the seeds off from their rind before popping them into my mouth. It wasn't the season for pomegranates but this one had ripened early and was sweet.

"You always love your wife . . . or husband, as the case might be," he said in that authoritarian tone that broached no further dispute.

But he knew just as well as I did that unlike his children and other grandchildren, that tone would not deter me. It had been that way since the beginning. I had had the most arguments with

Thatha, the most debates, and, ultimately, the most fights. We discussed various subjects and passionately argued our stance; even when I called him from the U.S., we'd get excited talking about something and our tempers would flare. I think he respected me because I was opinionated and not afraid to tell him how I felt and because I openly disagreed with him. Sometimes I felt that I argued a point just to earn his respect. He was important to me; his opinion mattered; he mattered.

The man was a bigot, a racist, a chauvinist, and generally too arrogant for anyone's liking, yet I loved him. Family never came in neat little packages with warranty signs on them. *Thatha* was all that I disliked in people, but he was also a lot more—he had a backbone of steel and an iron will to make the best of a bad situation. When *Thatha* joined the State Bank of AP right after Independence, he was just a lowly bank teller. When he retired he had been a bank manager of the large Hyderabad branch. His never-say-die spirit was also mine. I was his blood; there was no denying it and when our tempers flared I knew that I was a lot more like him than I would like to admit.

"In several arranged marriages, couples don't fall in love with each other, they merely tolerate each other," I told him. "I know some women who are unhappy with the husband their parents chose . . . but they can't do anything about it. Why condemn anyone to a lifetime of unhappiness?"

"Lifetime of unhappiness?" *Thatha* said loudly, mockingly. "Priya, you are talking like we marry our children off to rapists and murderers. Parents love their children and do what is best for them."

I shook my head. "I think a lot of parents don't know their children very well and if they don't know their own child, how can they know what would be best for them?"

"You think you're smarter than your parents?" *Thatha* asked pointedly.

"Sometimes."

Thatha laughed, a big booming sound, reverberating from inside his chest. "This hair didn't get white in the sun," he said, patting his thick white hair, which refused to give way to baldness despite his age.

"You think you are very smart?" I asked.

Thatha just grinned.

"Well . . . what do you think about Lata being pregnant for all the wrong reasons?" I asked because it was nagging me.

"I said I was smart, not broad-minded." *Thatha* arched his right eyebrow, in the way my mother could, I could. "But it also depends upon what your reasons are. I believe the family name has to be carried on."

"At any cost?"

"Not at *any* cost " *Thatha* said, and smiled.

"Neelima is pregnant, you know," I informed him, and saw his eyes darken with anger. "What if she has a son?"

"Then she has a son," he shrugged.

The calm way in which he declared a grandchild inconsequential to his plans angered me. "What if . . . *Nanna* was not a Brahmin? What if Ma and *Nanna* had fallen in love and had gotten married? Would you not be my *Thatha*?"

He stood up then and I knew I had crossed some imaginary line he had laid down. "We will never know," he said coolly, and then he broke into a smile. "You are here for another few days," he urged brightly. "I don't want to argue over something that does not concern you."

I was defeated but I knew I had to choose my battles. "Let's go inside," I suggested. "It's time for lunch, maybe I can help cook."

"Make some *avial*. You make the best *avial*, " he ordered sweetly.

Avial was the only South Indian dish I cooked that tasted the way it should. *Thatha* loved my *avial*, even more than he liked Ma's.

✳ ✳ ✳

To: Priya Rao <Priya_Rao@yyyy.com>
From: Nicholas Collins <Nick_Collins@xxxx.com>
Subject: Re: Re: Good trip?

Haven't heard from you. You must be at your Grandma's place making pickle. Just wanted to tell you that you are missed.
Nick

✳ ✳ ✳

Part Two

Oil and Spices

Avial (South Indian)

1 cup sour curds (for yogurt)
150 grams of yam or yellow pumpkin
2 raw bananas
2 drumsticks (an Indian vegetable available fresh or
    canned)
1 potato
½ cup shelled peas
½ teaspoon turmeric powder
¼ cup coconut oil
a few curry leaves
salt to taste

For Paste
½ coconut
6 to 7 green chiles
1 teaspoon cumin seeds

Grind together the coconut, green chiles, and cumin seeds to make a fine paste, adding very little water while grinding. Mix the curd with the ground paste and keep aside. Peel and chop all the vegetables and cook separately with a little water. Mix all the cooked vegetables and salt and turmeric powder. Add the paste to the vegetables and heat through—take care to prevent curdling. Remove from heat and add coconut oil and curry leaves, and mix well. Serve hot with rice.

Thatha and
His Merry Women

*T*hatha was not supposed to have married *Ammamma* in the
first place. It had happened by accident. *Thatha* had gone
to *Ammamma's* village with his parents to see *Ammamma's* cousin
and arrange a marriage with her.

"But I saw *her*," *Thatha* said, "and I wanted to marry her only.
What did I know? I was just fifteen."

"My father agreed to the proposal immediately," *Ammamma*
would say, giggling as if she were indeed thirteen years old and a
blushing bride. "Ratna, (the poor cousin), didn't speak to me for
five years after that. But she got married, too, and her husband . . .
He is a doctor, owns his own clinic in Vaisakh. What luck, enh?"

I was never sure if the story indicated that *Thatha* and *Ammamma* were pleased about being married to each other or if
Thatha felt he had been too young to have made the right decision
and *Ammamma* thought she could have married the doctor if
Ratna had married *Thatha*.

In any case, happiness and love was not the point of their marriage. They had two sons and two daughters and now they were trying to have a son's son; they were living the righteous life and no one could tell them otherwise.

"Eating pomegranates again?" Ma asked, as soon as *Thatha* and I entered the hall.

While I had been sneaking around fruit trees with *Thatha*, the others had done some major damage with the mangoes. Slices of mango were spread out evenly for different purposes. There were thick slices of peeled mangoes in a bucket alongside a big sheet of white muslin cloth. These I assumed were for making another type of mango pickle, *maggai*.

For *maggai*, slices of mango covered with turmeric, salt, and oil had to be dried for two days in the hot sun. After they were dry and almost brittle, they were marinated in a mixture of oil and spices. Another set of chopped mangoes languished in colored plastic buckets. The dark pink and yellow buckets were Lata's, the neon green and light pink ones were Ma's, the three red ones were *Ammamma's*, and the blue one was Neelima's.

The mangoes used for making *avakai* still had their skin and stone casing intact. My lips twitched into a smile as I remembered how the remnants of mango pickle lay on discarded plates of food after a meal—the core of the mango stones lay in bloody red oil like dead and mutilated soldiers in a battlefield of yogurt and rice. I used to think it was barbaric, eating the pickle with bare hands, tearing into the fleshy part of the mango that stuck to the core. Now I thought it was exotic, as if from a different culture and therefore tolerable.

"Oh come on, Radha, I am seeing my granddaughter after seven years." *Thatha* put his arm around me. "And the pomegranates were ripe, she won't fall sick."

My mother smiled to my utter shock. There were perks to seeing my parents once in seven years—everything was easily forgiven, within limits, of course. Wanting to marry an American probably did not fall in the easy to forgive category. I smiled uneasily and *Thatha* tightened his arm around me.

"So, when are you going to get her married?" he asked as if he could read my mind and I shifted in his grip.

My mother's smile turned into a pout. "As soon as we find a nice boy. . . . Someone she can't find anything wrong with. Every boy we sent to her, she doesn't like. Like they have horns growing out of their heads or something." She sighed deeply. "*Nanna*, you have to talk to her now," she said as if he was her last hope in convincing me to get married. I wasn't listening to my own father, what made her think I would listen to hers?

Sowmya tucked the edge of her sari around her waist and picked up a bucket filled with thick slices of peeled mango, lying listlessly, squished against each other. Seeing it as a chance to avoid talking about my marriage I picked up the other bucket, which was filled with oil, turmeric, and salt.

"Neelima, can you bring the muslin cloth upstairs?" Sowmya called out when we reached the stairs to go up to the terrace. "So much to be done and Lata *and* your mother do absolutely nothing. They just sit around giving orders. Must've been queens, *maharanis*, in some past life."

I grinned. "*And* they take all the credit for the *pachadi*."

Sowmya snorted. "I make better *avakai* than both of them. You think they would come upstairs and strain their backs a little? Nothing. They will sit downstairs under the fan while we sweat up here."

On the terrace there was a coconut-straw bed that was used for the purpose of drying mangoes or any other fruit or vegetable that needed to get some sun. And it was a good place to get some sun—heat scorched the cement floor, burning everything in its wake.

"Ouch, ouch, ouch." Sowmya and I danced on the cement floor as the heat burned our bare feet. We reached the coconut-straw bed next to which tall coconut trees threw some shade on the floor, making it cooler, bearable to touch with the soles of our feet.

"Should've worn slippers," I said. "I'd forgotten how hot it gets."

"Ah, slippers are for babies," Sowmya said, laughing. "I don't know how you can stand the cold in the States. It gets very cold, doesn't it?"

I shrugged. "In San Francisco I think it's always cold. But it gets quite hot in the summers in the Bay Area and yes, a little cold, nothing drastic. It doesn't snow or anything."

"Why is it always cold in San Francisco?"

"It's by the bay. Lots of people joke that the coldest winter they endured was a summer in San Francisco."

"Then why do you live there?" Sowmya asked.

"Because I like the city," I said. I didn't tell her that it was Nick who liked the city a lot more than I did. I wouldn't mind living in the South Bay with the Indian restaurants and Indian movie theaters in arm's reach. But Nick liked the way he could just walk from our apartment and find a café to get a cup of coffee and a croissant.

"Can't have *tandoori* chicken early in the morning," Nick would say when I would complain about San Francisco, and how I hated to find parking when I got home every day from working in the South Bay, and how wonderful it would be to live close to all those Indian restaurants.

But my bitching and moaning aside, I liked living in San Francisco as well; not as much as Nick, but I certainly liked being able to live amidst the bustle of the city. I liked having an apartment from where I could look at San Francisco and know that I was *here*, in the U.S., in the land of opportunities. I had worked so hard to get here and nothing said America as clearly to me as standing in the balcony with a cup of coffee looking at the city of San Francisco.

Neelima came upstairs and spread the muslin cloth on the co-conut straw bed. We dunked the mangoes in the bucket filled with oil, salt, and turmeric.

It was great fun, just like the olden times when I was a child visiting my grandparents. My hands would smell of turmeric and stay yellow for days. I hadn't done this for so long and I was stung by the loss. I had lost so much since I had left India and I hadn't even thought about it. I had become so much a part of America that the small joys of dunking pieces of mango inside gooey paste were forgotten and not even missed.

It was as if there were two people inside me: Indian Priya and American Priya, Ma's Priya and Nick's Priya. I wondered who the real Priya was.

I had always thought that self-evaluation was nonsense. It didn't really mean anything. How could you not know yourself? I believe we know who we are, we know the exact truth about ourselves, and it is when this truth is not palatable that we want to dig deeper within our conscience to find something better, something we can live with. Did I need to dig deeper now, to ex-plore who I was beyond Nick's Priya and Ma's Priya?

We laid the oil- and spice-coated pieces of mango on the cloth, our yellow fingerprints marking the pristine white muslin.

"Did you tell your *Thatha*?" Neelima asked without looking at me, and suddenly I was face to face with familial politics again.

Everything was so complicated and it struck me like a sack of mangoes—I couldn't live here. Nostalgia for a mango and HAP-PINESS was one thing, living here on a day-to-day basis was im-possible. I didn't want to live close to my family anymore. I had been in *Thatha's* house just a few hours and I was already seething with feminine rage over half a dozen things.

I wanted to distance myself from India and my family; I wanted to feel nothing, pretend this was happening to someone else, not me; but I couldn't. I knew these people and they knew me; however dark and ugly it might get, I would still know them and they me. There was no delusional escape, this was the here and now, and whether I liked it or not, I was here now.

"I told him," I murmured softly.

Neelima wanted *Ammamma* and *Thatha's* approval but she was never going to get it, not complete and total approval. For that she would have to die and come back as a Telugu Brahmin. I felt sorry for her even as I felt annoyance. Why was she here? If Nick's family treated me the way *Ammamma* and *Thatha* treated Neelima, I would give Nick hell and make sure I didn't deal with his family.

As it was, Nick's family was wonderful. Whenever we went to visit them in Memphis, they were all hugs and acceptance. When I went with Nick the first time, it was for Thanksgiving and I was very nervous. What if they didn't like me? I was an Indian and I wondered if they would hate me for that as my parents would hate Nick for being American.

Nick's mother didn't care about my ethnicity but she was undoubtedly fascinated by my Indianness. When we met for the first time she told me, "I've never spoken to an Indian before, but I love curry."

And over curry powder and turkey, Nick's mother—Frances—and I became friends. She was an adorable woman who always remembered my birthday and sent me a gift, something she knew I wanted. She would investigate, harass Nick for information and try to find out from conversations with me what I wanted and then she would ensure that the birthday gift reached me wrapped and packed and on the mark. She always talked about our "impending" wedding and changed the reception dinner menu regularly—her way of asking us to hurry up and tie the knot and of course give her grandchildren.

Nick's father had died five years ago and from what Nick told me about him, I was sorry to have not met him. He used to be a high school football coach and apparently never held a grudge when Nick became an accountant and his brother, Doug, a sous-chef in New Orleans.

"He used to joke that we were sissies," Nick said when I asked him about his father. "I miss him. He never told us what to do. I think if I wanted to be a ballet dancer, Dad would have called me a sissy and then would have driven me to ballet lessons."

Frances had called me before I came to India. "Tell them you're pregnant. They'll want you to marry my Nick right away, " she joked when I told her that I was more than a little nervous about telling my family about Nick.

"So what did your *Thatha* say about the baby?" Neelima asked demurely.

"Nothing," I replied, and sat down cross-legged, my right hand still inside the pink bucket. "Why do you keep coming here, Neelima?" I asked bluntly, and her eyes met mine with shock.

"Priya!" Sowmya gasped.

I shook my head and put my hand on the cloth and made a yellow handprint. "I didn't mean it that way, " I said finally. "I mean, they treat you . . . well, they treat you like they don't like you."

"How will they like her if they don't know her?" Sowmya jumped to Neelima's defense.

"Do you really believe that knowing her will make them like her?" I asked slightly irritated. "Anand keeps sending her here and they . . . they don't want to like her, Sowmya."

Neelima sniffled and we both turned our attention to her. Lord! Did the woman have to cry? I disliked women who cried incessantly over one thing or the other. Neelima had been bawling or on the verge of doing so ever since I met her.

"Come, come," Sowmya nudged her sister-in-law with her elbow because both her hands were drenched in turmeric.

"Crying is not going to solve your problem," I admonished,

and they both looked like two little puppies I had kicked with high-heeled boots.

"Don't be mean," Sowmya said sternly. "You don't know what she has been through."

I shrugged. "Does it matter? So she has been through hell, I understand, but I don't see why she should keep coming back here for more of it."

"Because Anand wants me to," Neelima said, and wiped her tears with the sleeve of her red blouse. "He keeps making me come here so that his parents will . . . accept us. But they don't, do they? Priya is right, Sowmya. They just don't want to."

"It takes time," Sowmya said solemnly.

"How much time?" Neelima demanded sarcastically. "We have been married for over a year now; I am going to have a baby soon. How will they treat my child?"

"You may have a son and Lata may have a daughter," I said, trying to lighten the atmosphere just a little.

Sowmya and Neelima smiled.

"How about your parents?" I asked. "Are they okay with Anand?"

Neelima nodded. "They like him very much. They even tried to get friendly, but they don't want to have anything to do with my parents. We tried, you know; we called them all to our house so that the parents could meet and everything. But they didn't even come, called at the last minute making up an excuse about some water problem in the house. My mother was so upset and my father . . . bless that man, he told me to be careful and that he would support me through anything."

Sowmya glared at her. "Meaning?"

Neelima stuck her hand inside the pink bucket and laid out the remaining fistful of mangoes on the muslin and started to spread them.

"Neelima?" Sowmya persisted, and Neelima threw the last piece of mango down forcefully.

"Just that," she retorted angrily. "Your parents treat me like garbage and mine treat him so well. If things don't work out and if Anand persists on making his parents happy, what choice do I have?"

I was shocked. Divorce! Was she talking about divorce and being a single mother?

"But I am pregnant now," she added, and then shook her head. "Anand and I are very happy together."

Sowmya was pleased with that answer. "My parents will come around."

It was a hollow promise. They would finally, someday, accept her, but she would always be the woman who stole their sweet, little, innocent boy.

"Let us get out of here before one of us gets a sunstroke," I advised the duo, and we went downstairs to cook lunch.

Lata and Ma were already in the kitchen chopping vegetables, talking about a wedding they had attended a couple of weeks ago.

"She was fat . . . so fat," Lata was saying. "And he . . . What a catch!"

"I heard that they gave thirty *lakhs* in dowry, and that was just hard cash, plus a new Honda," Ma said conspiratorially.

"Thirty *lakhs* . . . So much money they have and they bought her a nice husband with it," Lata shrugged, and they both looked up at us when we entered the kitchen.

"Can I help?" Neelima asked politely, and was immediately shooed away. She didn't cry this time; just twirled around and asked Sowmya to show her the new saris she had bought at a sari sale last week. I sat down on the floor next to my mother and looked at the vegetables in steel containers that were strewn around.

"There is half a coconut in the fridge," Lata informed me. "You will need it for the *avial*."

I got the coconut out and attached it to the coconut scraper and churned the metal handle. Thin coconut slivers started to fall into a steel container.

My mother got up to leave. I knew she was not happy that my grandfather wanted me to cook. I didn't know when I joined a race with my mother, but I felt like she charted everything that *Thatha* said on a scoreboard and the score today was: Priya—one, Ma—zero.

"My back hurts," Ma complained unconvincingly, even as she rubbed her hand on the small of her back. "I will go rest with your *Ammamma*. You can take care, can't you?"

I made an assenting sound but didn't look up from my coconut.

"She is unhappy with you," Lata said, as she brushed an errant hair from her perfect, heart-shaped face.

"She's always unhappy," I said sulkily, and she laughed.

"You have to eventually get married," Lata said. She pulled a flat block of wood toward her and tugged out the folded blade that sat on it. She leaned her perfectly pedicured right foot on the block and started slicing potatoes on the sharp knife. Her gold toe ring and the bright red nail polish glimmered against the worn wood.

"Eventually, I will get married," I said. "I never figured out how to use that knife. I was always scared that I'd walk into it."

"It is easy," Lata said, and sliced another potato with a flourish. "So, do you have a boyfriend? Is that why you keep saying no to marriage?"

Was she being perceptive or merely voicing a popular familial opinion that my mother had failed to tell me about?

"I'm just twenty-seven, plenty of time to get married," I evaded. "And please don't tell me how when you were twenty-seven you were married with kids."

Lata dropped another sliced-up potato into the big steel bowl of water to keep it from changing color. "I won't tell you that because you already know it. But twenty-seven is late. When will you have children? The sooner the better, otherwise . . . you may not be able to have children."

"Maybe I don't want any children," I said annoyed. Was there no originality among the women of my family? One aunt said I should learn to cook so that my husband won't starve, while the other wanted me to get pregnant in case my reproductive organs gave up on me. And adding insult to injury was my mother who wanted me to marry any man who made what she considered "good money."

"All women want children," Lata said negligently. "So, my brother who lives in Los Angeles told me that nowadays Indians— not those foreigners, but Indian girls and boys—live together . . . do *everything* when they are not married. Why can't they simply get married?"

"Because they want to live together for a while, not spend the rest of their lives together. Maybe they just want to test the waters. Marriage is serious business. You don't marry the first guy you sleep with or live with for that matter," I said for the sole purpose of scandalizing the living daylights out of her.

From her shocked facial expression, I knew I had succeeded. But I knew she would mention this to my mother, or worse, to *Thatha*, and then there would be questions galore.

She looked at me sharply. "Would you live with a man without marrying him?"

Talking to Lata felt akin to walking into enemy territory where booby traps lay everywhere. "Does everything have to be about me?" I commended myself on the poker face I wore.

Lata continued to chop potatoes. "You know, Anand and Neelima . . . they did *it* before marriage. I think that is why they got married."

"Because they had sex?" I stopped scraping the coconut and then started again.

Lata picked up a bottle gourd, as green in color as the cotton sari she was wearing, and started to cut it into big chunks to make it easy to peel and then chop for the *pappu*.

"We are not like all those white women who have sex with hundreds of men. We marry the man we have sex with. Neelima trapped him," she said.

"Why would he marry her because he had sex with her? How should that matter?" I knew it was pointless to discuss Neelima or the institution of marriage with Lata, but my mouth ran away before I could put a leash on it.

"Anand is a nice boy," Lata explained her twisted logic. "Neelima seduced him and he had to marry her."

"So they're not a happily married couple?" I asked over the sound of the scraper rolling inside the now bare shell of coconut. I discarded the shell and ran my fingers through the white slivers of coconut lying in the steel bowl.

Lata placed a yellow pumpkin lying next to her in front of me. I put it on top of the elevated wooden chopping board my mother had been using. I then rose to pick out a large, smooth-edged knife from the knife holder standing by the sink.

"Anand seems happy," she remarked. "But you can never know for real. You can't, you know, judge a book by its cover."

I agreed with her. But if I were to go by covers, Lata and Jayant appeared to have a lousy marriage. They were perpetually at each other's throats. There was no blatant fighting; it was more the bickering, the constant animosity. One look at Jayant and Lata was enough to put anyone off of arranged marriage. Their marriage was obviously not working but they were still together in what appeared to be a stifling relationship, while baby number three was on the way. I wondered whose decision it had been to have another baby, Jayant's or Lata's. Who had given in to the pressure I am sure *Thatha* had firmly put on the couple?

"How are Apoorva and Shalini doing?" I changed the topic to her children as I cut through the large yellow pumpkin.

"Very well," she said with pride. "Shalini started *Bharat-natyam* classes and she dances with so much grace, and Apoorva is learning how to play the *veena*. I always say it is important for girls to know some classical dance or music."

"How do they feel about getting a little brother or a sister?"

She raised her eyebrows holding a piece of bottle gourd in midair. She slid it on the blade and put two pieces of the gourd in the steel bowl by her side. "Who told you? Neelima?"

"Not Neelima," I lied, as I started parting the peel of the pumpkin from its flesh.

Lata picked up the pieces of peeled pumpkin and sliced them on the blade jutting out of the wooden board and dropped them in another steel bowl.

"They made me," she said. "First, it was just *Mava* and then it was *Atha* and then Jayant started. What could I say? I have some duty toward my husband's family."

"What if you have another daughter?" I asked what was probably the most taboo question.

"I won't," she told me with fervor, as if even thinking about it would make it happen. "I know I could, but I hope I won't. All this for nothing, then."

"What will you do if it's a girl?" I persisted.

Lata smiled softly and met my eyes without flinching. "I love my children. I don't care if they are girls or boys. And I will love this baby, too. I only want it to be a boy so that *your Thatha* will be happy."

I didn't believe her.

"We will find out next week whether the baby is a boy or girl," she added. "They can tell in the sixteenth week itself these days with that amnio test."

"And then?"

"Then we will know."

I didn't care to ask her if she would have an abortion at that point; somehow, I didn't want to know the answer.

All this for nothing, then, she had said, and her words echoed in my brain for a long time.

✳ ✳ ✳

Lunch was served at the large dining table that filled the entire dining area next to the kitchen. Steel plates clinked on the Formica table and steel glasses tried to find a foothold. The table was in disharmony with its surroundings. The Formica clashed with the red and yellow window frame against which the table leaned; it took up too much space and didn't really match with the cane dining chairs that *Thatha* had bought years before he had the table.

The Formica itself was lumpy, marred by errors of placing a hot pot directly on it or spilling water that seeped in between the thin vinyl layer and cheap wood.

The new dining table had replaced a sturdy old wooden table, which was just a few feet high and required us to sit cross-legged on straw mats to eat. But that table had to be put away in storage when *Ammamma's* arthritis demanded something that would be easy on her knees. *Thatha* bought the table at a small furniture store in Abids that specialized in gaudy TV stands and sold other assorted items of the same low quality as the dining table.

Thatha had liked the size of the table and the shining top had appealed to him as well. It had taken only six months for the shining top to become dull and lumpy, but by then the small furniture store had closed down and *Thatha* got stuck with the table, lumps and all.

A mound of hot rice settled in the center of the table and around it dark bobbing heads joined steel utensils filled with *avial,* bottle gourd *pappu,* potato curry, and cold yogurt.

Two jugs of ice-cold water were emptied in little time and the ceiling fan rattled endlessly, providing little surcease from the interminable heat. But I was getting used to it.

"Have you been to *Noo Yark*?" my grandmother asked as she attacked her food, her mouth open as she chewed.

"Yes," I said, and dropped my eyes to my plate where my fingers danced with the rice and the creamy bottle gourd *pappu*. How easy it was to eat with my fingers again. I had forgotten the joys of mixing rice and *pappu* with my fingers. Food just tasted better when eaten with such intimacy.

"Very good *avial*, *Priya-Amma*," *Thatha* remarked, and I nodded, pleased with the compliment.

"*Noo Yark* is a dangerous place, it is," *Ammamma* said, smacking her lips together and mixing the rice with *avial* on her plate with her fingers.

"The white people are just . . . crooks," she continued, and my head shot up. "And the black people . . . those *kallu* people are all criminals."

My eyes widened with shock.

"And how do you know this?" I asked, unable to completely submerge my instinct to get on my antiracism soapbox. Nick would love to be in on this conversation, I thought.

"I see Star TV," *Ammamma* said proudly. "All black people are doing drugs and they kill on the street. Vishnu . . . you remember him?"

I didn't, but I nodded.

"His son was mugged by a *kallu* person in *Noo Yark*. A black man"—she dropped some food into her mouth—"put a gun to his head." She spoke with her mouth full and I grimaced at her words and the half-chewed visible food. "All black people . . . dirty they are."

And what had my grandmother done—smelled their clothes? Frustration warred with the reality of the situation in front of me, and reality won.

"That is right," *Thatha* spoke up, and exhibited his ignorance. "All white people do is exploit the others. And the black people kill. That country is just . . . no family values, nothing. All the time they get divorced."

"They have a moral structure, *Thatha*." I could hardly sit silent in front of such blatant disregard for the facts.

"What moral structure?" Ma glowered. "Your friends . . . what, Manju and Nilesh, they were fine when they were here and they would have been fine if they had not gone to America."

Manju and Nilesh were classmates from engineering college in India. They started their romance in the first year of college and survived as a couple through four years of engineering college, two years of graduate school in the United States, and a year or so of working in Silicon Valley before getting married. But happily ever after had evaded them. They had recently divorced and I made the big mistake of telling Ma about it. She immediately decided that it was because of the evil American influence.

"These friends of hers got married," Ma explained to the others. "Same caste, same . . . real good match. They went to America and now they are getting a divorce after four years of marriage. What happened? If they were in India, it would have never happened."

She was absolutely right. They definitely would not have gotten a divorce in India. After all, divorce was still not commonplace. The pressure from their families would have kept them together even as Nilesh screwed everything in a skirt including Manju's older married cousin.

"Why did they get a divorce?" Neelima asked softly.

"Does it matter?" my mother launched into a tirade. "They got a divorce and they would have been married if they were here in India. There . . . no one cares. Women have three, four marriages and all the men cheat on their wives. They all sleep around."

This was why I knew it was going to be a tough, tough thing

to tell the family about Nick. They had condemned the entire Western world to being immoral criminals and crooks. What chance did poor Nick stand in getting a fair trial?

"They don't *all* sleep around," I defended. "In the South, couples don't have sex until they get married. They're very religious there."

I don't know how and why this discussion was taking place. I couldn't remember discussing sex in any fashion with my family ever before. Sowmya and I would talk about it once in a while, but that was girl talk. This was simply too weird.

"And then there are those religious fanatics," *Thatha* added, and I lost it.

"And here there are none?" I demanded. "How can you say that about the West when you know nothing about it?

"Damn it, this country has its own screw-ups. Men beat up their wives and the wives stick to their marriages. At least in America they have a way out. They can walk out of their sick marriages. Here people don't decide who they should marry, spend the rest of their lives with—their parents do. That seems okay to you?"

Silence fell like rain in monsoon. *Thatha* looked at me with the look reserved for the belligerent or the retarded—I wasn't sure which.

"You only *live* in the States. It is not your country. They will never accept you. You will always be an outsider there, a dark person. Here they will accept you and don't use foul language in this house," *Thatha* said.

"Accept me?" I was on a roll so I stepped into cow dung, big time. "I apologize for the foul language, but, *Thatha*, you don't accept Neelima because she comes from another state. You don't accept Indians and you expect me to believe I'm accepted in this society. How long will this society accept me if I want to live by my own rules?"

"All societies have rules," Lata launched into the discussion. "You have to follow American society rules, don't you?"

I smiled that sick sarcastic smile I was warned against by Ma all my life. "Yes, but in that society no one can pressure me into having a child so that a family can have a male heir and—"

"*Priya.*" My mother silenced me with that one sharp word. "You don't know what you are talking about."

Silence fell again. Except for the chewing of food and the movements of steel utensils, no one said anything.

Now I had done it and I wanted to kick myself. This was not how I was going to soften the blow—this was how I was going to make it more severe. Of all the stupid things to do I had to go and try to change my family's mind about the evil and corrupt Western world. I might as well have tried to climb Mt. Everest in my shorts.

❊   ❊   ❊

To: Nicholas Collins <Nick_Collins@xxxx.com>
From: Priya Rao <Priya_Rao@yyyy.com>
Subject: Re: Re: Re: Good trip?

I found an Internet cafe, just down the street from *Ammamma*'s house. Small place, charges Rs. 30 for 15 minutes and the connection is sooooo slow, it crawls. Nevertheless, it exists and seven years ago it didn't. I'm constantly surprised at how some things have changed and how some things are exactly the same.

Just met with *Thatha* and, Nick, the man is a chauvinist. I mean, the man is a freak, out of a museum. And the rest of them are equally bad. I told you about Anand and how he married Neelima. Well, you should see how everyone treats the poor girl—slapping her across the face repeatedly would be kind.

AND YOU WON'T BELIEVE THIS, BUT LATA IS PREGNANT AGAIN. *THATHA* WANTS A PUREBLOODED BRAHMIN GRANDSON AND ANAND'S SON, IF HE HAS ONE, WON'T CUT IT. NEELIMA ISN'T A TELUGU BRAHMIN, YOU SEE, JUST A MAHARASHTRIAN ONE. THIS FEELS LIKE A BAD TELUGU MOVIE; ALL THE CHARACTERS ARE THERE IN DIFFERENT SHADES OF GRAY: THE INTRACTABLE MOTHER-IN-LAW, THE VILE SISTER-IN-LAWS, THE SPINELESS HUSBAND, THE PATRIARCHAL FATHER-IN-LAW, AND, OF COURSE, THE POOR DAUGHTER-IN-LAW FROM THE OTHER CASTE.

I'M NOT GETTING ALONG WITH MA EITHER. I'M TRYING HARD AND FAILING. FOR ONCE I WANTED US TO BE FRIENDS AND I THOUGHT THAT NOW THAT I'M OLDER, WE WOULD BE FRIENDS. NOT HAPPENING FOR US. AND IT HURTS. I HAD THIS FANTASY OF US GETTING ALONG ONCE I GOT BACK. BUT TIME HAS HAD ABSOLUTELY NO EFFECT ON OUR RELATIONSHIP.

NATE HAS GONE HIKING WITH FRIENDS AND I'M STUCK HERE WITH THE RELATIVES FROM HELL. I WANT SO MUCH FOR THEM TO BE DIFFERENT, MORE ACCEPTING, LESS JUDGMENTAL, LESS RACIST, MORE TOLERANT. I WANT THEM TO ACCEPT YOU. BUT THE MORE I SEE, THE MORE I REALIZE THAT IT ISN'T GOING TO HAPPEN.

HOW AM I GOING TO TELL THEM, NICK? HOW ON EARTH AM I SUPPOSED TO TELL THEM ABOUT YOU? IT'S GOING TO BREAK MY HEART TO BREAK THEIRS. BUT I LOVE YOU AND I CAN'T DREDGE UP AN OUNCE OF GUILT . . . AND THAT MAKES ME FEEL GUILTY. I'M SUPPOSED TO FEEL GUILT, RIGHT?

ANYWAY, GOT TO GO. THE MAN AT THE FRONT DESK IS

LOOKING AT HIS WATCH AND THEN AT ME . . . SUBTLE AS A
CHAINSAW. I'LL COME BY AGAIN AND CHECK EMAIL.

AND, I AM NOT GOING TO MARRY SOME INDIAN
BOY!! HOW CAN YOU THINK THAT, EVEN IRRATIONALLY?

AND I'M COMING HOME AS SOON AS I CAN.
PRIYA

* * *

Swimming in Peanut Oil
and Apologies

Ma all but dragged me out to the back yard after lunch. "You might be here just for a few days but you *will* behave yourself," she said, gripping my arm tightly.

I jerked her hand off and rubbed the small bruises her fingers left behind. "I will say what I feel like saying. If you don't like it, I can pack up and leave." That was not what I really wanted to say, but I was angry and furious at being treated like a five-year-old. I was a twenty-seven-year-old woman; I was not a child. When would they learn that? And then again, when would I learn to act my age? Why did I have to go off the deep end over matters that did not concern me? I knew that; I knew that it didn't really matter what *Thatha* or *Ammamma* thought about black people or white. Yet I couldn't help myself and couldn't regret what I said. Somehow I felt justified in taking umbrage at what they had said because I was *right*. But that didn't change the fact that I had behaved badly and hurt my grandfather, my aunt, my

grandmother, and my mother. Now if only I could find some beg-
gars on the street to kick, I could call it a day.

"Are you threatening me?" Ma demanded, and I just gave her
a "yeah sure" look but didn't say anything.

"Are you?" she asked again, her eyes boring into mine.

I didn't look away. Sometimes it was better to face the demons
than ignore them. All that was left now was to purse my lips in a
pout to look like a recalcitrant adolescent. Just the image I was
trying not to portray. How could I convince them to trust my
judgment in men if I was pouting like a child?

"All the sacrifices we made for you," Ma said in disgust. "And
this is how you repay us?"

I raised one eyebrow negligently and the little guilt I was feeling took a nosedive. "Ma, put a sock on the sacrifice routine," I said
with belligerence, all my vows of being the perfect daughter for the
two week trip vanishing completely. This "you owe us" line was
not one I liked, not one I believed in. I hadn't put a petition to my
parents asking them to give birth to me. It was their choice and
since they made that choice I couldn't owe them.

My mother's eyes raged at me and she was about to say something when Sowmya came into the back yard with the dirty dishes
in a blue plastic tub for the maid to clean. She set the tub down
next to a plastic bucket that lay directly beneath a leaky water tap.
For a while there was just the sound of the drops of water, drip-
drip-drip, landing on a steel plate recently rinsed by Sowmya.

She looked at both of us and put a hand on my mother's
shoulder. "We are getting the oil and spices together," she said
calmly.

Ma nodded vaguely, obviously shook up by my statement. I
refused to feel guilty. All my life my mother had been drilling in
me the "we sacrificed for you, so you have to be our slave" line and
I had had it up to here. If I would think about it calmly I would
see that I was exaggerating. My parents had given me a lot of
leeway compared to so many other parents. They had afforded me

a good education. They had spent a decent amount of money to send me to the United States and make a better life. Sure they always tried to get me married but they never forced a decision on me as I had seen other parents do.

A classmate of mine in engineering college had ended up marrying a man she didn't even like the look of because her parents insisted that it was the best match she could get. He was not asking for any dowry—it was her lucky day!

"All this is the influence of America," Ma concluded. "You were never such a bad or rude girl before."

She went inside and I curbed the impulse to run behind her with apologies. The love-hate relationship I shared with Ma was peppered with guilt and seasoned with the need for acceptance, I think from both sides. I wanted—no, sometimes needed—acceptance from Ma, but I wanted her to accept me the way I was, not the way she envisioned me to be. I wanted her to love Priya the person, not Priya the daughter who didn't live outside of her imagination.

"Priya." Sowmya tried to soothe me and I raised both my hands to silence her.

"She doesn't want to believe that I am who I am, so she blames America for it," I said caustically. "She doesn't want to believe that I don't really like her or care that she and *Nanna* made a thousand sacrifices for me."

Lies, all lies. I did care, how could I not? But like gifts that become uncouth burdens when pointed at with ownership by the giver, Ma and *Nanna's* sacrifices seemed to be uncomfortable loads that I didn't want to acknowledge because I was being asked to.

"But they did," Sowmya argued.

I twisted around and faced Sowmya. "And that makes me what? Their property?"

"Just their daughter."

I shook my head. Sowmya knew better than anyone that a daughter was a piece of property, something you unloaded after a certain point. Sowmya had already become excess baggage and my grandparents were waiting to get her married and out of their house.

In Telugu, the word for girl is *adapilla*, where *ada* means theirs and *pilla* means girl. In essence, the creators of the language had followed the rules of society and deemed that a girl was never her parents', always the in-laws', always belonging to someone else rather than to those who birthed and raised her.

"But I'm not just a daughter, I am me," I said wearily, trying not to sound like a cliché. "No one seems to give a damn about me. Everyone is interested in their daughter, granddaughter . . ." I let my words trail away as I wiped from my face tears that had fallen, unbeknownst to me.

"Let us go inside," Sowmya suggested, uneasy I believed with my show of emotion. "We have to put the mango pieces in peanut oil."

We sat down again in the living room. My grandfather was taking a nap in the adjoining bedroom and *Ammamma* was snoring softly on the sofa. Ma was pounding on mustard seeds in a large black stone pestle; runaway mustard seeds that had jumped out of the pestle were evidence of the indelicate force she was using to powder them.

I sat down next to Neelima who was pounding dried red chili. Her eyes were watering and I held my breath. There was red hot chili pepper in the air.

Lata was putting fenugreek seeds in another pestle. No one was speaking. I felt I had silenced them all, blown up a bomb, and everyone was now quiet in the aftermath.

"Lata, I'm really sorry," I said humbly. Now that the blood was not roaring in my ears, I knew that I had no right to judge her. She had made the choices she wanted to make and I who claimed that personal choice was of great importance should respect that. Lata gave me a tremulous smile and shrugged. It was more than I deserved.

"Ma," I called out but she didn't even look at me, "I'm sorry, Ma. Really."

She didn't acknowledge the apology and I sighed. There she was again, sulking like a five-year-old, instead of behaving like a grown woman.

Just like me?

"Ma, I'm really, really sorry," I repeated, and she continued to pound on her mustard seeds, probably to drown out my voice.

Sowmya was visibly disturbed and she sat down next to my mother on the floor and spoke softly to her. I couldn't hear what she was saying but, whatever it was, my mother was obviously displeased.

"You stay out of it," Ma bellowed, and Sowmya immediately moved away from her. "She is my daughter and I will do as I want to do."

"*Akka*, she is just here for a few more days," Sowmya said. But her *Akka*, my mother, was in no mood to listen to Sowmya.

"She thinks she can say anything she likes," Ma rattled away as her hands powdered mustard seeds. "So she is in America . . . as if that should impress us." She looked at me and stopped pounding for an instant. "I don't care. If you don't treat me with respect . . . I am your mother after all." She continued the pounding.

"Then you have to learn to treat me with respect, too," I told her very gently, and the shit hit the fan.

"You are too young to gain my respect and you have done nothing so far to gain it," she raged. "Respect! Children respect their parents . . . and that is all there is to it. You have to learn to behave yourself. I am not your classmate or your friend that you can speak to me like this."

The eternal problem! My mother wanted to be a textbook parent while I felt that I was old enough to warrant being treated as an equal. We had had this particular flavor of fighting many times in the twenty years I had lived in her house.

"I said I was sorry, what more do you want?" I demanded in frustration, not using an apologetic tone, not even by a long shot.

"You always say sorry, but you do the same thing again. You don't mean it."

My temper flared once more. "So now I'm a bad and rude person *and* a liar?" I asked petulantly.

"Priya, shush," Sowmya pleaded. "Please don't fight. She is here for such a short time. If you fight like this, she might never come here again."

My mother's eyes blazed at that. "She doesn't have to come here. She is not doing us any favors by coming here. She has done nothing but made our lives miserable." Ma stopped pounding on the mustard seeds and went to work on me instead. "She is twenty-seven years old and she won't marry. Our neighbors keep asking us and we have nothing to say. You are an embarrassment, Priya. You have done nothing to make us proud. So if you don't come back, it won't kill anyone here."

That hurt!

I walked out of the living room in a daze. I reached the veranda and slipped my feet into my slippers, slung my purse on my shoulder, and shakily got the hell out of my grandparents' house.

✳   ✳   ✳

Yellow and black auto rickshaws drove noisily on the thin, broken, asphalt road as I walked on the dirty roadside, sidestepping around rotten banana peels and other unidentified trash. A vendor was pushing a wooden cart on the uneven road as he announced to the world he had fresh coriander and spinach. I walked past the vendor and kept walking. The roads became familiar as they flipped past my eyes.

I wish I had never come, I thought, as I blinked the tears away. I wished Nick was here, just to tell me that everything was okay with my universe. I felt like I was a little girl again, scared that mummy didn't love me. And she didn't, she had just said so. Fresh tears sprang in my eyes even as I brushed the old ones away.

I stopped in front of a small *paan* and *bidi* shop where they sold soda, cigarettes, *bidis, paan,* chewing gum, and black-market porn magazines, the covers of which you could only see through shiny plastic wrappers. They were hidden, but not completely; you could once in a while catch a naked thigh or a dark nipple thrusting against the plastic wrap. A man sat at the hole in the wall and looked at me questioningly.

"*Goli* soda, *hai*?" I asked.

"*Hau,*" the man said with a perfect Hyderabad Hindi accent. "Flavored, or plain?"

"Plain," I said, and dropped a ten rupee note in front of him.

The first time I had *goli* soda, I was five years old. I remember going for a movie with Jayant and Anand; it was an old black-and-white movie made in the thirties called *Mayabazaar,* the bazaar of illusions, a Telugu movie, which I watched even now, whenever I could get ahold of it. It was a magical movie, a small, obscure story plucked from the great epic *The Mahabharata.*

I had seen some other children drink the soda before the movie and I threw a tantrum to get one too. We had been given strict orders by my mother that, no matter what, I should not eat or drink anything at the cinema theater because the food and water was not good there and there was a good chance I would fall sick.

The soda came in thick green bottles and the gas of the soda was blocked inside with a marble. The bottle was opened with a black rubber opener that sucked the marble out with a big popping sound. As a child I could hardly resist the sound of the marble popping out of place and landing inside the neck of the bottle, or the fizz that appeared on top.

After I threw a mile long tantrum, Jayant relented and bought both Anand and me one soda each and made us promise on the top of his head (the theory being that if we went against our promise, Jayant would die) that we wouldn't tell anyone he let us drink *goli* soda. Unfortunately, Jayant had been found out because both Anand and I came down with dysentery and the blame was placed squarely on the unhygienic *goli* soda.

As soon as the shopkeeper opened the bottle I grabbed it eagerly and put it to my lips even as warning bells rang inside my head. This could be a really bad idea if I fell sick for the rest of my visit.

"*Chee*, Priya," Sowmya called out from behind me and I almost jumped at her voice. "Can't you drink a nice cool drink or something? Why does it have to be this . . . *chee* dirty stuff you drink?"

I drank the entire soda before speaking. "It's good stuff," I told her and she sighed.

"Two *meetha paan*," Sowmya said to the shopkeeper and I pulled out money from my purse.

"Can we go sit somewhere?" I asked as I waited to put the *paan* in my mouth and relish the sweetness and taste of it.

Sowmya looked around and pointed to a dilapidated road that had been trampled on by numerous feet and automobiles over the years. We took that road and came close to the Shiva temple our family frequented often because of its proximity. We sat down on a cement bench that had a worn campaign poster on it.

We both chewed noisily on our *paans*. Juices threatened to drip from the corner of my mouth to embarrass me.

"They make the best sweet *paan* at this place near the university," I said, remembering my old engineering college days. "And there is another place in Koti," I added, "where they sell used textbooks."

Sowmya smiled. "Remember when we went there in your final year and drank so much coconut water?"

"Hmm," I said as the forgotten taste of coconut water

streamed through my lips. "Why do Ma and I never get along? I always think I try but . . . in retrospect I can feel that I don't. She makes me feel like a little child and I start to behave like one."

"Maybe you want too much," Sowmya said, plucking a leaf from a bougainvillea bush growing by the bench.

"You don't see too many of those in the U.S.," I said, pointing to the paperlike purple flowers. "Whenever I see a bougainvillea I'm reminded of the house we lived in in Himayatnagar where there were so many of those bushes."

"And your mother had half of them cut down when she found that snake in the bathroom," Sowmya remembered, laughing. "Remember how big the snake was?"

It was a black, thick, coiled cobra that had managed to get inside the bathroom. And Ma had walked in on it when we were all watching TV. The scream she rendered when she saw the snake gave all of us goose bumps and for a second we were a little afraid to go into the bathroom and see the hair-raising monster Ma was crying out about.

"It raised its fangs and hissed," Ma had said hysterically, even after the snake had been killed and burned. "Those bushes, that's where they hide," she told *Nanna*. "You have to cut them all off."

So the bougainvillea bushes went, but *Nanna* left just a few by the gate of the house and Ma always insisted that they should be cut down as well. What if another cobra was lurking there? "They live in pairs." She was fearful until the day we moved out of the rented house into the house Ma and *Nanna* constructed in Chikadpally.

"There are some good memories," I said to Sowmya. "I'm sure there are. . . . I just can't remember them. When it comes to Ma, I can't remember any of the good times."

"I sometimes feel the same way," Sowmya said and patted my shoulder sympathetically. "Want to go inside the temple? It's closed but they got a new *Shivaling*. It is very beautiful, made of black marble, with gold work done on it."

This temple had seen several *pujas* conducted on behalf of and by several of my maternal family members. In the seven years since I had seen it last it hadn't changed much. *Thatha* had brought me here in the morning, the day before I left for Bombay where I caught the 2 A.M. flight to Frankfurt and then onward to the United States.

Thatha had some *puja* performed then. All I could make out from the Sanskrit words mumbled by the *pandit* were my first and last names, and *Thatha's* family name. The old *pandit* with a large potbelly hanging behind his thin ceremonial thread that languished across his chest had seemed grouchy. He had a hoarse voice and he had coughed half a dozen times through the *puja* that *Thatha* had paid for in my name.

"To bless you," *Thatha* said, patting my head fondly. "To wish you the best in your long journey to a whole new world."

There had been quite a crowd that morning. It was just 8 A.M. but several people had already lined up to have *pujas* performed for their loved ones, their cars, computers, children, et cetera.

Thatha and I had taken some consecrated white sugar, *prasadam,* and found a quiet corner in the garden in front of the temple to sit and watch the people, dressed in bright colors, moving with the purpose of God. As we ate the *prasadam* from our hands, the sugar melted in the May heat and made our hands sticky.

"Now don't forget to call . . . often . . . as long as you have the money," *Thatha* told me. "And if you need money, you are really short, then call. . . . I will send you some."

I nodded. I had promised myself that once I left home I would not take any money from my parents or my family. Independence was not just a word to me, I wanted to stand on my own two feet, not run back to *Thatha* and *Nanna* at the first sign of trouble, financial or otherwise.

"I have a tuition waiver," I said to *Thatha*. "I will get some kind of assistantship. I will find a job . . . anything . . . I will be okay."

"Pay attention to your studies," *Thatha* said sternly. "And don't take up some stupid job in some restaurant bussing tables. Okay?"

I had known even then that it wouldn't make any difference whatsoever to *Thatha's* mindset regarding what he thought were lowly jobs for those of a higher caste and I hadn't bothered to convince him otherwise. But now I felt compelled to talk him out of his beliefs about black and white people, Americans, love marriages, and compulsory heirs. Why was it important to me now what had been understandable then?

I didn't know why I had changed from accepting *Thatha* the way he was to a *Thatha* who I wanted to change.

"Look." Sowmya pointed to a thick gold chain studded with diamonds that circled the top of the *Shivaling* inside a cage within the temple. "They say it costs one *lakh* rupees."

"Is that why they have it so nicely locked up?" I asked, barely able to see anything through the thick, closely aligned metal bars between us and the Gods.

"Ah, you know people, they will steal anything, even God's jewelry," Sowmya said. "So silent it is, but in another few hours, there will be so many people here. Are there temples in the U.S.? I know there is one in Pittsburgh; everyone says it is a big temple. All Indians get married there."

I laughed. "I don't think all Indians get married there. But yes, I've heard it's a big temple. There are a couple in the Bay Area. There is a huge one in a place called Livermore and there is another one in Sunnyvale, close to where I work."

"Do you go there often?"

I shrugged. "I've been there a couple times . . . I don't have the time, Sowmya."

I didn't add that I was not particularly religious. I didn't go to any temple because I didn't feel compelled to go.

"Do you go to church, then?" Sowmya asked, and I was taken aback.

"Why would you think that?"

Sowmya shrugged. "Got to follow something, right?"

"No," I shook my head. "I don't go to church."

"I just . . . thought maybe you've changed that way as well," Sowmya said.

"I have changed?" I didn't think I had changed at all.

"Yes," Sowmya said. "You are more . . . stronger. You stand by your opinions a lot more than you used to and you don't let your *Thatha* get away with everything."

I laughed softly. "But my relationship with Ma is still in the same pit."

"Nobody can fix that one, " Sowmya declared, and brought her hands together in prayer with a clap. "Maybe he can"—she pointed to the *Shivaling* with folded hands—"but I don't think so."

We laughed together and then she held my hand and squeezed it. "I am so happy to see you, Priya. You are a welcome change and I have missed you so much." Sowmya hugged me then. "It is so good to talk to someone like this again," she said, and sighed. "But you'll be gone soon."

"I'll come more often from now on," I said impulsively. "Maybe you can come and visit me?"

Sowmya made a face. "Yes, your *Thatha* is waiting for me to go gallivanting around the world unmarried."

"Maybe," I said.

"Maybe," she agreed, and pushed her glasses up her nose.

I was seeing this world, my ex-world from my Americanized vision. This ex-world of mine was different to me now from what it had been before. I saw some things better, while other things had blurred beyond recognition.

Thatha was not my hero anymore because I saw him in a harsher light, an American light that didn't condone men like *Thatha*. I had changed, I agreed with Sowmya. I hoped it was for the better.

✳　✳　✳

Ma wasn't in a better mood when we got back. Despite bad tempers, upset moods, and the exhausting heat, the work in *Ammamma's* pickle sweatshop continued.

Lata was barking orders, while Ma was telling Lata how she was doing everything wrong. Not out of love was this food made, but out of need to prove superiority.

Ammamma was also saying her piece but no one was listening to her. We all listened to Lata and Ma and I felt like a yo-yo doll giving in to whoever spoke the loudest.

For the first time I realized that this mango pickle–making ritual like everything else was a power game. *Ammamma* had lost the battle a long time ago; my mother had been winning, but now Lata had thrown in a googlie—a cricket ball with a spin—by getting pregnant to please the old ones.

Lata and Ma were the contenders while Neelima, Sowmya, and I were spectators. *Ammamma* sometimes played a biased referee while other times she tried to recapture her days of glory.

My relationship with everyone in this room was in some way or the other fractured, but it was my relationship with my grandmother that was the most superficial. *Ammamma* was a feeling, a smell, a memory, not a real person. I knew little about her. I knew who her favorite film star was and which movie she watched repeatedly ever since *Thatha* bought a VCR, but I didn't know how she felt one way or the other about her life, about having given birth to her first child when she was just fifteen years old.

After Ma, it took *Ammamma* ten years to conceive again and I could only imagine how hard those years must have been. It would have been imperative to have a male child, especially for *Thatha,* and it must have been pure torture to wait every month to see if she had a period or not.

Jayant's birth was a miracle, or so everyone claimed. After that *Ammamma* didn't get pregnant for eight years but it hadn't mattered since she'd already delivered the son.

Anand was born when *Ammamma* was thirty-two years old. "I didn't even think I could get pregnant and boom . . . suddenly my belly was growing. Your *Thatha*, he was so happy," she had told me, smiling fondly at Anand.

After Sowmya was born two years later, *Ammamma* started to have uterine problems. When Sowmya was a year old they found a tumor in *Ammamma's* uterus and they had to perform a hysterectomy.

They had also found a tumor in Ma's uterus when I was fifteen. Ma again put the blame squarely on that quack doctor and the birth control pills, but *Ammamma* told me that it was hereditary. Even Ma's *Ammamma* had had a tumor.

"So you have children fast," *Ammamma* always advised. "God may take your womanhood away and then where will that leave you?"

For *Ammamma*, having children was an achievement, something she was proud of. How did she feel today when all her children were grown and most of them ignored what she had to say?

I had asked her once how she felt about being married off so early. "It was the way it was those days," she replied but never told me how *she* felt about following tradition, accepting her fate. I knew nothing about her true feelings, she was just *Ammamma*, the woman who sat on the sofa all day long watching television and eating *paan*.

I didn't know the woman behind the relationship I had with her.

And neither did *Ammamma* know the woman behind her granddaughter.

I looked at all the women in the room and wondered if behind the facade all of us wore for family occasions we were strangers to each other.

I was trying to be the graceful granddaughter visiting from America but my true colors were slipping past the carefully built mockery of myself I was presenting. Maybe the masks worn by the others were slipping, too. Maybe by the end of the day I would know the women behind the masks and they would know me.

I tried once again to talk to Ma but she shunned me and I concluded that she didn't want to look behind the label: DAUGHTER, and didn't want me to look behind the label: MA. If she wouldn't show me hers, how could I show her mine?

✳   ✳   ✳

"We just add these in?" I asked, looking skeptically at the chickpeas soaking in water. Lata pulled a yellow bucket filled with spices close to her and dumped all the chickpeas in. Then, when her arm was up to her elbow she asked me to pour oil and the pieces of mango in for her to mix.

Lata always made the chickpea *avakai*, *Thatha's* favorite. When I was little I used to pick the chickpeas out of *Thatha's* plate as my palate was not ready to endure the chili and spice of the *avakai*. *Thatha* would wipe away traces of spices and chili from a chickpea and line it up with others for me to nibble on. Ma would tell *Thatha* he was spoiling me, that I should learn to eat spicy food and not eat out of other people's plates, but *Thatha* continued and I continued.

Even as an adult I could never eat food that was too spicy. When Nick and I went out to Indian restaurants he usually handled the hot food better than I did.

"Who's the Indian here?" Nick would ask, as he wiped moisture from his forehead. He would continue to eat, despite getting soaking wet with sweat, while I would give up on the really hot food.

"My mother would like you . . . well, your eating habits at least," I told Nick. "She believes that food isn't real food if your nose and eyes don't water a little while you eat."

Ma and Lata ordered us around like slaves to bring the big pickle jars from the kitchen. Sowmya and I demurely went and got six huge glass jars. Neelima started to cut muslin cloth into large squares. The pickle went inside the jars and then the muslin was tied to the mouth of the jar after which the lid was tightly closed.

We all worked as if we were on automatic pilot, abiding orders and following the leaders blindly. The last of the pickle was being put into the jars when *Ammamma* decided to stir up some conversation. "So tell us, Priya, do you have a lot of Telugu friends in the States?"

"A few."

"They say the Bay Area has a very big Indian population, especially Telugu," Lata said, as she used a wooden ladle to fill *her* jar with *her* pickle.

"Some," I said tersely.

"You don't like Telugu people?" Lata asked, when I seemed reluctant to expound.

"I didn't say that," I protested.

Lata shrugged. "My brother who lives in Los Angeles told me that there are some Indians who don't like other Indians who live in the States. They always stay away from them and only make friends with *white* people. I think that is a shame."

"I agree," I replied with affected sincerity. "The race of a person should be of no importance when you make friends. I have several American and several Indian friends. I also know some people from Turkey."

Ammamma's eyes popped out. "What? You have friends who are white? Who are black?"

She could as well have been saying that my friends were little green men from Mars.

"What can you talk to them about?" *Ammamma* asked. "They are not really friends, are they?"

I gaped at her. Was the woman really stupid, or was she merely pretending?

"What do you mean?" I asked, unsure of her question.

"She means what do you have in common with these white

people," Ma piped in. "You should stay with your own kind. These white people will always swindle you."

"And how do you know that?" I sighed, first my grandfather and now my mother. It was a family thing, probably embedded in the genes.

"You think I am fifty years old and I know nothing?" Ma demanded harshly. "I know enough and I am telling you that you should only make friends with Indians, preferably our kind. Nice Brahmins . . . they will always be there to help you. You have to work with these *other* people, why should you spend your spare time with them?"

How was I supposed to argue with that?

"I have friends from different races and different countries. I don't care where they're from. If they're good people . . ." I began, once again a futile gesture.

"White people are never good," *Ammamma* announced emphatically. "Look what the British did to us."

I rolled my eyes. It was ridiculous the way my family thought and felt about the West. Ma would always show off about her daughter in the United States, but she didn't quite like the idea of her daughter even having friends who weren't Indian. This did not bode well for my revelation regarding Nick this evening.

I was relieved of pursuing the discussion when a car honked and Ma asked me to go open the gate.

My father was finally here—it was the best diversion I had had all day.

✳   ✳   ✳

To: Priya Rao <Priya_Rao@yyyy.com>
From: Nicholas Collins <Nick_Collins@xxxx.com>
Subject: Re: Re: Re: Re: Good trip?

Sounds like you're having a regular great time! I'm

GLAD YOU DON'T FEEL GUILTY ABOUT ME—I'D HATE IT IF YOU DID. SO TO ANSWER YOUR QUESTION, NO, YOU SHOULDN'T FEEL GUILTY FOR BEING IN A HEALTHY RELATIONSHIP. YOU CAN'T PLAN RELATIONSHIPS, IF YOU PLAN THEM THEY ARE CALLED ARRANGED MARRIAGES AND HONESTLY, I THINK THAT'S A TAD COLD-BLOODED.

YOU'VE MADE YOUR OWN LIFE HERE IN SAN FRANCISCO, WITH ME, AND YOU DON'T OWE ANYONE ANYTHING. KEEP THAT IN MIND. NO MATTER HOW YOUR CULTURE TELLS YOU THAT YOU OWE YOUR PARENTS, YOU HAVE TO REMEMBER THAT CHILDREN NEVER OWE THEIR PARENTS. YOU DON'T OWE YOUR PARENTS ANYTHING BUT YOU'LL OWE YOUR (OUR!) CHILDREN COMPLETE LOVE AND LOYALTY BUT THEY WON'T OWE YOU ANYTHING—AND SO THE CYCLE SHALL CONTINUE.

I'M TEMPTED TO FLY DOWN AND CARRY YOU AWAY—WARRIOR STYLE. I KNOW YOU CAN TAKE CARE OF YOURSELF, BUT I KNOW YOU'RE GOING TO GET HURT AND I FEEL IMPOTENT SITTING HERE IN OUR HOME WAITING FOR YOU TO BE STUNG BY YOUR FAMILY. JUST TRY AND STAY CALM.

CALL ME IF YOU CAN, IT'LL MAKE US BOTH FEEL BETTER. NICK.

✳ ✳ ✳

Part Three

In a Pickle

Mango *Pappu* (lentils)

4 cups yellow *gram pappu*
8 cups water
2 raw sour mangoes
5–6 curry leaves
2 teaspoons chili powder
salt to taste
2 tablespoons peanut oil
1 teaspoon black mustard seeds
3 dried red chiles
1 teaspoon red *gram pappu*
5 curry leaves
¼ cup chopped coriander

Soak four cups of yellow *gram pappu* in eight cups of water for half an hour. Chop the raw mango in small pieces. Add mango, yellow *gram pappu* with the water, curry leaves, chili powder, and salt in the pressure cooker and cook until two whistles. In a small frying pan, heat oil until sizzling. Add mustard seeds, red chile, red *gram pappu*, and curry leaves into the oil and fry for thirty to forty seconds (be careful to not burn the seeds or the leaves). Add the oil and its contents into the mango lentil mixture in the pressure cooker immediately and mix. Garnish with chopped coriander. Serve hot with rice.

Nanna's Friend's, Friend's Son

*N*anna enveloped me in a bear hug as soon as he stepped out of the car. I knew he didn't like to visit *Ammamma* and *Thatha* but came along because the alternative was listening to my mother complain about it for days, maybe weeks.

"That bad?" He grinned when he saw my drawn face and I shook my head.

"Worse."

"What is going on?" he asked when he sat down on the large swing on the veranda to remove his black leather shoes.

Sowmya stepped outside and smiled at him. "Coffee?"

My father nodded thankfully and she went back inside.

Nanna was a tall, lean man and his skin was dark. That was where I inherited the "wheatish complexion" that Ma complained about. He wore a small gray moustache. As his hair was growing white, he looked dignified and handsome. Ma tried to coax him into dyeing his hair as she did, but he refused, saying he had no issues with his age. I think he liked being in his fifties and looked forward to being sixty.

"No one has killed anyone yet?" he asked, rocking the wooden swing slowly with his bare feet.

I was sitting on a chair across from him and raised my eyebrows mischievously. "The night is still young. *Thatha* is very angry with me."

"*Thatha* is always angry with someone," he said negligently. "What happened?"

My father and grandfather did not get along. Even though Ma and *Nanna* had had an arranged marriage, *Thatha* never did quite like the idea of his favorite daughter being married to a man, any man. There was the age-old "he stole my daughter" thorn in the side of their relationship, which could never be removed.

"We had a fight," I had to tell him in case he misunderstood me. "They were lambasting the United States and I lost it . . . a little."

My father gave a long sigh as if he understood it was going to be a long night.

"I got angry," I continued. "And I said something about the States being different from India . . . in the sense . . . that there, no one is forced to have a baby to provide a male heir." My mouth twisted sheepishly and I waited for my father to admonish me.

He shrugged. "You are right."

"Really?" My eyes brightened.

"But you had no business telling that to him," he said, thwarting my hopes of finding an ally in the family over this particular issue. "He is old and set in his ways. Leave him alone."

"Leave whom alone?" A voice thundered from inside the house and both my father and I were startled like criminals caught in the act.

Thatha stepped outside in his white *lungi* and the thin ceremonial thread that ran across his chest as it did across every Brahmin man's chest. *Nanna*, who was hardly religious, kept losing his thread. It always amused Nate and I how *Nanna* scrambled to find the thread whenever he had to visit *Ammamma* and *Thatha*.

"As long as I don't take my shirt off, the nosey old bastard won't make an issue out of it," *Nanna* would say if he couldn't find the thread.

Even though my father disliked *Thatha*, he was always polite, always respectful. I think that annoyed *Thatha* more because he could not really point to any of my father's obvious flaws.

"*Namaskaram,*" *Nanna* said, and folded his hands in acknowledgment. "How are you doing?"

Thatha sat down beside me, his mouth twisted in a pout. "Sowmya has coffee for you inside, Ashwin."

My father looked at me with his kind soft eyes that twinkled from beneath his steel-framed glasses. "Want to come and have coffee with your old man, Priya?" he asked in an effort to save me.

"Thanks," I said gratefully, and smiled. "If you don't mind, I'll talk to this old man for a while," I said, inclining my head toward *Thatha*.

"I don't like being yelled at in my own house by my own granddaughter," *Thatha* started without preamble as soon as my father went into the hall. "I feel the way I feel and I will continue to feel that way."

I stared at the white cloth that was draped around his hips and wondered why south Indian men persisted to wear this garb in the twenty-first century. It was great during the summers, but still, a thin sheet of cloth wrapped around your legs was hardly protection. Added to that was how men did not wear any underwear beneath the *lungi*. One false, thoughtless move and all was open for public viewing. I had seen my share of penises because of the fascination south Indian men had for *lungis*.

"Are you listening to me?" *Thatha* demanded.

"I'm listening," I said a little cockily. "But I was not raised to keep silent when people unjustly—"

"You were not raised to raise your voice in the presence of elders," *Thatha* interrupted me.

"Well, everything that Ma and *Nanna* taught didn't stick," I said, and shrugged. "Come on, *Thatha*, what were you thinking? That I'm a little shy girl? I'm not. . . . You've always known that."

Thatha took my hand in his and nodded. "No, you were always the one with the sharp temper. Not a good thing in a girl . . . even an American-returned one."

"I'm sorry I raised my voice, but I'm not sorry about the male heir remark," I said in compromise. If the old man was going to meet me halfway, I could manage the other half.

"I need a male heir and I thought this discussion was over," he said.

"You brought it up again," I sighed, and decided to make some amends for my bad behavior. "*Thatha*, sometimes I don't like the way you think and sometimes I don't like the way my entire family thinks. You know what, it doesn't make a difference. I still love you all very much and I'll always love you. But that doesn't mean I have to nod my head when you say something wrong."

That seemed to get to him. I think the "I love you" part did it. He patted my hand and rose from his chair. "It is okay. Come inside and have coffee."

Just like that, *Thatha* forgave me.

Forgave me? What had I done that needed forgiving?

❋   ❋   ❋

The sun started to set, sliding slowly and lazily into the horizon as we put away the pickle jars in the storeroom next to the kitchen.

"Priya, I have to buy some coriander and some *kadipatha* for dinner. Are you up for a walk?" *Nanna* asked me. It was almost automatic for him to find some reason or the other to leave *Thatha's* house.

"Ashwin-*garu*, we don't really need the curry leaves and I can manage without the coriander," Sowmya said, worried that she was inconveniencing my father.

Ma looked at me sternly and then looked at Sowmya. "Let them go. You go with your father, Priya."

I raised my eyebrow and then looked at my father curiously. "What's going on?"

"We need *kadipatha*. *Rasam* without *kadipatha* . . . is like . . . the States without the Statue of Liberty," *Nanna* said. "Come on, Priya," he urged as he slid his feet into Anand's leather slippers, which were lying in the veranda shoe rack.

Before anyone could mount any more protest, *Nanna* and I were out of the house.

"Is it me or is that house very stuffy?" *Nanna* said, taking a deep breath.

"It's probably you," I said, and slipped my hand in his. "You think we can get *ganna* juice?"

"You will fall sick," *Nanna* warned, "but if you don't mind vomiting and having a stomach infection for the rest of your trip, definitely."

"I won't fall sick and I had *goli* soda today afternoon. Today morning I couldn't eat the mangoes Ma wanted me to taste but I've gotten over that now. . . . hygiene is not an issue anymore," I said.

"Let us hope that you don't fall sick," *Nanna* said, squeezing my hand.

"Why did Ma want us to go out?" I asked.

"I have no idea why your mother wants us to do what she wants us to do. Has been a mystery for twenty-nine years," *Nanna* said. "Now, you can have your *ganna* juice but no ice."

One of the less illicit things that I used to love doing and Ma warned me against was eating *chaat*, spicy food, from roadside vendors and drinking sugarcane juice. Sugarcane juice stands were scattered throughout the city of Hyderabad and came to life during the summer. Long stalks of sugarcane lay on a wooden stand on wheels next to a metal juicer. The juicer was two large wheels with spikes rolling against each other. The stalk of sugarcane along with a small piece of lemon and ginger would be squeezed through the twin wheels. The sugarcane vendor would run one stalk through and then roll the squished stalk and run it through the wheels again.

The juice would be poured into glasses that were probably not washed in clean water, ever, along with a lot of ice. It was my favorite thing to drink after a long day at college. Usually the sugarcane stands and *chaat* stands were lined up next to bus stops. So while I waited for my bus, I would shell out the two rupees it used to take to get *ganna* juice. I always asked the vendor to not put ice in my juice. I figured that way I would get more juice and I would not have to speculate where the ice came from. The rumor was that the vendor probably got the ice from a morgue.

"Okay, no ice," I conceded. "Any news from Nate?"

"No, Nate never has any news," *Nanna* said. "He may be back tomorrow but I doubt he will come here. You know he can't stand Lata or Jayant."

I shrugged.

"I think Nate has a girlfriend," *Nanna* continued and I stopped walking. "What?" *Nanna* asked looking at me. "Let us walk, we have to get *kadipatha.*"

I sighed.

"So you think Nate has a girlfriend," I said, playing along with him.

"Has he said anything about her to you?" *Nanna* asked, as we reached the small vegetable store at the end of the street from *Thatha's* house.

I looked at the various vegetables sagging in their small straw baskets at the end of the day and got a bunch of *kadipatha.* A few people milled around the baskets, picking up vegetables for the last meal of the day.

"They look half dead," I said about the coriander my father had in his hand.

"They will do," *Nanna* said, and put the *kadipatha* and coriander in front of the vendor and paid the ten rupees they cost from his old brown leather purse.

"You still have that purse?" I asked. "You're not using the one I sent for your birthday last year?"

"Nate took that," *Nanna* said. "And I am fine with this. So . . . did Nate say anything . . . about his girlfriend?"

"No," I lied smoothly. "Why?"

"Well, we would like Nate and . . . you . . . all our children, to understand that we are open to hearing the truth," *Nanna* said, subtle as the chili powder in Ma's pickles.

"Really?" I said, as we walked toward a sugarcane juice stand close to the vegetable store.

"So . . . do you have a boyfriend?" *Nanna* asked.

I ignored his question.

The light from the setting sun was still illuminating the skies; it wouldn't get dark for a while and in the summers it never really got pitch dark. The sky always looked a little blue, even in the dead of the night.

"*Amma*, want one?" the sugarcane juice vendor asked, holding a glass filled with frothy greenish brown juice.

"No, no," *Nanna* said. "No ice. Two glasses and wash them properly."

As if washing the glasses would make any difference whatsoever to whatever germs and bacteria we would ingest with the juice. I knew I shouldn't, but it was too tempting, just like the *goli* soda had been. I could taste the sweetness of the juice; the long-forgotten memories came rushing back to my taste buds and the desire to take just one sip became irresistible.

"More ginger," I told the vendor, as he went about his business.

"So, do you?" *Nanna* asked again.

"Do I what?" I evaded on purpose.

Nanna made an irritated sound.

"Is that why Ma asked me to go with you?" I questioned bluntly.

"Don't change the subject," *Nanna* said. "Tell us if you have a boyfriend. If you do, we will accept whatever . . . I mean as long as . . . you know . . . he has to be suitable."

"And what if he is, say . . . a *sardar*?"

"A *sardar*?" *Nanna* asked, the terror in his voice palpable. "Come on, Priya, have a heart."

I sighed. A Sikh would at least be Indian.

"So you wouldn't accept *any* boyfriend."

"We would, we would," *Nanna* said hurriedly. "I mean . . . you should at least tell us why you are stalling. You are twenty-seven and we would like to see you married. Play with some grandchildren."

Nanna was a sucker for children. When he built the house they were living in, he insisted that in all the bathrooms the latch on the outside should be slightly lower so that his grandchildren would be able to open the bathroom door to go inside and the latch on the inside should be slightly higher, so that the children would not be able to lock themselves in.

He had also purchased a beautiful wooden rocking chair. "Babies cry and if you rock them they stop crying and go to sleep," he would say.

He had been waiting for grandchildren for as long as I could remember and I felt sorry for him and guilty because children had not figured in my plans yet. I knew I would have children someday and I wanted to have children someday, but it was one of those "yeah, I also want to go to space" kind of thing you reserved for the indeterminate future.

"*Nanna*, I'll marry when I'm ready," I said, fearful now of telling him anything about Nick. If a *sardar* was going to give him heart palpitations, an American would give him a seizure.

"But you have to be ready sometime, Priya," *Nanna* said wearily. He gave the sugarcane juice vendor fifteen rupees and picked up his glass of frothy juice.

I tentatively sipped mine and sighed in pleasure. "This is what I really miss. This and *chaat.*"

Nanna drank his juice in two gulps and set his glass down. "We are not going to eat any *chaat.* Sowmya is making a nice dinner. Your favorite, mango *pappu.*"

I finished my *ganna* juice slowly, savoring the taste through the last sip. As we started to walk back I quietly waited for *Nanna* to say whatever else he had to tell me before we reached *Thatha's* house.

"We are staying here tomorrow. I am taking the day off," he said over the sound of honking cars, sidestepping trash on the pavement.

"I know, I brought a change of clothes. I'm planning to sleep on the terrace tonight like Nate and I used to when we were kids," I said.

Nanna held my hand tightly in one hand and a plastic bag with the coriander and curry leaves hung from the other.

"Do you remember Mahadevan Uncle?"

Mahadevan Uncle is one of *Nanna's* friends. In India, I have no idea why, but all of my parents' friends are called uncle and auntie. For the longest time I had trouble calling Frances, Nick's mother, by her name because she was so much older than I and I felt I was being disrespectful calling her by her first name.

"Sure, I remember Mahadevan Uncle. He has two sons, doesn't he?"

"Yes, both married," *Nanna* said, and then crushed my hand some more. "Mahadevan Uncle has a friend. His name is . . . well, everyone calls him Rice Sarma."

"Rice? Why?"

"He works at ICRISAT and he has done some big-time research in rice. Has won some major awards; the President gave him one just last year," *Nanna* continued. "Good people."

"Hmm." I refrained from saying more. I could see where this was going.

"Rice Sarma has a son," *Nanna* said, and then waited for a while to see how I would respond. When I didn't say anything, he continued. "His name his Adarsh. We saw his pictures. Good-looking boy. Lives in Dallas. Works for Nortel Networks. Is it a good company?"

"Yes," I said tightly.

"He is a manager there," *Nanna* said. "He did his engineering in BITS Pilani."

BITS Pilani was a very good school for engineering in India and I could see my father was laying it on thick. Producing the perfect groom for me. My heart sank. How was I going to get out of this one without telling him about Nick? How could I now not tell him about Nick?

"Oh."

"And he did his master's at MIT and has an MBA from Stanford," *Nanna* said, as he measured my facial expression for results.

"Impressive," I said. Good God, what next? Would he tell me that the man was six feet two and looked like Adonis?

"He is six feet two inches tall," *Nanna* continued as if on cue. "Your mother thinks he looks like that movie star Venkatesh."

Venkatesh was a Telugu film actor I used to be fond of seven years ago. I hadn't seen a movie of his since I left India, but I was impressed that Ma was using him as bait.

"So what?" I pretended ignorance.

"We showed him your photo—"

"You did what?" I extricated my hand from his and faced him. We had reached *Thatha's* gate and we stood there, I angry, he contrite.

"Well, what did you want us to do? Wait until you are fifty to get you married?" *Nanna* went on the offensive even as his face remained defensive.

"He seems perfect. Maybe Ma should marry him," I quipped.

Nanna opened the gate. "He is here on vacation. Tomorrow afternoon, they will be coming here, at *Thatha's* house for tea."

I stared at my father. "You are not putting me through one of those cattle-seeing ceremonies."

"You are *not* cattle and stop overreacting."

"Overreacting? His family will show up . . . that's why Ma packed my silk blouses. Damn it, *Nanna*, you've known all along. This isn't news. You've known since I got here." I was appalled that my father had joined my mother in tricking me.

"Don't use words like *damn*," *Nanna* said, and shrugged. "Like I said, we can't . . . *won't* wait till you are fifty."

"I *won't* sit there and be watched by him and his family like I'm a cow for sale," I said sharply.

"It won't be like that, Priya Ma," my father tried to console.

I brushed past him and marched into the house. I flung my straw slippers from my feet onto the veranda and went inside the hall.

I barely acknowledged Jayant who had arrived while my father was sticking the knife in my back.

"I'm not going to be here tomorrow afternoon," I told my mother. She was sitting on the floor, leaning on a cushion, and I towered over her, my hands at my waist.

"You will be here," Ma said without even flinching. "None of these shenanigans will work with me. Your father will put up with this—"

"Really? What will you do if I leave tomorrow afternoon when *Nanna's* friend's friend and his oh-so-perfect-son arrive?" I demanded.

"Priya," *Thatha* said sternly. "Calm down and don't yell in my house. Why don't you go help Sowmya in the kitchen?"

I almost raged at him but bit my tongue back. This was not the time to get on the feminist soapbox.

I wanted, I so very much wanted, to stay and fight but I didn't want to behave like a child and prove their point that they didn't think I could take care of myself, find my own husband.

"You should've at least asked me before you invited them," I told Ma in a soft voice. She shrugged again and looked away from me.

It was on the tip of my tongue to tell Ma that this was why it was so hard to respect her. Respect was a two-way street and if I didn't get any, I couldn't give her any either. Feeling utterly betrayed by both my parents and my grandparents—my entire family—I walked out of the hall.

In the kitchen, Sowmya was soaking lentils in water for the mango pappu.

"Can I help?" I asked sourly, and she smiled gamely.

"Peel the mangoes, will you? I have to cut potatoes for the curry," she said, handing me a peeling knife and two green mangoes.

I stood on one side of the sink and she on the other as we worked on our respective vegetables.

"They've set up a *pelli-chupulu* for me," I said bitterly.

Sowmya nodded. "Radha *Akka* told us when you went to the vegetable store."

"How can they?"

"Come on, he sounds perfect. I have someone coming tomorrow evening and he is a lecturer in a private college and looks like Brahmanandam, not Venkatesh," Sowmya said with a broad grin.

Brahmanandam was a comedian in the Telugu film industry. He made people laugh but didn't have anything going for him in the physical attributes department.

"That's not the point," I said.

"You think that you are too good for a *pelli-chupulu* and only people who look like me have to go through it?" she asked quietly, and my eyes flew wide open, denial dancing on my tongue ready to pour out.

But she was right. That was exactly what I thought.

I wanted to make an excuse, a good one, and that was when it slipped out; I was busy trying to make Sowmya feel better about her several *pelli-chupulus* and my belief that I was much better than she was.

"I have a boyfriend . . . a fiancé," I blurted out.

"What?" The potato Sowmya was holding rolled away from her into the sink. She grabbed it and stared at me through her nine-inch glasses.

"Yes," I said. I had stepped in it with one foot so I might as well dip the other one in. "He's American."

"Your father will kill you and, if not, your *Thatha* will," Sowmya said as she clutched the knife she was using to peel potatoes against her chest. "When . . . how . . . ? Priya? What were you thinking?"

"He's a nice guy. I love him," I said and it sounded like such a line, even to me. "I didn't plan it." Another line. "It just happened." I felt like I was tripping over clichés, one after the other.

"No, Priya. You can't do this to us. Anand . . . that was bad enough, but this, this will destroy your *Thatha* and your father," Sowmya said.

"What do you want me to do? Dump Nick to marry some guy my parents think is good for me?" I demanded.

"Yes," Sowmya said firmly. "That is our way."

"Oh, screw our way," I said, and threw a raw mango on the counter.

"What will you do?" Sowmya asked, picking up the mango I had thrown and checking to see if it was bruised.

"I don't know," I confessed and had an overwhelming desire to cry.

✳ ✳ ✳

To: Nicholas Collins <Nick_Collins@xxxx.com>
From: Priya Rao <Priya_Rao@yyyy.com>
Subject: Re: Re: Re: Re: Good trip?

You won't believe this but some nice Indian boy is coming over tomorrow afternoon to "see me." Bloody hell! How dare my parents do this to me, Nick? This is humiliating. They expect me to participate in this barbaric ritual of allowing some man to come and assess my worthiness as a wife.

What hurts is that my father is in on it, too. I expected this from my mother, but *Nanna* . . . he was supposed to be on my side.

I am going to try and call you as soon as I can. But don't worry about anything. It is just . . . damn them. I have never been this angry before. I have to tell them about you now, before they put me in a spot with this idiot Indian boy they have decided is just perfect for me.

I wish I wasn't here. I wish I were back home. I wish my parents cared more about me than what the neighbors will think.

Priya

✳   ✳   ✳

To: Priya Rao <Priya_Rao@ yyyy.com>
From: Nicholas Collins <Nick_Collins@xxxx.com>
Subject: Re: Re: Re: Re: Re: Re: Good trip?

Sweetheart, I am so sorry. But you were expecting this, weren't you?

I don't mean to patronize (and you sound slightly melodramatic!), but I'm sure your parents care

MORE ABOUT YOU THAN WHAT THE NEIGHBORS THINK. REGARDING YOUR FATHER, GIVE HIM A BREAK. HE WANTS TO SEE HIS DAUGHTER MARRIED AND HE WANTS HER TO GIVE HIM SOME GRANDKIDS. HE DOESN'T KNOW YOU'RE ENGAGED TO A HANDSOME AMERICAN, SO HE'S TRYING TO DO HIS BEST.

I KNOW IT'S HARD TO TELL YOUR FAMILY SOMETHING YOU KNOW FOR SURE THEY DON'T WANT TO HEAR AND IF IT'S TOO MUCH PRESSURE, DON'T. JUST DON'T MARRY SOME INDIAN GUY WHILE I WAIT HERE TWIDDLING MY THUMBS. PLEASE? WE HAVE A JOINT MORTGAGE! IN SILICON VALLEY THAT'S AS SOLID AS A MARRIAGE!!!

IT'S OKAY IF YOU DON'T WANT TO TELL THEM ABOUT US. JUST RELAX. I DON'T WANT YOU TO HAVE AN EMBOLISM BECAUSE OF ALL THIS STRESS. DO WHAT YOU'RE COM-FORTABLE WITH.

TAKE CARE, SWEETHEART, AND CALL ME.
NICK

✳ ✳ ✳

Confessions and Lies

Anand was one my favorite relatives. He was five years older than I and we'd spent many summers together in *Thatha's* brother's house in our village near Kavali.

The last summer we spent there had been quite an adventure. *Thatha's* brother, who we called *Kathalu-Thatha*, had been trying to track down the thief who was stealing from his mango orchard and we were convinced that we could be just as good as writer Enid Blyton's Famous Five heroes. Anand was thirteen, Sowmya eleven, and I was all of eight years old; we thought we made a dashing Thrilling Three.

Thatha's brother told the best stories and that was why we called him Stories-Grandpa, *Kathalu-Thatha*. We would all gather around a fire and *Kathalu-Thatha* would tell us about the ghost who lived in the old well in the middle of his sugarcane field, the old-old man who still lived in the shack by the stream at the end of the village and the tigers that would come out only in the night to take away little naughty children. Some stories scared us, others made us laugh, but all of them brought us closer to *Kathalu-Thatha*. My memories of sitting by the fire, sipping hot sweet milk from silver tumblers while *Kathalu-Thatha* wove tall tales that were rich, still had the ability to brighten my day.

✳   ✳   ✳

Anand gave me a hug as soon as he saw me. "You took too long, Priya," he said. "And now you are all grown up."

"All grown up and single," Ma muttered from behind us. "And making *nakhras*, throwing tantrums like a spoiled brat."

I sighed.

"Let it be, *Akka*," Sowmya said, wrapping the edge of her sari around her waist. "Why don't both of you go and bring the mangoes downstairs while I get Anand's tea ready?"

It was a good escape route—neither Anand nor I needed to be told twice.

"I hear a boy is coming to see you tomorrow," Anand said, as we went up the stairs. "Two boys in one day. . . . My mother must be in heaven."

"Yup," I said sarcastically, "one for me and one for Sowmya. Just a regular meat market."

"Oh, it won't be so bad," Anand said, and patted my shoulder.

"And so says the man who fell in love, *eloped*, and married," I pointed out. "And there is *big* news as well."

Anand smiled from ear to ear. "I can't believe it. Can you believe it? I am going to be a father?"

I shook my head and laughed. No, I couldn't believe the Anand who had spent an entire night atop a mango tree waiting for *Kathalu-Thatha's* mango orchard thief to make an appearance was now old enough to be a father.

"I was thinking about our last summer at *Kathalu-Thatha's*

house," I said, as we started folding the muslin cloth on which the now dried and wrinkled mangoes lay.

"Oh yes," Anand said, rubbing a scar over his left eye. "*Amma* refused to ever let me go there again."

It had been late in the night. Sowmya and I kept guard at the end of the orchard, looking for the thief. We'd sneaked out of the house, adamant at finding the thief to impress *Kathalu-Thatha*. Sowmya had been reluctant, but Anand and I had been persistent. Unable to bow out in the face of our enthusiasm, Sowmya came along, her forehead wrinkled in a worried frown.

Anand was on sentry duty atop a mango tree along with a steel flashlight. "I will have a better view," he said.

It surprised all of us when the thief turned out to be a monkey who freaked out when Anand flashed a light on its face and attacked him. Anand fell from the tree and hit his head on a stone, its sharp edge just missing his left eye.

Sowmya and I, sick with worry, ended up screaming for help like the girls we were.

We were all reprimanded the next morning and unfortunately that had been the last time we had gone to the orchard on vacation. *Kathalu-Thatha*, did not make it through the coming winter and *Thatha*, his only next of kin, sold the family house and leased the orchard to some jam and juice company.

After we folded the two muslin clothes with the mangoes, Anand looked around stealthily and pulled out a pack of cigarettes. "Don't tell anyone," he said. "If *Nanna* found out . . . he will kill me."

Here was a grown man, about to become a father, who was still afraid of his father.

I shook my head. "Just don't smoke around Neelima."

"Of course," Anand said, and sat down on the cement floor. He leaned against the cement balustrade and sighed. "I have been waiting all day for this."

"Neelima is not the happiest person in the world," I told him bluntly. "You keep bringing her here and they're all so mean to her."

"They are just getting to know her. . . . You know how they are when someone new comes in. Remember how both my *Amma* and your *Amma* made Lata's life miserable when she and Jayant *Anna* got married?" Anand said.

"Lata is very different from Neelima," I reminded him. "Neelima feels really bad, Anand."

"She would tell me if she felt bad," Anand said, looking up at the sky. "See the *Saptarishi*?" he asked, pointing at the constellation of seven stars shaped like a question mark. "For the longest time I couldn't see Arundhati," he said.

The *Saptarishi* were the seven *Maharishis*, great holy men, who were created by the vision of Lord Brahma. They were learned beings to whom the *Vedas* had been revealed and they represented the seven powers of life and consciousness in all of God's creation. The seven *rishis* were married to very nice-looking women and once when they were performing a *yajna*, Agni, the God of Fire, saw the women and immediately fell in lust with them. Agni's then-girlfriend, Svaha, wanted to please her lover and took the form of all the *rishis*' wives in bed. She could, however, take the form of only six of the wives. Arundhati was such a true wife that Svaha, no matter how hard she tried, couldn't change her body to look like Arundhati. Thanks to all this shape-shifting and sex, Svaha got pregnant, and the rumor that traveled around the Godly circles was that one of the six *Maharishis*' wives had a baby with Agni. All the *rishis*, except for Vashishtha, who was married to his true wife, Arundhati, kicked their wives out for being not-so-true wives.

In the *Saptarishi* constellation of stars, the last but one star at the bottom, which is Vashishtha, has a small star revolving around it, and that is Arundhati. The myth is that if you cannot see Arundhati, you will have bad luck . . . lots of it.

"And now you can see her?" I asked, avoiding looking up to

find out if I could see Arundhati. It was a silly superstition, but I didn't want to put it to test.

"Not really," Anand said, "but I am getting there. Neelima will adjust, Priya." He took a deep puff and blew out small rings.

I put a finger through one dissolving ring of smoke. "You should tell *Ammamma* and Lata and the rest of them to stop blaming her for marrying you."

"It is not something you should *have* to tell your own family," Anand said bitterly. "And I can't just walk up and tell them . . . can I?"

"Of course you can," I said. "Be a man, Anand, stand up for your wife. Or is *Thatha* still controlling you like a puppeteer?"

I was being a little harsh. . . . Well, I was being very harsh, but Anand's nonchalance at what his wife was going through at the hands of his family had increased the temperature of my blood. And Anand and I were close enough that I knew I had a right to be direct with him. As I guessed, Anand didn't take offense but he was a little miffed.

He crushed his cigarette on the cement floor and glared at me. "You want me to take on my big bad father?"

"Yes," I said.

"Really?"

"Yes, "I repeated.

"So when are you going to tell him about your boyfriend?" Anand asked.

"What?" I asked aghast. Sowmya would never tell anyone about Nick. Would she? How could Anand know?

"Oh, you're telling me you are against arranged marriage as an institution because you like being single and alone?" Anand demanded. "It is easy enough to guess. So who is the boyfriend?"

I felt the bile rise up to coat my throat with fear. Was I wearing a neon sign that said I HAVE A BOYFRIEND IN AMERICA?

"Come on, Priya," Anand said. "I know these things. I am not stupid."

"This isn't about me," I muttered. "This is about Neelima."

"You don't have the guts, do you?" Anand smirked. "So you shouldn't—"

"If they were ill-treating my boyfriend, you bet I'd take issue," I charged at him.

"So there is a boyfriend," he grinned, and lit another cigarette. "Tell, tell."

I sighed. "You're not going to like this."

"Hey, I married Neelima."

"At least she is Indian."

The cigarette in Anand's hand dropped. "No . . . you don't have an American boyfriend."

I nodded.

"Oh *Rama, Rama . . .*"

"I know."

"What will you do?"

"I don't know," I said honestly. "I have to back out of this stupid *pelli-chupulu* first."

"You can't, not now," Anand said, sounding worried. "Not without telling them about Mr. America."

"Forget about me; are *you* going to do something about how everyone is treating Neelima before she divorces you?"

Anand picked up the cigarette he had dropped and put it in his mouth. "I will see what I can do."

"As soon as Neelima said she was pregnant Lata talked about miscarriages in the first trimester and—"

"That bitch, how dare she?" Anand burst out and the cigarette he was holding fell on the cement floor yet again. "I don't know how Jayant can stand her. And now they are pregnant again. Wants to give *Nanna* a pure-blooded *Brahmin* heir."

"What will you do?" I asked.

"I don't know," Anand said.

✴ ✴ ✴

When we came back downstairs, my father was in a heated discussion with Jayant about nonresident Indians, NRIs. Jayant sincerely believed that those who left India were betraying their motherland and my father was convinced that those who stayed were missing out on opportunities to grow and develop.

"The world is everyone's oyster," *Nanna* was saying. "We should think of ourselves as citizens of the world not just as Indian or Korean or Malaysian."

They were sitting at the dining table sipping tea as Sowmya bustled around them setting the table for dinner.

"Ah, Priya," Jayant said and extended both his hands to hold both of mine in a warm clasp. "You have grown up. And getting all set to be married I hear. This Sarma boy seems to be very ideal. What do you say?"

Anand cleared his throat while Sowmya glared at me. I smiled uneasily. Jayant patted my hands as if he could feel my tension.

"She is angry with us for setting this up," *Nanna* said, obviously enjoying the position I was in.

"Angry, nothing," Ma said, as she came into the dining area from the kitchen carrying a big steel pot with hot *rasam* in it. "They will be here tomorrow and once she sees the boy . . . ah, she will thank us. He is earning hundred thousand dollars a year, fifty *lakh* rupees."

"Money isn't everything, you know, Ma," I said sitting down beside Jayant. "And I haven't said yes to being here tomorrow for this . . . humiliating experience you want me to go through."

"Humiliating?" *Nanna* asked, his voice thick with emotion. "What, Priya Ma, you are talking like we are demons torturing you. We love you; we are doing this because we love you."

"Don't break our hearts now, Priya," Ma said suddenly serious. "We have waited this long. You said you were not ready and we waited for all these years. What more do you want from us?"

If they had yelled at me, scolded and admonished, coerced and coaxed, I would've known how to deal with it. This quiet remonstration was alien, their behavior strange, and because of it all the fight left my voice.

"It isn't like that, Ma, *Nanna*," I said softly. "I just don't think that getting married like this is . . . It isn't dignified . . . no, no . . . it just isn't for me."

"Everyone else is doing it," Ma said in a low voice. "You think Sowmya and Jayant are not dignified?"

That was hardly fair. How could I answer that when both Sowmya and Jayant were looking at me waiting for me to reply?

"No . . . that's not what I meant," I said lamely.

"So you'll be here tomorrow?" *Nanna* asked.

It was a goddamn ambush!

"No one will force you into marriage," Ma said eagerly. "Just look at the boy and if you don't like him, you don't have to marry him. But if you don't see him you will never know."

Oh, I'd know! But they were all looking at me with quiet desperation on their faces. They were so enthusiastic to see me married, settled, as they believed I should be. And what child could hold out against parental desperation?

"I'll be there," I said defeated, before leaving the kitchen.

I walked past the hall where *Thatha*, *Ammamma*, and Lata were watching the evening Telugu news and found Neelima and Anand talking to each other in the bedroom next to the veranda. She was crying, yet again, and he was holding her hand. They both looked incredibly cute and very much in love with each other. I felt a pang of envy. They were already married, while I didn't have the guts to tell my parents about Nick. My cowardice knew no bounds because now I had even agreed to sit through a bride-seeing ceremony.

I felt my empty ring finger with my thumb and then clenched my fist. I had taken the ring off in the plane before it landed in Hyderabad. I had hidden Nick from the start. Maybe I had known even before I left that he would continue to be my dirty secret.

I picked up my purse, which was lying next to the shoe rack

on the veranda, and leaned over to find the slippers I had thrown from my feet a while ago. I slipped out of the house without telling anyone to look for a telephone booth. I found one a street away from the *goli* soda shop. I dialed Nick's cell phone number and he picked up the phone almost before the first ring ended.

"Hi," I said, and I could hear his relief even before he said anything.

"How are you? Where are you?"

"At my grandma's house," I said.

"How're you holding up?" Nick asked.

"Okay."

"You don't sound okay."

"I'm fine," I said, trying to inject some false joy into my sagging voice. "It's just the whole . . . the boy they want me to see . . . It's just tiring."

"You're not going to go through that bride-seeing ceremony . . . are you?" Nick asked softly.

I paused for a microsecond before lying confidently. "Of course not."

"Are you sure? I mean, do you want to? I . . . This is hard, this is very hard. I am . . . Are you having doubts?" he asked, his frustration hitting me squarely on my conscience.

"Doubts about us?" I asked, swallowing hard. "Of course not, Nick. How could you even think that?"

"Well, it makes me wonder. You're so reluctant to tell them about us. I'm not a serial killer or rapist. I'm a pretty decent catch. . . . Don't you think? My mother thinks so," Nick said, laughing a little at the end.

"Oh, you're better than decent. You're the best catch this side of the Mississippi," I said, joining him in trying to lighten the air, letting the doubts slip away.

"I wish I'd come with you. I wish I was there with you now," he said suddenly in exasperation.

I wished he had, too. It would've made everything twice as

difficult but at least I wouldn't have been alone and my parents would never have tried to set me up with some friend's, friend's son.

"I want to tell them about you. I *will* tell them about you, today, soon, now," I said, lying again. I had never lied to Nick before, this was akin to cheating on him but I couldn't do anything about it. I was caught up in a tornado and I had left Kansas a long time ago.

"I'll tell them tomorrow," I lied yet again. I had no intentions of telling them about Nick anymore. I couldn't. I would just have to kill myself on the way back home to Nick so that no one would be the wiser about my deception.

"Tell them . . . don't tell them; just don't stress too much. You're on vacation, you should enjoy yourself," he said and I wondered if he knew I was lying.

"I *will* tell them. I love you, Nick," I said almost desperately.

"And I you."

"I've got to go back now. I'll call you again. Send me email . . . lots of email. I like to read."

He said he loved me again before I hung up. A gloom settled upon me. I didn't have the raw guts to tell my family about Nick. It was not to protect them from pain and hurt, it was to protect myself. I was afraid that if I told them about Nick, they wouldn't love me anymore. I was afraid that if I didn't tell them and went back, Nick wouldn't love me anymore. It was not a fair bargain. I could keep either Nick or my family.

I cried all the way back to *Thatha's* house, feverishly wiping my tears with both my hands.

✳ ✳ ✳

Dinner was boisterous as *Thatha* talked about how we could have a double marriage. "What do you say, Priya, you and my Sowmya getting married in the same *mandap*?" he asked, slapping a hand on his thigh.

I scooped out some mango *pappu* from a steel bowl onto my plate and mixed it in with rice.

"*Nnayi?*" Sowmya held up a small steel container with clarified butter and I shook my head. I should never have come to India—I was convinced of that. Now I had more problems than I could solve.

"Priya? " *Thatha* questioned. "What, *Amma*, you don't want a double wedding? "

"Maybe we should just have one wedding in one *mandap*," Ma said as if it was all a done deal and she didn't want *Thatha* to get the wrong idea. When her daughter would marry, it would be in her own *mandap*; Sowmya could get her own.

"Let's not count the chickens before they hatch," Lata said and for once I was thankful. "Anand, pass me the *rasam*."

Anand and Neelima were sitting next to each other and they had been quiet ever since dinner began. He looked up at Lata and then at the *rasam* and took a deep breath.

"Lata, did you say Neelima would have a miscarriage when she told you about her pregnancy?" he asked, a small quiver in his voice betraying the straight face he was trying to wear.

Silence fell so soundly that the echo of voices past crashed against the steel glasses standing on wobbly feet on the Formica table. Anand's fearless voice clamored to rise above his usual calm, comfortable, fearful, and almost silent voice. He was not one for confrontations, that was why he told the family about Neelima after they had married.

"What?" Lata asked, her hand covered with mango *pappu* lying listlessly on her plate.

Anand was silent for a minute. I could see his Adam's apple bob in and out—his nervousness had tentacles that reached out to everyone in the room.

"Anand, we don't need a fuss now. Lata didn't say anything," *Ammamma* warned, not wanting to witness a fight.

"There is no fuss," Anand said and stood up as if towering over everyone at the table would make it easier for him.

Nanna, who was sitting next to me, lifted his eyebrows in query. I shook my head. I knew what Anand was about to say, though I wondered if he had the courage to go through with it.

"Ever since Neelima and I got married, you all have been treating her really badly," he began.

"Badly?" *Thatha* demanded, his voice thunderous. "What nonsense! You are imagining things."

"Not nonsense, *Nanna*," Anand said, his voice for once confident as it measured up against his indomitable father. "Neelima is my wife, she deserves respect. If as a family you all have decided to ill-treat her—"

"No one is ill-treating her, Anand," Lata interrupted him. "I was simply telling her to be careful. The first trimester is always a delicate one. I don't know why she misunderstood what I was saying."

Neelima started crying softly. It was partly the tension in the room and partly because her hormones were raging. "I am sorry," she whispered.

"No, I am sorry," Anand said, sitting down to hold her hand. Such display of emotion between couples was not commonplace in our family and again I felt envy raise its head inside me. They loved each other, they were married, they were going to have a child; I was in love with a man who had the wrong skin color and nationality, I was living in sin with him and I had just lied to him.

"I keep sending her here"—Anand looked at *Thatha* when he spoke—"so that you will accept her. You will get to know her, see what a wonderful person she is and love her, treat her like a member of the family. But . . . if you don't want to do that, she won't come here. . . . I won't come here . . . and neither will our child."

The line had been drawn. Anand had just crossed over and become a man. I couldn't have been prouder.

Ammamma was about to say something but stopped when *Thatha* raised his hand.

"I agree, she is a daughter-in-law of this house and as such she deserves respect," *Thatha* said somberly. "But it will take time before we love her. She will never be our choice for your wife, Anand. What is done is done; I can't change the past or our past behavior. But from now on we will treat her like a member of the family."

Ammamma looked away and Lata made a small clicking sound. My mother pursed her lips and then shrugged.

"Are we clear?" *Thatha* repeated, looking at the women of his house.

"Yes," *Ammamma* finally said, speaking for everyone.

"Good," *Thatha* said, and nodded toward Neelima. "Congratulations on the baby. We can't wait to hold another grandchild in our arms."

By now Neelima's tears were racing down her face with the speed of a heavy waterfall. Anand looked at me and mouthed "Thank you." I nodded, feeling like a total fraud.

✳ ✳ ✳

To: Priya Rao <Priya_Rao@yyyy.com>
From: Nicholas Collins <Nick_Collins@xxxx.com>
Subject: Phone Call!

It was wonderful talking to you.

I know you are under a lot of pressure and I wish I could find a way to ease it. I don't understand the intricacies of your relationship with your family and sometimes that makes it hard for me to understand why you do the things you do.

But I do understand that you have to follow your intuition and your heart to keep your family happy because that's how you can be happy. I realize now that maybe the detachment you felt for them when you were here isn't easy to feel when they're next to you. Here you could see yourself telling them about me easily because I was with you, now you're with them and you find that it's not easy.

I won't like it but I'll understand if you find that at the end of the day, you can't tell them about me. I won't like it at all because I want you whole, not divided as the daughter or granddaughter and wife and lover.

But ultimately, I'll take you any way I can get you.

Take care.
Nick

✳　✳　✳

I couldn't sleep.

Sowmya, Anand, Neelima, and I were spread out on the terrace on straw mats, *chappas*. I lay my head on a flat cotton pillow and looked up at the stars. For the past half an hour since Sowmya had fallen asleep, I had been staring at *Saptarishi* and, just my luck, I couldn't see Arundhati.

Instead, the vultures were circling.

The last time I had slept on this terrace, I had been twenty years old, ready to face the world with the strength of the innocent. I was gearing up to go the United States; I had gotten my F-1 student visa and my bags were packed. I was spending a last weekend at *Ammamma's* house before heading over across seven seas to the land of opportunities. I had been so eager to leave, so excited that I had never thought that when I came back everything would be different to me and for me. I had never thought about how it would never be the same again, about how the cliché "you can never really go back home" would stand true.

This was not home anymore. Home was in San Francisco with Nick. Home was Whole Foods grocery store and fast food at KFC. Home was Pier 1 and Wal-Mart. Home was 7-Eleven and Star-bucks. Home was familiar, Hyderabad was a stranger; India was as alien, exasperating, and sometimes exotic to me as it would be to a foreigner.

I heard the gate opening and got up to see who it was. A lanky figure with a backpack stepped into the yard and then under the small yellow light that glowed with a flicker under the carport. He looked up and waved. I had never been happier to see Nate.

"I'm starving," he said, as soon as I came down. "You guys sleeping upstairs?"

"Yes, and there's plenty of food in the kitchen," I said. "Let's go in from the back door."

"Good idea, last thing I need is Ma waking up and going, 'oh my son is home,' " he said with a grin.

I hugged him tightly then. He was taller than me now, I realized as he stroked my hair.

"Hey," he said, and pushed me away after a moment, "I'm a man, this hugging thing is for sissies."

"Ah," I said and tweaked his nose with my fingers.

Nate left his sneakers outside the back door before coming inside the house. We turned the light on in the kitchen and Nate flopped down onto the floor.

"What're you doing back?" I asked, as I picked out a plate from the cabinet for him.

"Got bored," he said, and then shrugged. "I wanted to be here for the bloodshed. Or has the fat lady already sung?"

"What fat lady?" I demanded, and filled a glass with water

from the earthen pot next to the stove. "*Pappu* with rice work for you?"

"What kind of *pappu*?"

"Mango?"

"Sure. Sowmya makes this spinach *pappu* that's painful to swallow," Nate said. "You think you can heat the rice a little? Fridge-cold rice makes my hair in all the strange places stand up."

I pulled out some rice and *pappu* for Nate from the fridge. I mixed them both with my fingers and put the mixture in a frying pan to heat.

"This house so needs a microwave," I said.

"The American-returned daughter brings in some fancy ideas," Nate said with affected mockery. "So . . . when're you going to tell them?"

"I'm not," I said, not looking at him. "They set up a *pelli-chupulu* for me."

"Rice Sarma's Venkatesh type."

"You know?"

"Not really. It isn't like Ma discloses all to me. But in all fairness, the boy—ah, man—is very handsome, has a good, stable job. Don't know about the smoking and drinking part, though his mother claims he is a *gudu-baye*," Nate said.

"A good boy, my ass," I muttered. "Remember the *gudu* boy from Chicago?"

"Oh, the *Cheee-cah-go baye*, you mean?" Nate imitated Ma. "He was a prize, Priya."

"He was also screwing another woman."

"Details, details."

I put the now warmed rice and *pappu* on a plate and placed it in front of Nate along with a glass of water. I sat in front of him on the floor and drank some water from his glass.

"There is also some HAPPINESS in the fridge," I told him. "I asked Sowmya to save it from the mango she cut for dinner."

"And you don't want to fight over it?" Nate asked suspiciously.

I shook my head. I didn't even want to fight over HAPPI-NESS. This was an all-time low.

"What, not feeling well?" Nate put a hand against my forehead as if checking my temperature.

"I lied to Nick," I confessed. "I told Nick that I wasn't going to go through with the *chupulu* and that I was going to tell everyone about him."

"Nick is the man's name. Do we have a photo?"

"Photo? I have bigger problems, Nate."

"So tell him the truth and don't go through the *chupulu*," Nate said as he chewed on his food. "Then tell them all about Nick. And I'd still like to see my future brother-in-law, if not in the flesh, at least in Kodak color."

"I'll send you a picture later." I said. "And what does it matter how he looks? Lord, Nate, this stress is going to give me a coronary."

"You're not going to have a—"

"Nate?" *Nanna's* voice filtered into the kitchen.

"Hey, *Nanna*," Nate called out and winked at me. "At least *she* didn't wake up," he added on a whisper.

"Nate is here?" Ma's voice chimed in on cue.

"Well . . . can't have it all, can we?" Nate sighed as my mother's shrill voice came in through the hall, she was saying, just as Nate had predicted, "Oh, my son is home."

Part Four

Old Pickle, New Pickle

Rava Ladoo

1 cup semolina (*rava/sooji*)
1 cup sugar
3 tablespoons *ghee*
1 cup milk
1 tablespoon cashew nuts
1 tablespoon raisins

Fry the semolina in a saucepan on low heat till it turns slightly brown in color. Then add sugar, *ghee*, milk, and fry till the mixture becomes sticky. Chop the nuts and add them, along with the raisins, to the mixture. Remove the pan from the heat and form the dough into small balls. Serve when dry.

Aloo Bajji

1 cup chickpea flour (*besan*)
water
salt to taste
1 teaspoon chili powder
1 cup peanut oil
4-5 large potatoes, sliced

Mix the *besan*, water, salt, and chili powder until the consistency is runny. Heat the oil in a deep frying pan. Dip thinly sliced potatoes in the chickpea flour mixture and fry in peanut oil until golden brown.

The Similarity Between Cattle and Women

S owmya added the *rava* for the *ladoos* to the hot frying pan in which the *ghee* was sizzling. She used a steel spatula to coat the semolina with the *ghee* and lowered the flame on the stove.

"I can't believe Anand said that to *Nanna*," she said. The family was still buzzing with the way Anand had stood up for Neelima and how *Thatha* had accepted Neelima as his daughter-in-law, finally.

I was standing by the sink peeling potatoes to make potato *bajji*, dazed that I was allowing this atrocity of bride-seeing ceremonies to not only be perpetrated, but to be perpetrated upon me.

"I can't believe I'm getting snacks ready for that stupid *chupulu*," I said angrily, ripping away some skin from the potato.

"Maybe you should forget about this American and marry this nice boy—" Sowmya started to suggest.

"What do you mean 'forget', Sowmya? I'm in a relationship, not some dream I can wake up from," I said in exasperation. "I live with Nick. I share a home, a bed, a life with him. What am I supposed to do, just walk away?"

Sowmya's lips shaped into a pout and she sighed before slowly adding milk into the fried *rava* from a steel tumbler.

"And I love him," I said softly. "I love him very much."

Sowmya shrugged and put the tumbler down on the counter with a sharp sound.

"What's that supposed to mean?" I demanded.

"Nothing, Priya," Sowmya said, and then sighed again.

"Why don't you just say what you have to say and stop with the shrugging and sighing?"

Sowmya measured sugar with her fingers and dropped a few handfuls into the frying pan. She rubbed her hand against her sari to shrug off the remaining particles of sugar and picked up a spatula.

"I don't know how you can love an American. I mean . . . what do you two even talk about?" she asked as she slowly stirred the *rava* and sugar in the pan.

"What do you mean, talk about? We talk like everyone talks," I said, as I bit back the few topics that had collected on my tongue as an automatic response to her question.

"But . . . he is not even Indian," Sowmya said, as if that explained it all.

I dropped the potato I was peeling and put my hands on my face. If Sowmya, who was more my generation, had trouble comprehending my relationship with Nick, I could only imagine how the others would react.

"Priya, they'll be here in an hour," Ma said, bursting into the kitchen. "Have you at least taken a bath?"

"Yes," I said. "First thing in the morning, Ma. After all that's what a *Gangiraddhi* does, isn't it?"

Drawing an analogy between a "dressed-up" cow for a *puja* and me was probably not a wise thing to do, but I was prepped up for a fight like a homicidal bull being made to do something against its will.

"A *Gangiraddhi* doesn't have the choices you do," Ma said angrily.

"What's the boy's name, *Akka*?" Sowmya asked before I could tell Ma what she could do with what she thought were my choices.

"Adarsh, a nice name. But probably not good enough for Priya *maharani*, our very own high-and-mighty queen," Ma said sarcastically.

"The name is fine," I muttered.

"I have put out some saris with blouses for you on *Ammamma's* bed along with some jewelry; go and pick what you like. I don't want to battle over this with you, Priya. . . . Just choose anything you want. I don't want to interfere," Ma said, picking up the potato I had let go.

"I'm not going to wear any heavy jewelry," I warned.

"You don't have to do anything you don't want to do," Ma snapped. "Don't do us any favors. We find an excellent boy for you to see and . . ." She threw the potato in the sink and said, "I can't deal with this anymore," before she stormed out of the kitchen.

Lata came into the kitchen in Ma's wake and asked us what was going on. I followed my mother's example and stormed out myself.

* * *

When Nick first suggested we move in together, my answer had been an unequivocal "no." Unmarried couples living together was exactly the kind of thing I had been raised not to do.

"But you're here all the time anyway," Nick said about his apartment. "How would it matter if we were officially living together?"

"It'd matter . . . to my family," I'd told him honestly. A week later I agreed to move in with him because I realized that I had to stop worrying about what my family would think and start living my own life on my own terms. After that I had been determined not to let Ma or *Nanna* or *Thatha* decide my fate for me. But now when they were so close, the ties that bound me to them grew tighter, biting through my skin and conscience.

The saris strewn on *Ammamma's* white bedspread were so laden in embroidered gold that they made my eyelids heavy to just look at them.

"The blue one," Nate said, as he sauntered in, biting into a carrot. "And this," he said, flicking his finger over a heavy sapphire necklace-and-earrings set.

"I'll look like someone's grandmother," I said.

"So, big deal. Who are you trying to impress?" Nate asked with a smirk.

"Stop being such a wiseass, will you," I said, and smiled despite myself. Ah, vanity! Even though I didn't care for Adarsh Sarma's marriage proposal, I still wanted to look my best.

"If you really want to look nice, I say the yellow one with the red border. Classic Telugu movie sari, with that ruby necklace," Nate said. "My girlfriend looks great in the classic yellow and red sari."

I sat down on the bed and picked up the sari. "What's your girlfriend's name?"

"Tara," Nate said without hesitation. "She's doing her degree at St. Frances in Begumpet. Her father is an ex-army officer. They live in Sainikpuri and yes, her parents have met me and think I am the next best thing since instant coffee."

I nodded. "*Nanna* was asking me about her."

"*Nanna* knows about her," Nate grinned. "He saw me with her once. We were having lunch at Ten Downing Street and *Nanna* came in with a colleague. We both saw each other and pretended we didn't. Never talked about it. I guess *Nanna* didn't want me to ask him what he was doing in a pub and didn't want to know what I was doing there. Don't ask, don't tell, a good philosophy."

"Does Ma know?"

"If Ma knew everyone would know," Nate sneered. "Tell Nick about this *pelli-chupulu*. If Tara went through one of these ridiculous ceremonies without even telling me about it, I'd be pissed as hell for a very long time."

When he left I sat amid the beautiful silk saris and contemplated my options. I had to go through with this afternoon. If I tried to back out now, it would reflect badly on my parents. And I had to tell Nick the truth. And I had to tell Ma, *Nanna*, and *Thatha* the truth.

It was very simply really. I just had to tell everyone the truth and hope that they'd still love me.

✳   ✳   ✳

By the time the Sarmas were about to arrive, I was feeling like an object instead of a person. Ma had pulled and yanked and tucked and arranged for the nth time since I picked the blue-bordered sari to look like someone's grandma.

"There," she said with a satisfied glint in her eyes. "This boy is perfect, Priya. Even you can't find anything wrong with him."

"Wanna bet?" I felt like asking.

Sowmya came giggling inside *Ammamma* and *Thatha's* bedroom where I was getting ready.

"They are here. Drove in a Mercedes," she said with a big smile, unable to contain her joy at seeing me about to be fixed up with some loser who looked good on paper.

"They are very well off," Ma explained, arranging *Ammamma's* sapphires to her liking on my neck. "I wish you had worn the yellow sari. This is . . ." she clicked her tongue and then sighed.

"You look very nice, Priya," Sowmya said and I smiled uneasily. I felt like a trussed up turkey with a timer that could go off at any time now.

I heard the voices of the guests from the hall in the next room—I closed my eyes and silently apologized to Nick. "I'll make this up to you," I promised him fervently, but I had no clue how I would go about doing so.

"If you both want to *just* talk a little, go sit on the swing in the veranda," Ma instructed. "And don't swing your legs like a *junglee* when you sit there. Be ladylike."

"Do you want to tell me how to walk as well? Maybe you would like to continue giving me instructions after my marriage to make sure my husband doesn't leave me?" I demanded sarcastically.

"With your attitude I may just have to," Ma replied promptly. She was after all my mother, and my sarcasm had been inherited from her so my abilities were therefore diluted.

"You bring the *ladoos*, Priya, and—" Sowmya began and I raised both my hands in protest.

"I'll go there and sit and talk like a normal human being but if you want me to demurely carry food around for them while they look me up like I'm cattle for sale, you're both very mistaken," I said in a soft, ominous voice. I realized that even at this late stage, I wanted them to protest, say something that would make it justifiable for me to walk away from this. Because if this didn't happen there would be nothing I would not have to tell Nick about.

"Okay," Ma sighed. "Sowmya, you just put the *ladoos* and *bajjis* on the center table along with tea. This *maharani* here can just sit there like a big lazy blob."

I refused to be paraded around like meat for sale, so I casually walked into the hall as if I didn't know who was there and why.

This time, I had to admit, Ma had pulled out all the stops. The boy—the man—was very handsome and if I were single, I would've probably agreed to an arranged marriage to this hunk without even speaking with him. Where were these handsome men when I was going to college in India? But as things were, he didn't compare to the hunk I was already engaged to.

"My daughter, Priya," my father introduced me. "Priya, this is Adarsh, Mr. Sarma, and his wife."

"*Namaskaram*," I said, folding my hands. "Hi," I said to Adarsh. He smiled back. He had a dimple on his right cheek. Nick had a dimple on his left.

"How are you finding everything?" Mr. Sarma asked conversationally once I was seated by Ma in a lighted spot where everyone could see me, my sari, and all my jewelry to the best advantage. "It has been seven years, I hear, since you came back to India."

"Everything is the same . . . but not the same," I said enigmatically.

"Our son Adarsh feels the same way," Mr. Sarma said enthusiastically, and smiled broadly. "He says how nothing has changed and then he says that everything has changed. Looks like both of you cannot make up your mind."

"Have you ever thought about moving to *Tek-saas*?" Mrs. Sarma asked.

"I like living in San Francisco," I replied, now very uneasy with this whole bride-seeing business. I avoided looking at Ma who was glaring at me and smiling at our guests alternately. Telling them that I was not ready to move was an obvious sign of reluctance on my part.

"Adarsh is planning to move to the Bay Area," Mrs. Sarma said. "We have lots of family there and he is starting a business, too."

"Actually . . . I'm not," Adarsh corrected his mother uncomfortably. "I'm joining a friend's start up . . . or, rather I'm thinking about it."

"Really, what does your friend's company do?" I asked.

"They make—" Adarsh began.

"Oh, all this business *gup-shup*," Ma interrupted. "Why don't you kids sit outside on the veranda and talk while we old people eat some *ladoos* and *bajjis*."

Oh, what I wouldn't give for Ma to be just, just a teeny-weeny bit subtle.

"What, no *ladoos* and *bajjis* for us?" Adarsh asked mischievously.

"Of course." Ma flushed and held up a plate of *bajjis*.

Adarsh picked up a *bajji* and we both sauntered out to the veranda. I sat down on the swing and he sat across from me on a chair eating his *bajji*.

"I just got back from Dallas yesterday evening," Adarsh said. "So maybe I'm jet-lagged, but you don't seem all that eager to be married."

The bluntness of his question, imparted in a casual manner, instantly put me at ease. "I didn't come back home for seven years to avoid this," I said frankly.

"I know the feeling. I'd managed to stay away for almost six years . . . but now, my grandmother's health is failing, so I thought, what the hell, how bad can it be," he said with a shrug. "My friends who got married like this seem happy enough."

"Doesn't it seem a little barbaric to come and see a bunch of girls while you're in India and pick one to marry?" I asked.

Adarsh shrugged again. "Not really . . . Well, it did early on, but now, the girls looks at the guys, too, you know. It works both ways."

"You're right," I conceded, now fidgeting with *Ammamma's* sapphire necklace.

We both fell silent. This was awkward. Did this happen with everyone who sat through one of these bride-seeing ceremonies? Or did things change for a veteran like Sowmya?

"I want it all," he said suddenly. "The wife, the children, the house . . . you know what I'm saying?"

"Well, I'm no Sherlock Holmes, but the fact that you're here is a good indication that you're looking for a wife," I responded, smiling at his enthusiastic honesty. He was as unsure as I was about what needed to be said to know if the person you were speaking with for just a few minutes would be the person you'd want to spend the rest of your life with.

He grinned. "I could be here under parental duress. I just want to make sure you want the things I want."

"I want a husband and children and that house in suburbia. . . . well, maybe not suburbia," I said. It was not a lie. I did want those things. I just wanted those things with Nick.

"I'm glad," Adarsh said. "I don't know much about you and you don't know much about me. And in another ten minutes my mother or your mother will come and interrupt us because it's still not right for us to be talking so freely for too long."

"My mother will come out of curiosity, not out of some sense or propriety," I corrected him.

He smiled again and the dimple on his cheek deepened. Telugu film star, Venkatesh, had nothing on Adarsh Sarma, son of the eminent Rice Sarma. Any girl in her right mind would grab this guy, hope that he would grab her as well, but I was contemplating whether or not to tell him about Nick.

"I'd like to be honest with you," he said. "It's important to be honest I feel because we have to make a rather large decision based on a very short conversation.

"I was dating a Chinese woman two years ago. We broke up after a three-year relationship. That was when I realized that I wanted to marry someone from India."

This was an unusual boy . . . man. I had never heard of anyone discussing ex-girlfriends at a *pelli-chupulu*. It was simply not done and even though it gave me an opening to talk about Nick, I was reluctant. India was still a man's world and it was still okay for Adarsh to talk about his ex but taboo for me to mention my current or ex. In any case, I didn't have the guts.

"How did a bad relationship with a Chinese woman convince you that Indian women were the right variety for you?" I asked.

"I wouldn't use the word *variety*," he said, visibly flinching at my description. "I'm just doing what you're doing, looking for a life partner who'll make me happy and will make my family happy. With my ex-girlfriend it was great, we got along well, but Chinese New Year never started to mean anything to me and she never figured out *Ugadi*," he said. "Can you understand that?"

Actually, I couldn't. Nick and I hadn't had any problems on that front. I celebrated Christmas and Thanksgiving with him and he celebrated *Diwali* and *Ganesh Chaturthi* with me. But we were hardly religious and all festivals on either side were about good food, spending time with friends and family, and alcohol.

"It appears that you're looking for someone traditional," I said, and rose from the swing. "I'm not traditional."

He shook his head and gestured me to sit down. "Not traditional, just Indian."

"I'm not very Indian either," I told him evenly, still standing. "Don't be fooled by the sari and the *bindi* and the jewelry. I work hard and I play hard. I'm not even going to remember when *Ugadi* is unless someone will tell me. I drink an occasional glass of wine and I'm known to smoke a cigar to bring in the New Year . . . I—"

He lifted his hand, a big grin on his face. "I'm not looking for some *gaonwali*. I'm not interested in some village-type; I'm looking for a peer. It doesn't bother me if you want to drink a glass or two of wine, or even a bottle on occasion, I really don't give a damn. I simply want someone I can share Hindi movies with, be Indian with. Someone who understands the jokes, you know?"

Now I did understand what he was saying. I had lost count of the times I'd translate something to Nick and he'd sit there with a wrinkle on his forehead, unable to comprehend the Indianness of what I was telling him. But I needed more from a relationship than the understanding of a joke or an Indian cliché. I needed so much more. I needed Nick.

"Priya Ma," *Nanna* came outside then, obviously at the urging of my mother, "why don't you offer our guest a cup of *chai?*"

"Of course," I said, and looked at Adarsh. The meeting as such was over. Now we'd have to make a decision based on this small conversation. A decision of a lifetime!

"How much sugar would you like?" I asked him.

"I don't drink tea," Adarsh replied.

"Coffee?" I asked.

"No thanks, I'm fine," he said. "It was nice talking to you," he added.

I smiled at him before walking away.

Even before I entered the kitchen, Ma descended upon me. "So what did he say? What did you say? You didn't make any *pitchi-pitchi* remarks, did you?"

"No, Ma, I didn't make any insane remarks," I muttered, and sat down on a dining chair instead of going inside the kitchen. My heart was racing at a hundred miles a second. I had gone through with this demeaning ceremony. I, who was already spoken for, had talked to another man who considered himself a potential husband to me. I had insulted Nick, our relationship, myself, and, ultimately, even Adarsh.

"So . . . how did it go?" Sowmya asked.

"Okay," I said, as tears threatened to fall like little hard pebbles of hail.

"Do you like him?" she asked.

"Of course she likes him," Ma said. "What's not to like?"

"Radha," my father called out from the living room. "They're leaving. Come here, will you?"

I joined my mother to bid our guests farewell. Adarsh smiled at me, and his parents grinned knowingly at mine when they saw their son smile at who they thought was their future daughter-in-law.

✳ ✳ ✳

To: Nicholas Collins <Nick_Collins@xxxx.com>
From: Priya Rao <Priya_Rao@yyyy.com>
Subject: I'm so sorry!

Nick, I am so so so so so sorry!

I told you I wouldn't go through with the bride-seeing ceremony but I did. I sat through the damn thing and even talked to the husband-not-to-be. This doesn't mean anything. I hope you understand that. I couldn't back out. My parents . . . *Thatha*, everyone . . . Lord, I'm sorry.

I'm so scared that now you won't love me anymore and that now when I tell my parents about you, they won't love me anymore. I feel very lonely, very confused, and very angry.

I'm really sorry that I couldn't find a way to extricate myself from this. I'm going to tell them about you tonight, right after dinner. I promise.

I do love you.
Priya

* * *

To: Priya Rao <Priya_Rao@yyyy.com>
From: System Administrator
<postmaster@yyyy.com>

Subject: Undeliverable: I am so sorry!
Your message
To: Nicholas_Collins@xxx.com
Subject: I'm so sorry!

SENT: SATURDAY 14:02:21 -0800
DID NOT REACH THE FOLLOWING RECIPIENT(S):
NICHOLAS_COLLINS@XXX.COM ON SATURDAY
14:02:21 -0800
ERROR: RECIPIENT SERVER NOT RESPONDING.

Number 65 and
the Consequences of
Confessions and Lies

S owmya looked into the mirror, the blue-bordered sari that I had worn just that afternoon draped over her shoulder. "Do you think I will look as nice as you did?" she asked.

"You'll look better," I said.

"You think he'll like me the way Adarsh liked you?" she asked, her eyes glittering behind her thick glasses. "Maybe I shouldn't wear my glasses, huh?"

"Wear them, don't wear them, it doesn't matter," I told her. "And Adarsh does *not* like me. There's nothing to like," I added.

Sowmya put the sari down and picked up the sapphire jewelry I had also worn to parade in front of Adarsh and his parents. "*Amma* said that she will give these to me when I get married. If this boy likes me, you and I can have a double wedding. What do you think?"

She was trying so hard to make Nick disappear that I couldn't take offense, but I couldn't let it slide either. Guilt sat steadily in my throat like the taste of the bitter soft stone of a raw mango; no matter what I ate or drank after biting the soft stone, its taste stayed with me.

"I'm not going to marry Adarsh, Sowmya," I said quietly.

She sighed and put the jewelry away and turned from the mirror in *Ammamma's* room to face me. "You can't marry a foreigner, Priya," she told me calmly as she picked up the blue sari again. "You just can't. They will all disown you. You will have to choose."

I shrugged. "It's no contest, Sowmya," I said with certainty. "I will always pick Nick."

As soon as I said it, I wondered. If push came to shove, which it would when I told my parents and *Thatha* about Nick, would I just walk out and fly away to the United States to be Nick's wife? What about the daughter, granddaughter, cousin, niece inside me? Would I happily sacrifice all those identities to be Nick's wife? I knew I would, I was sure I would, but it would be a sacrifice, and a big one. And did relationships based upon sacrifices truly work?

Maybe in a few years I would miss my family and they still wouldn't want me; would that make me resent Nick? No, I told myself confidently, nothing would make me resent Nick. He was everything I wanted in a man, a husband, a friend. He was it. If he were Indian instead of American, or even better, if he were a Telugu *Brahmin*, my parents and grandparents would've jumped at the idea of our marriage and would've paid for a lavish wedding, inviting everyone they knew.

None of that would happen now. My wedding would be an almost clandestine affair that'd take place far away from India and its mores in the United States, which my family would believe to be more suited for our unholy matrimony. There wouldn't be hundreds of Ma's and *Nanna's* and *Thatha's* friends and my family, there would be Nick and his family and our friends. Would it matter that I would be without my family, the family, which had been part of my weekends by phone for the past seven years?

Every weekend I would call home, or if my parents were at *Thatha's* house, I'd call there and we'd talk. I looked forward to calling my family on Saturday nights, sometimes on Friday nights if Nick and I were home. Would I miss that large telephone bill at the end of the month?

Ma walked into *Ammamma's* room and threw her hands up in exasperation. "You also want to wear that hideous sari, Sowmya?" she asked. "She looked like someone's grandma; you will look like her grandma's grandma. Wear that yellow sari with the red border."

Sowmya's face fell. "But, *Akka*, I like the blue—"

"Wear that red border one," Ma said forcefully. "Or do you want to go through another sixty-five of these?"

"Ma!" I cried out at her rudeness, but Ma just waved a hand and said, "Hush, what do you know? You just got here, *maharani*, and you are lucky that Rice Sarma's son was in India at the same time. Sowmya doesn't have those benefits."

Sowmya pushed her sliding glasses up her nose.

"*Ma*," I protested again, now embarrassed, and Ma shushed me again.

"Mahadevan Uncle called your father. Looks like they will make a proposal by tomorrow morning," Ma said, gleeful triumph in her eyes coupled with a challenge for me to refuse this prize stud she'd found me.

I looked at her with wide eyes. "What proposal?"

"Farming proposal!" Ma said indignantly. "Marriage proposal, Priya. That is what we do. We see a family and the boy and then they make a marriage proposal and we accept."

"Whoa . . . who said anything about accepting?" I demanded.

Sowmya raised both her hands. "*Akka*, they'll be here soon and I need Priya to help me get ready. Neelima left with Anand, and they won't be back until tomorrow, so I really need Priya."

Ma looked at me and then at Sowmya. "I told you, Priya, no *nakhras*, your father might tolerate that nonsense, but I will take my slipper and beat the living daylights out of you if you continue to misbehave."

I blinked and shook my head. I was not going to dignify that lame threat with a response.

"Remember that," Ma added ominously before she left.

"She thinks that I'm still ten and she can hit me," I muttered. "Why do Indian parents think they can beat their children into submission?"

"That is how it is," Sowmya said wisely. "Now tell me, will I look good in this yellow and red sari?" she asked, as she draped the sari in question over her shoulder.

✳ ✳ ✳

The "boy" who came to see Sowmya was definitely not a prize stud. His name was Vinay and he was soft-spoken, true to his name, but the rest was a far cry from anyone's Dream Man. He was extremely dark (even darker than I), a little on the short side (but still taller by at least a couple of inches than Sowmya); he wore glasses, which were as thick as Sowmya's, and to add to the interesting mix of physical traits was the small patch of balding hair that he was trying to hide with the classic and unsuccessful combover.

Sowmya served him and his parents the *bajjis* and *ladoos* while I served them tea, happy to be of help, since Vinay was Sowmya's suitor, not mine. Vinay's parents seemed like very nice people, polite and nonconfrontational. Vinay was thirty-five years old and was looking for someone who was homely and religious. Not too religious, though, just enough—should know how to do *puja* and keep *madhi*. Sowmya was par excellence at both. While Sowmya's grandmother, my great-grandmother, was alive, Sowmya was asked time and again to keep *madhi*; that is, to cook right after she took a bath before touching or doing anything else and preferably in wet clothes. Sowmya flat out refused to cook in wet clothes as great-grandma expected, but she knew the ins and outs of all the religious nooks and crannies.

They didn't want a working daughter-in-law, Vinay's parents said. They wanted grandchildren soon. Oh, Vinay is still single because he was so busy with his career. Couldn't be that busy, I thought cynically, after all he was just a small-time lecturer at some out of the way engineering college.

While I served tea, Sowmya sat demurely looking at her painted nails as her fingers fondled the yellow tassels at the edge of the red border of her sari.

"Do you play any instrument?" Vinay asked Sowmya and she nodded.

"I play the *veena*," she said.

Jayant had brought the *veena* out from storage just that morning and Sowmya and I had dusted it clean. *Thatha* had been informed from a good source that the "boy" liked music and since Sowmya could play the *veena*, everyone thought it would be a good idea to keep it handy.

I slipped out of the living room into the backyard when Sowmya started playing. As the notes filtered through the house, it was obvious that the *veena* idea was a bad one. It had been almost three years since Sowmya had touched the musical instrument; she needed practice and a lot of it.

I found Nate in the backyard tying his shoelaces by the *tulasi* plant.

"Where're you going?" I asked.

"Home," he said without looking at me.

"Oh."

He stood up and then looked me in the eye. "You should tell him, Priya. You should tell him."

"I have told him," I said, and when he looked at me suspiciously, I spilled the truth out. "The email bounced back, but I will send him another one. I will call him and tell him. *Ottu*, promise. I will."

Nate shook his head.

"And even if I didn't tell him, I don't see what the problem is. It's not like I'm going to marry Adarsh or anything," I said belligerently.

"No, but you definitely gave everyone the idea you would marry him," Nate pointed out. "Look, none of my business, but I just think that . . . I don't know what you're waiting for. They're going to make a proposal, what do you plan to do then? Not say anything?"

Sowmya stopped playing the *veena*, just as I got ready to lay it on Nate. Who did he think he was? Some *laat-sahib*, some big shot who could tell me what to do and when?

"I just feel bad about all of this," he said before I could yell at him. "I wish I could help, Priya, but I'm just going to go home and enjoy the house without Ma."

"I'll call you, as soon as . . . ," I said. I knew he was being honest with me because he cared about me.

"You're going to break *Nanna's* heart," Nate said. "That's going to be hard."

"Yes, and *Thatha's*," I said. "But what has to be done—"

"Priya?" Lata came out and I bit my lip. How much had she heard? Did we say anything incriminating?

"They're leaving and your mother wants you there," she said, and then smiled at Nate. "Going, Nate?"

"Yes," Nate said casually. He winked at me before leaving.

"He is so aloof," Lata complained. "As if we are not good enough."

"He just likes his own company," I defended Nate immediately. "And he is *not* aloof."

"Oh, come on, he has always been in his own world, not interested in the family or anything," Lata said, and then sighed. "Of course, you don't see anything wrong because you are his doting sister."

"There *is* nothing wrong with him," I said annoyed.

The family was not fond of Nate. It was as if he was more *Nanna's* son than Ma's. Even *Thatha* was more close to me than to Nate. It probably was because Nate spent more time with his friends and on his own than with the family. *Nanna* always said that he didn't blame Nate. "He isn't married to your mother, he doesn't have to be in her parents' house all the time," he would say.

And to be honest, Nate didn't even try to get along with *Thatha* or *Ammamma* or anyone else. He spoke to Anand once in a while and got along reasonably well with him, but the rest of the family could go hang itself and Nate wouldn't give a damn, as he always said.

❋ ❋ ❋

After the guests left, everyone congregated in the living room. *Thatha* opened his pouch of tobacco and started rubbing some in the palm of his hand. "Nice family . . . enh, Sowmya?"

Sowmya nodded.

Ammamma banged her hand against the arm of the sofa she was sitting on. "Very nice. If this works out . . . a big burden will be off our heads. I can't wait for this marriage to take place. Ten years . . . ten long years . . . Now I want to see my Sowmya married."

"They will definitely ask for dowry," Jayant said. "Do you know what they want?"

Thatha put the tobacco inside his lower lip and sucked the tobacco into his mouth. "From what I hear they are not greedy people. And whatever they want, we will give . . . within reason, of course."

Sowmya fidgeted with the gold bangle she was wearing. "He lives with his parents," she said quietly.

"And . . . ?" *Thatha* demanded immediately.

Sowmya just shrugged.

"Why? You don't want to take care of his parents?" *Thatha* asked, chewing the tobacco noisily. "Sowmya?" he asked again when she didn't respond.

"No, nothing like that," she all but whimpered.

"So, do we have a problem, Sowmya?" *Thatha* asked.

"No," she said after a minute's hesitation.

We all knew she was lying.

✳   ✳   ✳

"Grooms are not lining up outside the gate, you know," Lata said as nicely as she could to Sowmya when the three of us were in the kitchen. "And his parents seem like nice people."

Sowmya shrugged as she squeezed the pulp out of the tamarind, which was soaking in water. "Priya, large pieces, Ma. We need large pieces of tomato for the *sambhar*," she told me, and threw the pieces of tomato I had diced into the sink. "You don't even know the basics, Priya," she complained. "You have to learn to cook . . . And if you don't . . . just leave my kitchen."

I wanted to leave *her* kitchen as she suggested. It was there just for an instant, the prick of pride, piercing and slamming against ego. I let it pass.

"I'll do it properly," I said, and showed her as I cut the tomatoes into large pieces. "This will do?"

Sowmya nodded without looking at me.

"He is a nice boy," Lata said, looking up from the pearl onions she was peeling.

"He is thirty-five, dark, balding, and he wants dowry," Sowmya said, tears glistening at the edge of her eyes, threatening to fall. "And he wants his wife to take care of his old parents. Haven't I done enough? How many people do I need to take care of? What about me? Who will take care of me?" The tears fell.

I wanted to console her, but I didn't have the words. What would I say to her? Wait for number sixty-six; maybe that will bring better luck?

Sowmya sat down on the floor and buried her face in her hands. "He asks if there is problem." she sobbed, "There is always a problem. . . . I am the problem. Can't wait to get rid of me, she keeps saying."

"They don't mean it that way," I said lamely.

"What would you know?" Sowmya flashed at me. "You have Mr. Mercedes wanting to marry you and you have an American boyfriend who wants to marry you. You have all the choices and . . ." She stopped speaking as she saw the shock on my face and then on Lata's.

"American boyfriend?" Lata said, catching the most important part.

"I was just making a point," Sowmya tried to backtrack but it was already too late.

"Yes," I said boldly. No point in lying anymore, I realized. It was time. I should have done this as soon as I got to India. I shouldn't have waited. "But please don't tell anyone anything," I pleaded. "I want to be the one to tell them."

Lata nodded and then threw her hands up in the air. "You girls complicate your lives," she said in exasperation. "When I was getting married it was simple. The first groom who said yes, it was yes. With you—"

"It is not like I have been saying no, Lata," Sowmya pointed out.

"I know," Lata said, and sighed. "Our choices are so pathetic. Look at me, pregnant for the third time so that your father can have a grandson, so that Jayant can feel that he is for once closer to his father than Anand, so that when the old man dies he will leave something more to us than he plans to. Disgusting lives we women have to live."

"We make our own choices," I said.

"No," Sowmya said as she stood up. "No, we don't. If I had a choice, I would have gotten a job, gotten outside the house. Who knows, met someone. But *Nanna* wouldn't have it."

"*You* have choices," Lata said, looking at me. "And you are going to blow it. An American boyfriend?"

"I didn't plan it," I told her what I had told Sowmya. "It just happened."

"Have you slept with him?" Lata asked.

"None of your business," I said without thinking. "That's very personal."

"There is no *personal* for women," Sowmya piped in. "My father knows when I menstruate because I have to sit out, they know who talks to me and who doesn't, they know what movie I see and with whom, they know exactly, down to the *paisa* what I spend on anything. Personal! My foot!"

I had never seen Sowmya so riled up, but then I had never seen her as a real woman with feelings and emotions, always as Sowmya, everyone's punching bag. The one you could dump on, the one who put up with everything. I think all of us had forgotten that beneath the thick glasses lay the perceptive eyes of a woman. Not some bride-to-be but a grown woman who was as angry at the world as I was but had more of a right to be so.

I found Indian rituals appalling but I didn't have to live them; Sowmya and Lata did. My life was better and my choices infinitely more appealing than theirs. My parents had given me this and I owed them the truth about my personal life. They needed to know and soon that Nick existed and because he did exist, I could not marry Adarsh or any other good-looking Indian "boy."

✳ ✳ ✳

"Where did Natarajan go?" *Ammamma* asked. Both *Thatha* and *Ammamma* refused to call Nate anything but Natarajan. Nate they said was too anglicized and in any case why would you shorten a nice God's name like Natarajan?

"He had some studying to do, so he went home," *Nanna* made the excuse. "He wants to catch up with next semester's syllabus."

"What a hardworking boy," *Ammamma* said, buying into the cock-and-bull story. "See, Priya, that is the kind of boy girls want to marry. And Adarsh is like that. His mother told me that he used to study until four in the morning every day to pass the BITS Pilani entrance exam. Hardworking boys make good husbands."

First, BITS Pilani, unlike all other engineering colleges in India, did not have an entrance exam; admission was granted based on 12th class exam results. Second, I couldn't figure out the connection between hard work and good husband; I knew several hardworking guys at work who I was positive would make awful husbands.

"Pass the *sambhar*, Priya Ma," *Nanna* said, looking at me curiously. "So, what did you think of Adarsh?"

"What do you mean, what did she think?" Ma demanded. "She—"

"Radha, I want to know what she thought," *Nanna* interrupted Ma. It was a ploy; he knew I couldn't speak my mind here, in front of all these people.

"I don't know," I said honestly. "I spent all of ten minutes with him. It's hard for me to say what he's like."

Ma's face twisted and she glared at me.

"No, seriously," I said, "you expect me to marry this man and I don't even get a chance to talk to him before *Nanna* shows up asking if he wants *chai*."

"How much time would you need?" *Thatha* asked. "A whole day? A year? Priya, marriage is what all that time is for."

"Not in my world," I said easily. "I don't want to risk marrying the wrong man because tradition expected me to not know him before marriage. I can't take that chance."

"We all took that chance and we have done just fine," *Ammamma* said.

I shook my head. "Please, I don't want to discuss this."

"Why?" Ma asked.

I was about to tell her exactly why when in pure movie fashion, the phone rang. Sowmya got up and went into the hall to answer it. It was for my father.

Nanna came back, a 1,000-watt smile on his face. "They said yes," he said, beaming at me, and I felt as if a basketful of raw mangoes fell on top of my head.

You Can't Make Mango Pickle with Tomatoes

Everyone was very excited for the remainder of the dinner, making wedding plans and discussing how everything would have to be done fast-fast. Sowmya, Lata, and I sat somberly looking at each other. I had never expected it, but Lata and I were suddenly on the same side, while *Nanna* had joined the evil one on the dark side.

"They want to take the *tamboolalu* in the next two days and we can set the marriage date for . . ." *Nanna* said, looking at me, gauging my reaction.

"Ah, Priya can get more holiday," Ma said, overjoyed that finally all her efforts were coming to fruition. "What, Priya, your American boss won't give extra holiday for your own wedding?"

"Now all we need is for Vinay to say yes to Sowmya," *Ammamma* said, the loose skin around her jaw jumping around like Jell-O. "A double wedding . . . ah . . . a double wedding."

Ma leaned over to me and whispered, "They want a double

wedding so that they can reduce cost, but we won't have any of it, okay. Big wedding for my daughter," she said and then smiled. She kissed me on the forehead, pleased, I think, more with herself than with me. "Big wedding," she said, flushed, the happiness vibrating through her nauseating me with its consequences.

The blood roared in my ears; I could hear what everyone was saying but I couldn't quite comprehend anything. The boy said yes? Why on earth would he do that? Didn't I try my best to put him off?

"At that new reception hall," Jayant was saying, "where that actress . . . What's her name, Lata?"

"We have to shop for saris," *Ammamma* was saying. "Can't go to Madras, not enough time . . . Chandana Brothers will have to do"

"I have all the jewelry ready," Ma was saying. "Everything is ready . . . "

"Priya Ma," *Nanna's* voice reached my ear and something snapped inside me. This man loved me and he was entitled to the truth.

"I can't marry Adarsh," I said as the last hands were being washed in silver and steel plates. "Or anyone else you want me to marry," I spoke over Ma's tirade of objections and curses. "I came to India at this time to tell you all that I'm in love with an American and I plan to marry him. We're engaged." I showed them the winking diamond on my finger, which I put back on *after* the *pelli-chupulu*.

Silence fell in the room and then suddenly conversation rose like the small buzz of a mosquito raging into a zillion buzzing mosquitoes.

Nanna stood up unsteadily. "You hurt me, Priya Ma," he said and walked out of the dining room, the hall, and, finally, *Thatha's* house with the creak of *Thatha's* noisy gate and the small roar of his Fiat.

And with those simple words, *Nanna* broke my heart as well. The tears I had been holding back raced down my cheeks. Nate had been right; telling *Nanna* was very hard. It was harder to see *Thatha* sit rigidly, his expression unfathomable. I had opened all the doors to hell for my father and grandfather. That was the way they probably looked at what I am sure they saw as the ultimate defection.

"American?" Ma was dumbfounded. "American?" she repeated. She had already said that a few times, as if questioning it several times would change it.

I started to help Sowmya clear up the dining table while *Ammamma* just kept making sounds and Jayant sat quietly sipping water from a steel glass.

I knew that this was the lull before the storm. This was the quiet after which nothing would be the same again. It had been done and now I was scared that they would stop loving me. They would tell me to go away, like family did in movies, and never set foot in their house again.

I stood at the doorway between the kitchen and the dining area, while Sowmya and Lata rinsed the dishes, whispering to each other.

"Just because you are wearing some ring, doesn't mean you are engaged," Ma said, her voice strained and thin. "This boy . . . Adarsh is perfect. You will marry him before you leave and that is that. You will forget this American and—"

"It isn't that simple, Ma," I spoke over her words. In the kitchen, the sounds of water and steel clashing stopped and when I didn't say anything else the sounds resumed.

There was silence while Lata and Sowmya piled rinsed steel plates and glasses and ladles into the plastic tub for Parvati to wash the next morning.

I helped Sowmya carry the plastic tub outside into the back yard.

"Now what?" I asked unsteadily.

Sowmya just smiled. "Now we will have a family *Mahabharatam*."

I leaned against the cement base of the *tulasi* plant, not too keen on going back inside. The tension was flowing out of the house in small waves slowly coming together to form a tornado. I plucked a *tulasi* leaf and put it inside my mouth to stop tasting the rising bile of fear.

"They're going to kick me out or they're going to tie me up and marry me to this Adarsh fellow," I said. "What if they don't want to ever see me again?" I asked, my eyes filling yet again. "Will they just let me go?"

Sowmya took her hand in mine. "No," she said. "No one will let you go. They will be angry with you for a while but they will come around."

Lata came outside and asked if everything was okay.

"She is scared," Sowmya said sympathetically.

"So she should be," Lata said. "Once your mother gets over the shock, she is going to beat you within an inch of your life."

I sighed.

"And your *Thatha* is . . . Well, he is going to watch," Lata continued with a grin. "At least it is done. Now you can let what has to happen, happen."

"Let's go inside," Sowmya suggested. "Otherwise they'll think that you ran away."

Running away sounded like a real good idea, right about now.

✳ ✳ ✳

Everyone was sitting in the living room when we came back in. There was still no sign of *Nanna*. He never just left without telling anyone where he was going, no matter how upset he was or how big the fight he'd had with Ma. This was unusual but then it wasn't every day his favorite daughter not only broke his dreams but walked all over them with pointed shoes as well. Even though this was my life and I knew in my head that I had to live it the way I wanted to, I couldn't shrug the guilt away. It was there, rock solid, without give. And there was another form of guilt, the guilt for feeling guilty in the first place. Nick was part of my life, the man who had accepted all my flaws and I was feeling guilty about loving him, living with him. I was wishing, in a small corner of my mind, that he didn't exist in my life so that I could marry Adarsh or some other sap like him and not have this conflict with my parents.

"So we'll tell the Sarmas that you are saying yes, right?" Ma was agitated and her face was flushed, her tone flustered. She was scared, I realized, afraid that I had actually meant what I said about an American boyfriend. My heart went out to her. Like Sowmya, she was trying her best to make Nick go away.

"No, Ma, we can't," I said, and sat down beside her.

She slapped me across the face and tears streaked down her cheeks. "How could you, Priya? We taught you well . . . we raised you right and . . . How could you, Priya?"

I buried my face in my hands. This was just as bad as I had thought it would be. I stemmed my tears by pressing my eyes with my hands.

"I'm sorry," I said to Ma, facing her with clear eyes. "I didn't plan to fall in love with Nick, it just happened. And I can't *just* marry someone else. I don't want to marry anyone but Nick."

"Then you should have said something earlier," Jayant said, looking just as agitated now as Ma. "What will we tell the Sarmas? You have put us all in an embarrassing situation."

I wanted to remind them all that they had forced the *pelli-chupulu* on me, that I was not to blame for that, but I couldn't because a part of me blamed myself. I knew that if I had told them about Nick earlier, they would've put a stop to it. Even if Ma and *Thatha* wouldn't, I knew my father definitely would have.

"You have shamed us," *Ammamma* added her two cents. "An American? At least Anand married an Indian . . . but you have just ruined our good name. It is not too late, Priya. Forget this American, Nicku-Bicku, and marry that Sarma boy. Good boys like him don't come around all the time."

I waited for *Thatha* to say something but he was not saying a word. He was sitting as rigidly as he had before, looking into space. I wished he would say something, anything. The two people who I had been most afraid of hurting were hurt and they were the two who were saying the least; in fact, they had said nothing.

"When are you planning to marry this Nicku person?" Ma asked.

"Sometime this year," I said. "I know you don't approve—"

"Approve?" Ma charged at me. "You don't care if we approve. You don't care if our names are dragged through the mud. You are a selfish girl, Priya, only caring about yourself. We should never have let you go to America without marriage. Your father and I were too soft and you have taken advantage of us."

It was not like that hadn't crossed my mind and because it had, guilt, which was already lying heavily on me, increased in weight.

Several of my classmates from engineering school in India had married "boys" in the United States, while I and a few others had not. Our parents had not insisted that marriage be a criterion for leaving their home. They could have made it an issue but they hadn't. They had trusted me to take care of myself, to not fall in love with some foreigner, and I had betrayed their trust. That was what Ma had said when she had talked about Anand marrying Neelima, "What can we do when someone takes your trust and throws it away?" And I had done exactly that.

"I didn't do it on purpose," I cried out. "Ma, these things happen. I'm sorry that you don't approve, that you feel I've betrayed you, but this is my life and I have to live my life, you can't live it for me. I have to be happy and I can't let you be happy for me. And for me to be happy, I need to marry Nick. It's that simple."

"Nothing is that simple," *Thatha* finally spoke. "You think your marriage to a foreigner is going to be all roses?"

I shook my head. "All relationships have problems. That's a fact of life."

"But this relationship will have more problems than most," *Thatha* said assuredly. "You obviously will not have any support from your family. I don't know about his family but I am sure they are not completely happy about this. How can they be?"

"But they are, *Thatha*," I said. "They are. Nick's family loves me. They accept me and don't notice that I'm Indian."

"Then they are being dishonest," *Thatha* said confidently. He couldn't fathom that a world existed where people didn't notice skin color and differentiate on its basis.

"They will never accept you completely," *Thatha* declared. "And what will you be left with then? A marriage to a man who your family, your world, doesn't accept and his family accepts you, but reluctantly. I promise you that if you get married to this American, your marriage will end in divorce."

I was shocked at his cruelty. It was cruel to tell me that my impending marriage had no chance of survival. It was cruel to tell me that he would abandon me if I married Nick. It was cruel and unkind and he hit all the marks he wanted to strike with his words.

"Then it will be a risk I must take," I said bravely and got up. "Do you want me to leave your house now?"

"Priya!" Ma exclaimed.

Thatha shook his head. "No. You are still my granddaughter."

I nodded.

"It will never work, Priya. You cannot make mango pickle with tomatoes," he warned. "You cannot mesh two cultures without making a mess of it. I say this because I love you. Forget about this American. They are not our people. They will never understand us. Marry Adarsh. He is a good boy and it will make your family happy."

I shook my head.

"No, no . . ." *Thatha* said with a tight smile. "Don't make any rash decisions. Take your time to think about it. We don't have to say anything to Sarma-*garu* until tomorrow afternoon."

I didn't bother to tell him that I was not going to change my mind. Like my father had just a while ago, I walked out of *Thatha's* house into the warm night. No one called out after me to warn me how dangerous it was to be out at night, but it was just nine o'clock and the sky was still not completely black; hints of the sun still lurked in crimson streaks around sparse sickly clouds.

I went to the telephone booth from where I had called Nick just a few hours ago and dialed my parents' home number. Nate picked up the phone on the fourth ring.

I was sobbing and couldn't get any words out.

Nate was in front of the telephone booth on his motorbike within twenty minutes of my hysterical phone call. It was a Yamaha, which my father and paternal grandfather had given him for his eighteenth birthday a year ago against Ma's vehement objection. She was convinced that Nate would die in an accident on his Yamaha and hated it with a passion. I had shipped a helmet for him, which had annoyed Ma because she thought I was encouraging him but had pleased her as well, because she knew a helmet would keep her son safe.

"I know this great place where they serve very good ice cream," Nate said when I sat behind him on the bike.

"Nate, drive carefully or we'll die," I all but shrieked when Nate started driving on the bumpy roads of Hyderabad. Maybe Ma had a point!

The ice cream parlor was a cozy copy of a '50s Hollywood movie. There was a jukebox, a red jalopy in a corner, and Enrique Iglesias was telling some woman she couldn't escape his love at the top of his weepy lungs.

"Nate," I said mortified, "You've brought me to some teenage hangout?"

"Yeah," he said. "I thought you'd like to meet Tara."

I sniffled. "Tara?"

"My girl . . ."

"I know who Tara is," I said, not wanting him to think I had forgotten. "But I'm all blubbery and she'll think I'm a weepy hag."

"She already does," Nate said with a wink, and waved at a pretty girl sitting at a table right ahead of us. "Isn't she lovely?" he asked dramatically in a fake British accent.

"Yes, dear," I said with a grin. This was a side of Nate I had never seen before and it was charming.

"Hi, I am Tara," Tara said enthusiastically.

"Hello, Priya," I said, unsure of what I was supposed to say to her. I held out my hand and she shook it.

"So, how are you doing?" Tara asked. "Are your parents mad as hell about your American fiancé?"

Well, she sure got to the point, I thought critically. Now, as an older sister, it was my job to dislike any woman/girl Nate liked, was involved with, and/or wanted to marry

"Screw them," Tara said before I could respond. "You've got one life . . . no second chances, you know. *Kis-kis ka khyaal rakhenge, haan?* Who, who will we keep happy? So we have to make choices. You have to keep you happy."

"It isn't that simple," I repeated what I had been telling Ma all evening.

"Of course not, that would make it too easy," she said with a grin. "So, Nate tells me that you love *pista kulfi*. They make a wicked *kulfi* here. Why don't I get you one while you tell Nate what you think about me?"

Nate looked at me, his eyebrows raised. "She's very nervous. She blabs when she's nervous."

"She seems super-duper confident to me," I said. "And perky as hell," I added.

Nate's face fell. "You don't like her."

I smiled. "I don't know her and I have yet to make up my mind. So far so good."

Tara came back with *kulfi* for everyone and I got a chance to see how Nate was with a woman. It was a learning experience. He was so much my father in the way he talked and carried himself, always well behaved, always the gentleman.

"I don't want to argue about this, Tara," he said when Tara insisted that Nate wanted to go to the United States to do his masters.

"Well, why not," I said, finishing the *kulfi*. "It's a very beautiful place and you could do your masters in a really nice school there."

"See," Tara said, and put her hand on Nate's. "*Arrey, yaar*, it will be *mast*, a lot of fun."

"Why can't I just stay in India?" Nate asked belligerently. "Not everyone wants to run and join the Americans, *yaar*. I definitely don't."

"Well, I do," Tara said.

"Then you should find a nice boy. . . . Hey, why don't we hook her up with Adarsh Sarma?" Nate suggested jokingly and Tara threw her paper napkin at him.

"You dog," she complained. "But I can come and visit you, right, Priya?"

"Absolutely," I said.

They were so young, I thought. So very young! Was I ever that young? When I was in college, I didn't have any boyfriends. Well, I did have a crush on someone once in a while but no relationships. I had friends. Even now I had a good relationship with a couple of boys I went to engineering college with. With other classmates my relationship was limited to an occasional phone call.

I never had the easygoing teenage years that Nate was indulging in. There were no teenage hangouts, none that I visited, nor was Britney Spears part of my vocabulary. In fact, when I was in India I didn't know much about the pop music of the United States. Nate and Tara were aware of it all, their feet tapped to the music and Tara hummed to the lyrics. This was already another generation and in this generation girls could meet boys at a place like this after nine in the night. My mother would've hung me out to dry if I had tried to leave the house this late and especially to meet a boy.

"My parents adore Nate," Tara told me. "They think he is amazing. They want to meet your parents but Nate keeps avoiding it. But sooner or later, Nate, it will have to happen."

Nate shifted in his red plastic chair uncomfortably.

"You wouldn't like our mother," I said, and thought that Ma would simply hate Tara. Tara was what Ma would call a girl without a mother.

When Nate flipped through television channels to land on MTV, Ma would look at the gyrating, bikini-clad women in the videos and shake her head. "If you had shown up on television like that," she told me, "I would skin you alive. These girls . . . *chee-chee*, they don't have mothers; if they did, no mother, no mother and I don't care which country she is from, would allow this."

Tara definitely fell in the no-mother category in her tight yellow blouse and small black skirt. She wasn't different from a typical girl her age in the U.S. but for me it was a shock to see how much things had changed here in India. When I was this young, there was no way I could've walked out of my mother's house *alive* wearing what she was wearing. Ma would never have permitted me to bring a boyfriend home or even to have one to start with.

Nate and Tara were holding hands, touching each other with a familiarity I had not experienced until I met Nick. I wouldn't be surprised to learn that these two teenagers had had sex, even though it would make me queasy.

Yes, this was a different generation and they made me uneasy with their progressive ways. But who was I to speak? I was planning to marry an American who I'd been living in sin with for the past two years. I most probably made my parents' generation queasy with what they thought were my progressive ways.

"I'm going to put some money in the jukebox," Tara said, and walked toward the glittering music box.

"She is nice," I said because I knew Nate wanted me to like her.

"Yes, she is," Nate said. "Ma will absolutely hate her."

"Yes," I nodded, and we both laughed.

"You feeling better?" Nate asked.

I grinned and patted his hand. "This was a good idea, Nate. Thanks. I feel better. *Thatha* was . . . brutal. He said that we can't make mango pickle with tomatoes, that if I married Nick, our marriage would end in divorce."

"It could," Nate said. "There are no guarantees."

"I know. So, are you planning to marry this girl without a mother?" I asked, not wanting to dwell on my impending marriage and divorce as *Thatha* would like to have it.

Nate laughed. "Before I take her to meet Ma, I really need to get her into a decent *salwar kameez*."

Tara was definitely an independent woman of the twenty-first century. She zipped home on a white Kinetic Honda, waving, even as I gasped at her speed and lack of a helmet.

"She will be fine," Nate said when I voiced my concern, feeling like my mother. "She is always careful and . . . won't wear a helmet, messes up her hair, she says."

Nate and I drove to Tankbund instead of *Thatha's* house and sat down on one of the benches, right next to the statue of Krishnadeva Raya, the great king of the Deccan.

Krishnadeva Raya was part of my childhood; part of my knowledge of Indian history and mythology, of *Thatha* telling me rich, vivid stories of the king and his wise court jester, Tenali Raman. They were fables, part of folklore that had traveled generations to be revealed to me and hopefully to my children through me.

Thatha would sit me on his lap out on the veranda swing. He would fold one leg, which I would sit on, and keep the other leg on the floor to keep the swing in motion. He would then tell me a story.

My favorite was the story where corrupt Brahmins try to

swindle the king and both the king and the Brahmins are taught a lesson by Tenali Raman.

I would make *Thatha* tell me the story again and again of how, when the king's mother dies without her last wish of eating a ripe mango fulfilled, Krishnadeva Raya is filled with guilt and fear that his mother's *atma* is wandering around the earth because of an unfulfilled desire. The court priest, a horrible Brahmin, decides to take advantage of the grief-stricken king and tells him, "Since the Queen Mother died without eating a mango, her soul is lost, crying for closure." *Thatha* would say this in a sad quiet voice, imitating the Brahmin.

The king would then ask in *Thatha's* humble voice, "Mangoes were out of season, there was nothing I could do. What should I do, O great Pandit, to make this right?"

"You have to do a *puja*, a big *puja*," the Brahmin says. "And to ensure that your mother's soul rests in peace, you must give a golden mango to fifty noble Brahmins."

The king thinks it is a wonderful idea and decides to do accordingly, only he thinks fifty to be a small number and invites every Brahmin in his kingdom.

"Every Brahmin got a golden mango?" I would ask *Thatha* the same question each time. "How many gold mangoes would that be, *Thatha*?"

"Hundreds," *Thatha* would say and then would come to the part I loved the most.

Tenali Rama, seeing his Lord and Master being swindled, decides to teach the *Brahmins* a lesson. After the king's *puja*, Raman shows up at the temple and asks the Brahmins to come home with him as his mother had also recently died of an unfulfilled wish. Expecting more goodies the Brahmins follow Raman to his house.

When they get there they find several branding irons resting in hot fire. "What is that for, Raman?" the court priest asks and Raman folds his hands and raises them over his head (*Thatha* would do the same with one hand while the other would hold me), "My mother died of rheumatism and her last wish had been to be branded at her knees to ease the pain. But I am no king, I can't afford gold rods, so these will have to do."

I would cover my mouth with shock. "Did Raman brand the Brahmins, *Thatha*?"

"No." *Thatha* would laugh. "They all ran away, leaving their golden mangoes behind. Seeing them run, the king realizes that he was being conned and thanks Raman for showing him the truth."

"Are all Brahmins cheats?" I asked once, and *Thatha* had shaken his head violently. "No, Priya *Amma*, this is just a story. Brahmins are honest and good people. Tenali Raman was also a Brahmin . . . and he is good, isn't he?"

There were more stories, some about Raman, Jataka tales about Bodhisattva, stories about Jain and Buddha, about Lord Indra, *The Mahabharata, The Ramayana* . . . everything. *Thatha* had been my source of Indian history and mythology. He had been a great storyteller, just like his brother *Kathalu-Thatha* had been. But after I grew too old to sit on his lap, storytelling was replaced with discussions and now, finally, we had reached an impasse.

"I know I eventually have to go to *Thatha's* house and face the music, I just don't want to," I said to Nate.

"Then come home with me," he suggested. "Call and let them know you are at home. A good night's sleep will put everything in perspective for everyone."

"I don't know where *Nanna* went and . . ." I shrugged.

Nate nodded and put his arm around me. He pulled my head against his shoulder and kissed me on my forehead.

"Why is it that you are so close to *Thatha* and I am not?" Nate asked.

"I don't know," I said honestly, and turned to look at him. Objectively speaking he was quite a handsome young man and a wonderfully sensitive one as well. He got that from *Nanna*.

"Lata thinks you're aloof."

"Lata is a ditz," Nate said.

"She's not that much of a ditz," I said, remembering the conversation I'd had with Lata and Sowmya just that evening. "She's actually quite a woman."

"She is pregnant again," Nate said in disgust. "Ma told us and . . . it's just such a farce. The old man wants clean blood, and what the fuck does that mean, anyway?"

Unlike several boys his age, Nate's vocabulary was not littered with obscenities, so the fact that he was using one clearly told me about his strong feelings regarding the matter.

"They'll never give you their permission, if that's what you are looking for," he said, moving on to the topic I didn't want to discuss. "And why does it matter, Priya?"

"I don't know," I told him honestly. "I need them in my life. I need *you* in my life. You're family."

"Need is a very strong word," Nate reminded me.

"I know," I said. "Oh, how I know."

We sat in silence then and watched the cars pass by and for the first time since I had been back, I truly savored India. I had sat right here, on one of these benches seven years ago, watching cars pass by and the lights in Begumpet across Tankbund wink at me. I had sat here and wondered about my new life that awaited me in the United States, the land of opportunities. I couldn't wait to leave, to get on that plane and fly away from my parents' home and all the problems that came with it.

"Why don't you want to leave India, Nate?" I asked since I had been so eager to find the new world.

"I like it here," Nate said. "Why would I leave? Why did you leave?"

I wiped my sweaty hands on my *salwar* as I contemplated his question. "I left because everyone was leaving. All my classmates had written their GRE, some had married men in the U.S. and others were looking for a groom there. But I think the strongest reason was escape. I wanted to get away from here, from Ma and *Nanna* and *Thatha* and the whole family."

"But you still want their approval?"

"Yes," I said. "Ironic, isn't it? I spent so much time trying to get away and now I'm scared that I won't be allowed back in. They've always been my safety net. I have always been daughter, granddaughter, sister, niece just as I have been woman and fiancée. It is who I am. I can't divorce the family any more than I can myself. Do you understand what I'm saying?"

"I think so," Nate said. "I know it looks like I don't care about them, that I'm aloof. The ditz is right. I am aloof. I don't . . . You were always closer to them, Priya. I never thought I could compete. I never thought that *Thatha* would get close to me the way he was to you. Even with *Nanna*, I don't have that closeness you do. I envy you . . . a lot."

"Well, envy no more. I'm losing it all," I said, a little flabbergasted that the nonchalant Nate was after all not all that nonchalant. How we had all misjudged him.

"No, you're not." Nate sighed. "They'll never let go of you. *Nanna* loves you, he loves us both, I know that, but I know that he has this . . . this special relationship with you."

I didn't deny it. I had always known that *Nanna* and I had a closer bond. Maybe because I was the firstborn, maybe because I was a daughter, maybe because I was Priya.

"And how about Ma?"

"Ma will surprise you," Nate said, and smiled. "She may nag, she may be a real pain in the ass, but when the chips are down, she'll be there for both of us. No question about it."

"I wish I was that confident," I said. "She slapped me . . . twice in two days now."

"That's her way of showing love," Nate said, and we both burst out laughing.

"Why didn't you tell me about Nick earlier?" Nate asked. "You've been together for . . ."

"Three years and living together for two of them," I supplied. "I didn't want to tell anyone here. Frankly, I was scared what your reaction would be. An American, a foreigner! I . . . just didn't want to say anything to anyone about him."

"What's he like?"

"He's nice, a good guy. An accountant, how is that for stable and steady?" I said, and Nate grinned. "Accountant Nick! He is . . . he plays racquetball; it's like squash. You'd like him. He hates Madonna, loves Julia Roberts, thinks Salma Hayek is sexy and would like to sleep with Halle Berry. He's tall, dark, and handsome, at least I think so. He's stubborn, hates long lines, does this crazy thing when he has the hiccups. Drives me nuts."

"What does he do?" Nate asked.

"He drinks three sips of water from a tall glass and after each sip he holds the glass up and looks at the bottom of the glass. Apparently it stops the hiccups."

"And does it?"

"That's the weird part, it does," I said smiling. "I miss him. He wanted to come. Said it would be a *Guess Who's Coming to Dinner?* moment. I told him it would be more a *Guess Who's Getting Lynched?* moment."

"It would definitely have been interesting," Nate said, getting up from the bench. "You've got to believe, Priya, that love conquers all. You should've brought him along. Let the old people deal with it head-on."

"Oh, this is scary enough. That would've been worse and I don't need to be scared any more."

I got up and looked at the bench longingly. I would've been content to sit there all night with Nate, but it was time to go.

✳ ✳ ✳

There was still no sign of my father when I got back. *Thatha* and *Ammamma* had already gone to sleep; their bedroom lights were turned off and their door was halfway closed.

Ma and Sowmya were lying on straw mats in the hall talking. When I came and sat beside Sowmya, Ma turned away.

"I'll go and sleep up on the terrace," I told Sowmya, and she asked me to wait a second.

"*Akka*, I will go up with Priya. Is that okay?" she asked.

"Fine," Ma muttered and got up. "I will sleep in the veranda bedroom then and wait for Ashwin to get back. Where has he gone? All your fault, Priya."

I watched her walk out of the living room with detachment. I knew she was angry but now she was ready to blame me for global warming and war as well. I couldn't take her seriously when she was so excessive.

"Jayant and Lata went home?" I asked.

"Sleeping in the dining room bedroom," Sowmya said, and we rolled up the mats, gathered the pillows, and got ready for bed.

It was a beautiful warm night, despite the mosquitoes being out in the millions. We lit a mosquito coil close to our mats and lay down facing each other, our cheeks pillowed against our folded hands.

"Where did you go?" Sowmya asked.

"Nate took me to meet his girlfriend and then we sat at Tankbund," I told her.

"Is she nice-looking?"

"Yes, very cute. But North Indian," I said. "Ma will hate her."

"*Abba*, your Ma will hate anyone Nate marries, even if it is a girl she picks out herself," Sowmya said.

"I wonder where *Nanna* went." I sighed.

Sowmya sat up and looked at me. "I need your advice on something."

"What?" I sat up, too.

"I want to talk to Vinay . . . all alone. How can we do it?"

"Why?"

"They said they would make a proposal. They need to look through the horoscopes or something before they—"

"When did this happen?" I asked.

"They called right after you left," Sowmya said in exasperation.

"Things have never come this far before so *Nanna* is very happy, ready to give anything to get rid of me. But . . . I want to talk to him and if he is not to my liking, I don't want to marry him."

I stared at her and blinked. "What?"

"What do you mean, what? Just because I am thirty years old doesn't mean I will marry any man who comes my way. He is nice. He seems like a good person, but I want to talk to him," she said, strong determination in her voice. "What do you think?"

"I think you definitely should talk to the man before you—"

"I have his phone number. I need for you to call him and set up a meeting for tomorrow," Sowmya said, talking over me, as if she had it all planned. "We can meet at Minerva. And you will have to come along. I need you for support."

I sat up and blew out some air. "If they find out . . ."

"You are already in trouble, this won't make things any worse for you," she said with unfailing logic. "So will you call him?"

"Sure," I said. "First thing tomorrow morning."

"Good. It is a Sunday so he will be at home," Sowmya said, smiling. "I am going to change my life, Priya. I am going to change it. I am not just going to sit down and let them do what they want. . . . I am going to decide what I want to do."

I was amazed. This was not the Sowmya I knew. But the Sowmya I knew was seven years in the past. This Sowmya had had experiences and epiphanies I didn't even know about. This Sowmya was a revelation.

"What happened?"

"You," she said sincerely. "You are like me, Priya. We come from the same background, same place, but you have a different life. I want to have a different life, too. I don't mean I want to marry an American or anything, I just want to do the things I want to do."

"Like?"

"Work. I got a job offer to be an assistant at this doctor's office. She is a friend of mine and she needs help. *Nanna* said there was no way I could do it, but now, I think I will," she said, her face lighting up with the new life she was dreaming up. "And I want to stop wearing saris. I want to only wear *salwar kameez*. This sari is so uncomfortable. And I want to go to America to see your house and see that country."

"You are very welcome to visit," I said, enjoying this new Sowmya.

"So you will call him, right?"

"Absolutely."

Part Five

Leftovers

Perugannam (Curd Rice)

2 cups cooked rice
1 ½–2 cups thick curd (yogurt)
½ cup milk
salt to taste
½ cup fried peanuts
1 tablespoon finely chopped coriander leaves

Ingredients for the Seasoning
1 teaspoon oil
½ teaspoon mustard seeds
½ teaspoon Bengal *gram* (yellow *dal*)
½ teaspoon split black *gram* (black *dal*)
1 dry red chile, broken into bits
1 green chile, finely chopped
1-inch piece of ginger, finely chopped
5 curry leaves

In a wok, heat oil and when the oil is very hot, add the mustard seeds. Once the mustard seeds start to crackle, add the rest of the spices and fry until they are golden brown. Be careful not to burn the spices. Add the thick curd to the wok and stir until it liquefies and mixes well with the spices. Put all the rice inside as well and mix thoroughly so that it is completely coated with the yogurt and spice mixture. Garnish with peanuts and coriander. Serve warm or cold with lime or mango pickle.

Bridegrooms
and Boyfriends

I woke up to the sound of metal crashing against cement. I sat up, zombielike, when there was another sharp crash. I looked around with blind, sleep-ridden eyes.

Who the f——?

Sowmya was still sleeping and from what I could make out from my wristwatch, which wasn't much, considering I was still half-asleep, it was almost six in the morning.

I rose unsteadily and walked to the edge of the terrace and leaned over to investigate the noise and see if I could yell some sense into the noise-maker.

I smiled sleepily. How could I have forgotten?

Thatha was standing by the *tulasi* plant in his white *panchi* and looking like he belonged in the fifteenth century or some old-fashioned Telugu movie. His fingers were strumming the white thread that crossed his chest and hung loosely on his body, as if it were a guitar. Like every devout Brahmin, *Thatha* invoked the *Gayatri mantram* every morning to welcome the day. I watched him circle the holy *tulasi* plant and pour water into the cement pot with the offensive brass mug that had fallen on the cement floor and woken me up.

His deep voice boomed to me and even though I couldn't hear the words, I could feel them, words that were forbidden to women. Sanskrit, sacred words from the Vedas, passed from generation to generation, secretly, to men, by men.

Om

Bhur bhuva swah

Tat savitur varnyam

Bhargo devasya dhimahi

Dhiyo yo nah prachodayat

Om

The words were Sanskrit, unadulterated by bad pronunciation or lack of knowledge. He knew what he was talking about, but I don't think he really understood what the *mantram* stood for.

I knew; I had asked *Nanna* and he had explained to both Nate and me. The *mantram* stood for enlightenment. It was the way a Brahmin man could become a better person. It was to invoke the sun god and ask the light of the generous sun to enlighten the reader of the *mantram*, so that he could love all, wipe away hate, and start taking the journey that would bring him closer to the supreme god.

"Why can't girls say it? Why only boys?" I'd asked *Nanna*.

"I don't care if you want to say it," he said. "Do you want to wake up at six in the morning *every day* and say the *mantram*?"

Considering that waking up at seven-thirty in the morning to catch the school bus at eight-thirty was a trial, I shook my head and decided that maybe it was okay that Nate would have to be the one to wake up early, not me. As things turned out, Nate refused to have his thread ceremony done and was planning to never have it done.

"If I don't feel like a *Brahmin*, then why should I follow this farce?" he asked my mother, who had then blistered his ear about tradition and culture. He responded to that by saying that just yesterday he'd had beef *biriyani* at an Irani Café in Mehndipatnam and didn't care all that much about tradition and culture. Ma was so shocked she never brought the topic up again, mostly, we believed, out of fear that Nate would disclose the meat . . . no, no, that could even be overlooked, but the *beef*-eating incident to *Thatha* and the others. That couldn't and wouldn't be overlooked.

"Didn't the boy know that the cow was sacred?" Ma had demanded of *Nanna*, whose job it had suddenly become to instruct Nate on how to be a good Brahmin.

"Maybe if you read the *Gayatri mantram* like my father does, your son will learn something," Ma had told *Nanna*, who had turned a deaf ear to her demands and pleas in that regard.

But reading the *mantram* was just a formality. *Thatha* didn't really believe in what it was telling him, to hate none and love all. He did what he did because it was expected of him, because his father before him had said the same *mantram* in the same way with the same passion and lack of understanding. If *Thatha* understood and abided by the *mantram* he would not have a problem accepting Nick or anyone else that I might want to marry.

This was a man whose life was steeped in ritual. Life and tradition lay alongside each other and bled into each other. *Thatha* didn't question tradition but accepted it just the way he accepted waking up every morning at six to perform the *Gayatri mantram*.

He would never come around, I realized sadly. I would have to sacrifice the granddaughter to keep the lover.

✳   ✳   ✳

Needless to say, Vinay was shocked when I called him. It was just not done, but to his credit he stammered only a few times before saying, yes, he would be at Minerva at 11 A.M. sharp.

"He said okay? Really?" Sowmya asked, her fingers trembling on the piece of ginger she was holding.

"Yes, he did," I said, and stripped some curry leaves from their stem. "What will you say to him?"

Sowmya resumed grating the ginger. "I don't know, but I am sure I will be inspired once I sit in front of him. You will be there, won't you? All the time?"

"Yes," I said, and popped a peanut into my mouth.

"I can't believe it is going to happen. Marriage!" Sowmya sounded excited. "But I want to talk to him before I say anything to *Nanna*. Otherwise . . . life will be a waste, you know."

"You'll leave this house, your parents. Do you think you'll miss it?"

"I think so," Sowmya said, looking around the kitchen. "I like this house. It is nice and cozy. The tenants upstairs don't make too much noise; Parvati comes regularly, more or less, and yes, I am very comfortable here.

"But I am ready for the change," she said, and paused. She looked around to make sure no one was listening and then whispered, "You have had sex, right?" just as I put another peanut into my mouth. I all but choked on the nut.

"What?"

Sowmya gave me a look laden with curiosity. "You have, right? You live with this American and . . . you have, right?"

"I . . ." This was an intensely personal question, but she seemed so eager to know that I nodded.

"How was it the first time?" she asked.

I shrugged. I was mortified.

"Tell me," she demanded.

I watched her put a wok on the gas stove and fire it up. She poured oil into the wok and looked at me expectantly.

"I don't remember," was the best I could do on short notice. Sowmya gave me a "sell me another bridge" look and I grinned, embarrassed. "I . . . it was fine."

"Was it with this American?" she asked.

"Yes." Good Lord, this was not a conversation I was prepared to have.

Sowmya threw some mustard seeds in the wok, and they sputtered in the oil. Some sprang out and landed on the stove and counter. She stirred the mustard seeds for a few moments and then dropped some curry leaves with black and yellow *gram dal* into the wok and let them sizzle for a while. Then she broke two dry red peppers and plopped them into the oil with crackling fanfare.

"Oh, give me those *pachi marapakayalu*." She pointed to the green chilies by the sink, which I was leaning against.

She put green chilies inside the wok as well and sighed, spatula in hand. "I always wondered about it. And now it will actually happen. I am scared and excited."

I had never seen this side of Sowmya before. This was a dreamy Sowmya, not the practical mouse I had grown up with.

She piled a deep-bowled steel ladle with yogurt and thumped the handle of the ladle on the side of the wok to drop a dollop of yogurt in it. She dropped another dollop of yogurt alongside the first and stirred hard, forcing the thick yogurt to liquefy and mix with the spices already sizzling in the oil.

"I always liked curd rice," I said, as the familiar smell of burning yogurt filled the kitchen.

"This is the best thing to cook for breakfast," Sowmya responded. "Fast and easy and I can use all leftovers. Pass me that rice, will you?" She added the rice left over from dinner the previous night to the wok and started to stir hard again, mixing everything into a Telugu breakfast staple.

"Do you think he will say no because I am being so bold?" Sowmya asked, almost as if she were wondering aloud.

"If he does, to hell with him," I said.

She nodded, smiled, and turned the gas off.

Breakfast was ready.

Everyone in Ma's family drank filter coffee in the morning. Instant coffee was okay for any other time of day but for mornings it had to be filter coffee. The coffee was made in a steel filter where hot water was poured onto rich ground coffee and filtered to make a thick decoction. The decoction was then mixed with frothy, bubbling hot milk and sugar. I remembered waking up every morning to the smell of decoction. I never got hooked on coffee but I always drank it when I was at *Thatha's* house. No matter what Ma said about all filter coffee being the same—"You mix coffee decoction with milk, what skill do you need for that?"—Sowmya's coffee was way better and she didn't complain when I added five spoons of sugar to my coffee tumbler either.

Sowmya poured coffee in steel tumblers and put the tumblers in small steel bowls.

"Priya, I have a personal question," Sowmya asked. She topped the glasses off with the coffee left in the steel utensil after she had filled up all the glasses.

Asking me if I'd had sex was not personal enough anymore? "Sure," I said.

"Does it hurt a lot the first time?"

I shrugged. "Depends upon the . . . Sowmya, I can't talk to you about this."

"Then who should I talk to about all this?" she demanded. "Maybe your *Ammamma* would like to fill me in regarding the ins and outs of marital life. What do you think?"

I sighed. "It hurts, but it gets better."

"Really?" she brightened. "How much better?"

"A lot better," I said unable to keep a straight face any longer.

"But it depends upon the husband, right?"

"Yes."

Sowmya nodded. "But I can't test that."

"Not in India, you can't."

Sowmya sipped some coffee from a glass and nodded again. "That is okay. It is going to be okay. Right, Priya?"

"Right," I said, though I wasn't sure what she was talking about being okay.

✳   ✳   ✳

Minerva hadn't changed, even a bit. It even smelled the same way it had seven years ago. My mouth watered at the sight of long crisp *dosas* and sizzling *vadas*. It was hard to get good south Indian food in America. The chicken curries and *tandoori* places were in abundance but the all-out vegetarian, south Indian food was almost impossible to find.

"I'm going to get a *masala dosa*," I told the terribly nervous Sowmya.

"I am going to throw up," she said, as soon as her eyes fell on her husband-maybe-to-be. "I have never been this scared before, Priya. This is a really bad idea," she clutched my wrist. "Let us go back and we will pretend you never called him."

I unclasped the death grip she had on me and patted the offending hand. "You don't have to do this. But I think you need to, to be sure. It's okay. I'll be there."

"You are more interested in that *masala dosa*," she quipped nervously.

"Well . . . it is hard to get good *dosa* back home," I said with a smile. "Come on. You know you won't rest until you do this. And we have to get back by noon. *Thatha* wants me to let him know what my decision is."

"And what is your decision?" Sowmya asked, still rooted at a safe distance from Vinay.

"We're not here to discuss that," I reminded her. I raised my hand and waved to Vinay. "Hi," I cried out, and Sowmya closed her eyes.

She looked strange without her glasses. Vanity had taken over and she had abandoned the thick glasses for her seldom-used contact lenses.

"*Namaskaram.*" Vinay folded his hands and then gestured for us to sit down.

"*Namaskaram,*" Sowmya said. "Ah . . . *chala,* thanks, for coming here."

"No problem," Vinay said, and then smiled uneasily at me. "Would you like to eat something?"

"No," Sowmya said, but I nodded and said, "*Masala dosa.*"

Sowmya pinched my thigh and I stifled a yelp. "No, nothing, thanks."

"Coffee?" Vinay asked, sounding as nervous as Sowmya.

"No," Sowmya said, her head still bent. "I . . . wanted to talk to you," she raised her head and he nodded. Speaking of uncomfortable places to be, this one took the cake and the baker.

"So . . . is there a problem?" Vinay asked. "You don't approve of the match?"

"I . . . I want to marry you," Sowmya reassured him a little too curtly. "But I wanted to clarify a few things."

"Sure, sure. I am very happy that you want to marry me," Vinay said with a small smile.

Sowmya held my hand and almost broke my pinkie finger. "I want to work," she revealed sincerely. "My father didn't let me and they said that your family doesn't approve. But I want to work."

Vinay nodded. "No problem. I can handle my parents. I will explain to them. If you want to work, I fully support that and they will, too."

Sowmya smiled and I felt and heard her sigh of relief. "And . . . I want to have my own house. I know you care for your parents, but . . ."

Vinay smiled then. "The house is big. There are two kitchens and two everything. Old house, though. My grandfather, he built it. We will live separate, but they are still my parents."

Sowmya smiled back and nodded.

"Anything else?" Vinay asked.

"And that is all," she said.

"Now will you have coffee?" Vinay looked at me. "*Masala dosa*?" he asked.

Sowmya nodded shyly and Vinay signaled for a waiter to come to our table.

During the auto rickshaw ride back home, Sowmya was flushed with happiness. "He is nice, isn't he?" she said.

"Very nice," I agreed with her.

"I can work," Sowmya said almost giddily. "A job, Priya. A place I can go to every day, out of the house. I am so glad I did this. I feel so relieved. And"—she laughed softly—"I am getting married!"

"Congratulations," I said, and kissed her on her cheek.

"What will you tell them?" she asked me when we got off the auto rickshaw.

"The truth," I said easily. If Sowmya could take such a big chance to make a better life, I should be able to do the same. "I love Nick. I'm going to marry him."

Sowmya laced her fingers with mine after she paid off the auto rickshaw driver and squeezed gently. "I will be with you all the time. All right?"

"All right," I said. "I . . . am going to go and make a phone call."

"Isn't it late there?"

"Yeah," I said. "Around midnight, but he's usually awake late."

"Okay, I will make an excuse for you," Sowmya said and winked at me.

❋ ❋ ❋

I couldn't get ahold of Nick. His cell phone said he was out of range. I got our answering machine the five times I tried our home number and his work number said he was either out of his cubicle or on another line.

Panic set in! Had he received the email about my meeting Adarsh despite the server error and had just gone postal? Or maybe he had moved out of our home, changed his cell phone number and . . . didn't pick up his work phone either? All sorts of unhealthy scenarios emerged in my head. To quell the feeling of misery that was welling inside me, I dialed Frances's phone number from memory. I knew it would be really late in Memphis but if Nick had dumped me his mother would definitely know.

She was sleeping, but the minute she heard my voice she sounded wide awake.

"They're forcing you to marry some Indian man and you want me to say good-bye to Nick for you," she said as soon as she heard my "Hello, Frances."

I laughed. "No."

"Thank god, because my policy is that everyone does their own dirty work," Frances said and I could hear her smile. "How's it going, Priya?"

"I can't find Nick," I said, now feeling foolish for having woken her up. "I . . . thought he might be angry with me."

"Angry? No, I don't think so. I just spoke with him yesterday and he was fine. Was waiting for you to come back and get married to him," Frances said. "And speaking of marriage, I found the perfect place for you both. It's in midtown and it's beautiful. The gardens are lovely. And I was thinking, if we did it in the fall, *this* fall, we could have great pictures of the foliage and—"

"Frances, I'm worried your son has dumped me. I don't think I can even think about marriage," I said, half hysterical.

"What's one thing got to do with the other?" Frances demanded. "Find the right place to get married and I'll make sure he shows up. He's silly in love with you. Don't you have faith?"

"Plenty," I said. "Plenty back home. Here everything is murky and they made me go through this bride-seeing ceremony."

"Like they do in the books? Was he a suitable boy?" Frances

asked sounding excited. "Are you sure they made you go through it? Or did you want to?"

"Of course I didn't want to and he isn't suitable," I said.

"Are you saying that a grown woman like you couldn't stop something as simple as a bride-seeing ceremony?"

"I didn't have the courage to tell them about Nick. Now I have and they all hate me," I confessed.

"If this is all it takes to get them to hate you, you're better off without them," Frances said. "But they don't hate you. They're just mad and once they're over their mad, they'll be fine."

"Really?"

"Well, I would be, if you were my daughter," Frances said. "So . . . do I book this place for this fall or what? I was thinking early October. Not too hot, not too cold."

"And then I can be knocked up by December?" I asked sardonically.

"Would you?" Frances said. "That would be excellent. You could have a baby in September and . . . oh, that would be excellent. A September baby would—"

"Frances!"

"I'll tell Nick that you wanted to get in touch with him," Frances said, sounding very satisfied. "But don't worry about him. He isn't going anywhere."

We chatted for a while; Frances wanted to know how everything in Hyderabad was, including the weather. She had this romantic idea about India, the way it was shown in books as an exotic land. When I told her about the slums and the dust that settled on your entire body, even your eyelids as soon as you got here, she thought it was quaint. India was not just a country you visited, it was a country that sank into your blood and stole a part of you.

As an insider all those years ago I couldn't see it, but now after several years of exile I could feel the texture of India. It was the people, the smell, the taste, the noise, the essence that dragged you in and kept you. I hated this country for a lot of reasons, the narrow-mindedness, the bigotry, the treatment of women, but that was all on a larger scale, on a day-to-day basis. India still was *my* country.

I felt light-hearted, confident, and on top of the world after speaking with Frances. That changed when I got to *Thatha's* house.

I stepped into the hall and the earth shifted. This was classic Ma, classic Indian mother.

Ma and *Thatha* were sitting across from Adarsh on the sofa *Ammamma* frequented most.

"Priya," Ma stood up nervously. "Adarsh is here to see you."

"I can see that," I said, my lips pursued. "Hi," I said to Adarsh, and he nodded with a confused look on his face.

"Can you come with me?" Ma insisted, and then just in case I would say something contrary she grabbed my wrist and took me inside.

"We thought it best," she said as soon as we were in the kitchen.

"Thought what best?" I was now very confused and very suspicious. It was always a bad thing when Ma started thinking about my best.

Ma took a deep breath, her potbelly jiggled and her hands landed on her waist in an offensive gesture. "We asked Adarsh to come here saying that you wanted to meet him one last time before you made a decision."

I wanted to say something, anything, but the words were not forming. Each time I thought they couldn't surpass their previous nonsense, they did.

"We think you should talk to him and see what a good boy he is before you decide anything," Ma advised.

I shook my head as if to clear the cobwebs that had settled in as soon as I saw Adarsh. "Ma, I've already decided. Actually, there is nothing to decide."

"Just talk to him," Ma cried out. "What do you lose?"

"Does *Nanna* know about this?" I asked.

"No. Your *Thatha* and I thought it was a good idea."

I sighed. "I'll talk to him, but not here," I said even before she could let the triumphant smile form on her face. "We'll go out and I'll talk to him. You handle *Thatha* about that."

"And you'll be good to him? Right? Speak properly? No nonsense?"

I grinned; she had to push for that extra mile. "Ma, don't you think I'm doing enough?"

Ma frowned and muttered something that I thankfully couldn't catch. *Thatha* was called into the kitchen by Ma while I asked Adarsh if he wouldn't mind going out.

"Sure," Adarsh nodded and then followed me onto the veranda. I slipped my feet into the Kohlapuri slippers that I had just taken off. I had bought them a few days ago when I got home and they were already showing serious signs of wear.

While Adarsh buckled his leather sandals, I asked him if he knew of a place where we could have a cup of coffee and talk.

"Sure, we can drive," Adarsh said, pointing to a black Tata Sierra parked outside the gate that I hadn't noticed when I'd come back.

We didn't speak as Adarsh drove to a *chaat* place.

"I love *chaat*," he told me. "As soon as I got here I ate *chaat*."

"I lived on *chaat* and *ganna* juice while I was in college," I said. "When I got to the U.S. I was skinny. I looked like I was a refugee from one of those sad African countries."

"Can't bulk up just on *chaat* and sugarcane juice," Adarsh concurred. "But if you add beer to the mix . . ." We laughed, almost companionably.

The *chaat* place was a small restaurant. Not your regular roadside *chaat*, this one was a step up. There were probably fifteen tables covered with red-and-white checkered vinyl tablecloths. Each table had a small plastic vase where a dusty plastic red rose stood upright proclaiming its artificiality.

Adarsh asked for two bottles of water as soon as we got in. The place was practically empty except for a man sitting at a table in a corner reading a newspaper. We found a table by a window looking out at the busy road where Adarsh had parked the black Tata Sierra. A young boy of maybe ten or eleven years old, wearing a pair of oversized khaki shorts and a dirty white T-shirt, put two bottles of water on our table. A small white-and-red checkered towel rested on his shoulders and he took our order on a small notepad with a ballpoint pen that had been resting against his ear.

"Just *chai*? No *chaat*?" Adarsh asked when he heard what I wanted.

"I just had a *masala dosa* at Minerva. Went there with my aunt," I said, but my mouth watered when Adarsh ordered *pau bhaji*.

"The best *pau bhaji* is still in Bombay," Adarsh said when the busboy was gone. He then took a swig from the bottled water. "So, why did you want to see me?"

I rested my chin on the palm of my left hand, moving my head slowly as my hand pivoted around my elbow and smiled at Adarsh.

"You didn't want to see me," he deduced, and sighed. "Your mother and your grandfather—"

"Plotted behind my back," I finished. "Yup. I'm horribly sorry and to make up for it, *chaat* is on me and we can stop by this place I went to the other day and even have *ganna* juice."

Adarsh's eyes glinted with good humor. "You don't want to marry me. Is that it?"

"Well . . . " I started and paused when a big smile broke on his face. "I don't."

"Okay," he said, and took another swig of water.

"You don't seem too broken up about it," I said, slightly miffed that he was taking my rejection so well.

"I've seen five girls and I liked you the best, but I'm not in love with you," Adarsh said.

That was the good thing, I thought, about men like Adarsh. They treated arranged marriage exactly the way it should be treated, without too many emotions messing with their decision-making process.

"Any of the other four girls to your liking?" I had to ask.

"Yes," Adarsh said with a smile. "Her name is Priya, too, but she's shorter than you are and definitely has less . . . of that spark."

"Is that a polite way of saying I have a short temper?"

"Well . . . I just saw a spark of it here and there," Adarsh said with a grin. "So, your family forced you into that *pelli-chupulu*?"

"Yes and no," I confessed. "I could've—no, should've—fought against it but I wanted some peace and I didn't have the courage to tell them about my boyfriend."

Adarsh put the bottle down and made an annoyed sound. "You have a boyfriend? And why the hell didn't you tell me when I told you about my ex-girlfriend?"

He had every right to be mad so I continued humbly. "I was scared," I admitted the truth. "I was scared of hurting my family and I ended up hurting you."

"Humiliating me," Adarsh amended. "Goddamn it, what's wrong with you women? I mean, I agree that arranged marriage is archaic but, Priya, you work in the United States. You are a grown woman. Why the hell are you playing these stupid games?"

"Not games, Adarsh," I said, keeping my voice calm even though I wanted to rage at him. How would he understand how much I was afraid of losing my family? How could he understand that?

"Then what?"

"He is American," I revealed. "And I told them yesterday but they don't want to come to terms with it. They dragged you here hoping I would give in. Be charmed by your ultra-good looks and the rest of the package."

We fell silent when the busboy brought Adarsh's *pau bhaji* and my *chai*. He ignored his food while I blew at the hot tea to cool it.

"I'm so sorry," I apologized.

"I'm so fucking tired of women like you," Adarsh muttered.

"Women like me? Excuse me, but you don't even know me," I said, putting my cup down with force that caused some of the tea spill on the saucer.

"Why are you so scared? My ex-girlfriend wouldn't tell her parents about me. She was scared because they expected her to marry a Chinese guy. . . . And that's why we broke up, because I got sick of her not accepting me," Adarsh said.

"And you told your parents about her?"

"Yes," Adarsh said. "I told them when things got serious and we moved in together, but Linda just wouldn't do it."

"I'm sorry," I repeated sincerely. "I told my family yesterday night. I'm going to tell them again today. . . . I don't know what else to do. I'm scared that I'll lose them if I tell them and I'm scared I'll lose Nick if I don't."

"Oh, you'll lose him if you don't," Adarsh assured me and dug into his *bhaji.* "Want a bite?"

I shook my head. "So am I forgiven?"

"Hey, who am I to judge. I'm the one finding a wife like I would a job," Adarsh said, and then chewed on his food with relish.

"You think the other Priya will work out for you?"

Adarsh nodded, his expression amused as well as confident. "She's twenty years old, lives with her parents. Just finished her degree, so yeah, I think she'll work out. She likes to run and hike, I kinda like the same things, so . . . we'll go camping a lot."

"I'm glad and again, I'm really sorry for having put you through this," I said.

Adarsh shrugged nonchalantly. "As long as you pay for the *chaat* and provide me with the promised *ganna* juice . . . I have no complaints."

*　*　*

I tried to call Nick once more and still got the answering machine and voice mail. It was hard not to panic. I checked my email in the hope that he had sent something but I couldn't access the account as the ISP of the Internet café I was going to was down.

Not wanting to go back to *Thatha's* where I would have to deal with some unsavory questions, I decided to go to my parents' house instead. Nate was there and if he wasn't, I knew the neighbor always had a key to the house. I could sneak in and get some quiet time. And I could check email from Nate's computer.

Talking to Adarsh had raised some difficult issues; mostly I was feeling the garden variety, old-fashioned guilt. I started to wonder how Nick had felt about me keeping him a secret for the past three years we had been dating. I knew he thought it was silly not to tell my family about him, but now I started to realize that maybe he saw it as an insult as well, just like Adarsh had with his Chinese girlfriend.

But it was still a man's world and we women had to balance the fine line between familial responsibilities and our own needs.

I waved for an auto rickshaw to take me to my parents' house from the Internet café. I didn't barter with the *rickshawwallah*, just agreed to the forty-five rupees he asked for.

Maybe Nick was busy. My mind made up excuses for his not being available on any data line. What if he had had an accident? No, no, I told myself firmly, Frances would know if that happened and Frances had said everything was fine, that she'd just talked to Nick the night before.

What if he was with another woman? As soon as I thought it, I knew it was preposterous. Nick could never be with another woman. Whenever I joked that he should leave me and go away he would say, "Where would I go? No one will have me but you."

We both really had nowhere to be but with each other. Relationships bound people together to the point that home was a feeling and not a brick structure. I knew where home was and it definitely was not here in Hyderabad. These people were not family. How easily they had decided to give me up. Anger ripped through me. I don't conform to their rules, I don't exist, not important to anyone anymore. My own father walks out and doesn't bother to tell me whether he is dead or alive as if my marrying Nick is the end of the world.

I paid the auto rickshaw driver and opened the rickety metal gate that led to the grilled veranda of my parents' house.

"Priya?" Mrs. Murthy who lived across the street called out from her veranda.

I nodded and then waved to her. She stood up from the cane chair she was sitting on, fanning herself rapidly with a coconut straw fan. "Is your mother back, too?"

"No," I said. "She's still at *Thatha* and *Ammamma's* house."

"They took the light off again," she complained, vigorously fanning herself. "Why don't you come here and sit with me for a while until the light comes back, *hanh*? It is cooler here than your place. . . . I always told Radha, west-facing house, big mistake."

It would be rude to say no. On the other hand I could have a nervous breakdown in front of good old Mallika Murthy, mother of a brilliant son who had gone to the best engineering and business school in India and now worked for a big multinational consultancy. She also had a gorgeous daughter who was married to a handsome doctor in Dubai and made an insane amount of money.

Ma hated Murthy Auntie even as she spent all her afternoons gossiping with her. They both talked about their children and tried to one up each other. Nate was in an IIT and he had gotten a better rank than Ravi Murthy in the IIT entrance exam so Ma showed off about that every time Murthy Auntie brought up the topic of her daughter, Sanjana, and her amazing husband. They were expecting a child in six months and Ma was burning with jealousy. Maybe that was why she had tried to hook me up with Adarsh who had gone the BITS Pilani-Stanford-big-company-manager job route, which made him just as desirable as the doctor in Dubai.

"Come, come, Priya," Murthy Auntie insisted. "I have some *thanda-thanda nimboo pani*."

Well, cold lemon juice did sound good and there was probably just Nate in the house sweating like a pig. So I made the big mistake of going onto Murthy Auntie's veranda instead of my parents'. I should've known that she'd grill me about my personal life as she gave me the *nimboo pani*. It had never bothered me when I lived in India how everyone nosed around everyone else's life; now it was inconceivable.

I remember Sowmya asking me, when I first got a job, how much I was getting paid. After two years of graduate school in the United States I flinched at the question and didn't give her a number. I couldn't be coy with Ma who would beat the number out of me, but if I had been working in India, I would've probably not even thought twice about telling anyone who asked.

The *nimboo pani* was a little too sweet, but it was cold enough that I didn't complain. The heat was getting to me in more than one way. My *salwar kameez* had wet patches at my armpits, my back, and my stomach, and my thighs felt like they were plastered to any chair I sat on. My hair was matted against my skull and my head was starting to slowly ache because it had forgotten the taste and smell of a Hyderabad summer.

"Radha tells me that she has *the* perfect boy for you." Murthy Auntie didn't even bother to mask her curiosity. "So," she demanded, her eyes wide, "how was this Sarma boy? Did you see him? What did he say?"

I licked my lips and stifled a scream that was lodged in my throat, waiting to get out. "He was okay," I said, digging my nose into the lemon juice, trying not to look at her when I spoke.

"Really . . . just okay?" Murthy Auntie persisted. "Radha said that he was . . . as good-looking as Venkatesh. Personally, I don't even think Venkatesh is that good-looking. Aamir Khan any day for me. What do you think, *hanh*?"

"About Aamir Khan?" I looked up at her with innocent, wide-eyed confusion.

Murthy Auntie sighed. "So, he wasn't good-looking, *hanh*?"

"He was fine looking," I told her casually.

"So"—she cocked an eyebrow—"did they refuse the match? You can tell me, really. There is no shame. It happens all the time. Of course, with Sanjana, as soon as Mahesh saw her . . . clean bowled, he was. Married her within two weeks, would not let us delay an extra day."

"I heard Sanjana is pregnant. Congratulations," I said politely, hoping that this would veer her off my marriage path.

Murthy Auntie glowed. "It is a boy, they found out just two days ago. Mahesh is the only son so his parents are very happy that he is also having a son. Very rich family . . . The boy will be born with a silver spoon in his mouth."

"That's nice," I said, now uncomfortable. Added to the heat was the fact I had nothing in common with this woman and I had, really, nothing to say to her.

"So they refused, *hanh*? Did they?" she asked, her eyes jumping out of her skull, wanting to peep inside my head to find out the truth.

"No," I said in irritation.

"They said yes?"

"Yes."

"And *you* said no?" Murthy Auntie asked in disbelief. "You can tell me the truth, Priya. If they said no, that is fine, it is okay to tell me. I am not a gossip like all the—"

"I can't marry him, Auntie," I interrupted her and gulped down the whole glass of lemon juice. I put the glass on the cool marble floor and stood up.

"Why not? Sit, Priya, what's the hurry?" she said, tugging at my hand.

Just seven years and all this seemed alien. This browbeating and digging into personal lives seemed alien. But inside me I knew that this was the Indian way. I could turn my nose up at it and think it was uncouth but this was how I was raised, this was how things were. It was bloody high time I accepted it and did what needed to be done.

"No," I said and smiled at her. I was just about to make her day. "I'm already engaged. My fiancé is an American. We're getting married this fall, hopefully in October. I will definitely send you an invitation but the wedding will probably be in the U.S."

Her mouth stayed wide open for almost fifteen seconds. But for the fact that I had just ruined my mother's reputation and my apparent good name, I would've found it comical. It felt good, though, to have told her. I had stepped into the light, the light of truth, and it was a nice place to be.

I knew that even before I got inside my parents' house, Mallika Murthy would be dialing the phone number of ten of her and Ma's closest friends to inform them about my fall from grace.

I was smiling when I knocked on my parents' front door. The power was still off and the doorbell was useless. I was fully expecting Nate to open the door and was surprised to see my father, red-eyed, looking slightly sloshed at his doorstep.

"*Nanna*?" I asked, and he sighed deeply.

"I was hiding, but everyone seems to find me," he said, and stepped away from the door.

"Hiding in your own house, *Nanna*?"

Nanna shrugged. "Best place I could think of."

"Have you been drinking?" I asked, as I smelled whiskey in the air.

"Not really," he said, and pointed to Nate who was lying on a sofa sleeping, despite the heat. "We just drank a few pegs of whiskey last night."

"A few pegs?" I picked up an empty bottle of Johnny Walker

lying on the coffee table, surrounded with a few empty soda bottles.

"Well, after the first three pegs we lost count," *Nanna* said and sat down by Nate's feet on the sofa.

Nanna usually didn't drink like this, maybe a peg socially and never with his own son. Looked like they were connecting on the alcohol level—a whole new kind of closeness?

"How're you feeling?" I asked lamely.

"Hung over," *Nanna* said, leaning against the backrest and closing his eyes.

Father of the Bride

When Nate was little he had lots of ear infections. They plagued him until he was almost four years old and caused him such pain that to this day he remembers the earaches with fear.

I used to sit with him when he was a baby and sometimes even cry with him. Once, when I was nine years old, I couldn't watch Nate suffer and wished I could take some of his pain on me. I asked *Nanna* why we couldn't share pain. He told me, "If we could share other people's pain, mummies and daddies all over the world would die of pain because they would take all their children's pain."

Nanna always wanted to be a good father. I think it was one of the goals of his life. He probably had it written down somewhere:

1. Save enough for retirement at sixty years of age (two more years to go; clock is ticking, tick-tock, tick-tock).

2. Be a good father.
3. Avoid fighting with Radha.
4. Get Priya married before she becomes an old maid.
5. Die in a painless way.

Nanna was a meticulous man. When he packed something, it was done neatly and tightly. If he planned a vacation, he would plan everything, leave nothing to chance. He made notes constantly, and when I gifted him a PalmPilot for his fiftieth birthday, he had been deliriously happy. He never left home without the Palm and he always told anyone who'd listen that his daughter who was in America had given the wonderful electronic gadget to him.

He was very proud of me. Even when I was in high school and I would win silly awards for elocution or debate, he'd be on cloud nine, calling his parents in whichever country they were to tell them what a wonderful daughter he had. He would even call *Thatha*, who he rarely phoned, to gloat.

If I asked him for anything, his answer would always be "yes," regardless of whether he could comply with my wishes or not. "If your *Nanna* doesn't say yes, who'll say yes?" he would say. A father's job according to my father was to keep his children happy.

"When you were a baby," *Nanna* once told me, "all I wanted to do was make you laugh. You liked pulling my moustache a lot and whenever you did I would yelp and that would make you laugh out loud." Apparently, I pulled out several of *Nanna*'s moustache hairs when he and I were young.

✳ ✳ ✳

Nanna ran a finger over his moustache, smoothing it, and looked at Nate's lifeless body. He picked up Nate's left hand and let it drop. It fell limply on the side of the sofa.

"The boy can't handle his liquor," he announced, and stumbled as he tried to stand up.

"So you both got nice and drunk. . . . Do you do this often?" I asked, and picked up the day's newspaper to fan myself. "How can he sleep in this heat?"

"Your Ma keeps asking me to get a generator and an AC. I think it's too decadent for us simple folk," *Nanna* said with a lazy smile, as he leaned back into the sofa, giving up his feeble attempts to stand.

"If it wasn't this hot, I'd suggest coffee," I said, furiously fanning around my neck. I sat down on the rocking chair by the telephone and rocked gently as I fanned.

"Your Ma is looking for you," *Nanna* said after a little while. "She called. Very angry, she is. Mahadevan Uncle just called. Adarsh is very impressed with your honesty."

"*Nanna*—" I began.

"No, no, Priya Ma, you did what your generation always does, stab us in our hearts," *Nanna* said, clapping the left side of his chest with his right hand before letting it drop. "Adarsh said he holds no hard feelings, but you have left me with no leg to stand on with Mahadevan Uncle or Mr. Sarma."

"I was trying not to hurt Adarsh's feelings," I said. "And he was quite forthcoming about his ex-relationship with a Chinese woman."

Nanna shook his head. "Kids these days. I never thought I would say it, but I am: kids these days have no idea what is good for them. It will not work out, Priya." He used the exact same words as *Thatha* had. "Marrying someone who does not understand your culture, your roots, your traditions, it will not work out."

Before I could answer the ceiling fan began to whirr again and we both sighed in relief. "Someone needs to be shot for cutting power off like this," *Nanna* said, and got up to stand right under the fan.

As he pulled the cotton *kurta* that was plastered to his skin away from it, I contemplated how much I should tell him. Even as the thought came to me I decided that I had done enough filtering and that now was not the time to shield him or anyone else anymore.

"It has been working out for three years, *Nanna*," I said. "We've been living together for a while. . . . Two years, we're . . . together and we're happy."

Nanna stood still and then looked at me with his lips pursed. "You share a home with this man?" he asked.

"Yes," I said, and curbed the impulse to fall on my knees and apologize.

Nanna shook his head again. "And you've been living with him for two whole years?"

"Yes."

"And you didn't feel the need up until now to tell us about this important person in your life? Even when I asked you to your face you didn't tell me. Why? What's to hide?" *Nanna* asked angrily.

They were all valid questions and I realized then how much I had botched this entire announcement business. I should've told them before I came and I should've brought Nick along. I should've introduced him to the family instead of dropping a bomb on them.

"I was afraid," I told him frankly. "I'm still afraid that you all don't love me anymore, that you hate me. But there's nothing to hide. . . . I mean, he's a good man. He loves me, he takes very good care of me. And he wanted to be here, he didn't want to do it this way. I want you to know that this is on me. I made the mistake."

Nanna sighed, and sat down on an armchair on the other side of the telephone and turned to face me. "What's his name?"

"Nicholas, Nick. He's an accountant with Deloit & Touche. He . . . What else do you want to know?" I asked.

"His family? What's his family like?"

"They're good people. His father passed away five years ago. He used to coach football at a high school in Memphis, that's where Nick was born and raised. His mother, Frances, is a pediatric nurse; she works with children who have cancer at St. Jude's. It's a big children's hospital in Memphis. He has a brother, Douglas, Doug, who is a sous-chef at a very trendy restaurant in New Orleans." I gave him the list.

"How did you meet him . . . this Nicholas?" *Nanna* asked, his voice, cool, nonjudgmental, almost interrogatory.

"We met at a party," I told him. "A friend of mine knows a friend of his kind of thing. We met and we started seeing each other and . . . *Nanna*, I really didn't want to date or love or marry an American. I truly never believed I could have anything in common with someone like Nick."

Growing up, the West and Westerners were almost surreal beings. It was a given that "they" had different morals and values than "we" did and "we" were morally superior. Most first-generation Indians in the United States only had friends who were Indian. I had never thought I would be any different. I had started out with only Indian friends but my circle grew as I grew. Now I was in a place where I didn't think in terms of Indian friends and American friends, just friends. I had somewhere down the line stopped looking at skin color.

"He is a very, very nice person," I said. "He . . . makes me happy."

"I can't accept it, Priya," *Nanna* told me seriously. "Probably in a few years, maybe, but right now, I am very angry with you and I am very hurt, but I don't hate you. I am your father, I will always love you."

"And that's enough for now," I said. "I want more, but I understand, perfectly. In trying to protect you from Nick and Nick from you, I think I've ruined this big time."

We were quiet for a while and then *Nanna* shrugged. "I think you did what anyone in your place would do."

"It's hard," I said softly. "I wanted to be the perfect daughter, but I realized that in trying to be the perfect daughter, I wasn't trying to be happy."

"I never asked for perfection, Priya Ma," *Nanna* said.

I nodded. "Yes, you never did but I wanted to give it to you anyway. I wanted to have your love and have Nick's love and *Thatha's* love. I'm selfish, maybe a little greedy; I didn't want to lose anything or anybody. But I find that it's not as easy as I thought it would be and maybe not as difficult as I told Nick it would be either.

"You are my favorite man, *Nanna*. I just didn't want to lose you because I was in love with another man, the man with the wrong nationality and race. I know *Thatha* is going to disown me and—"

"He is?" *Nanna* interrupted me.

"It's a gut feeling, not anything he said, but I know him and I know that this is not what he wants for me. That's a battle I have lost. I'm worried that Ma will turn her back on me as well," I confessed. "And even though she and I have never been best of friends, I came here to tell you all. I wanted so much for you to accept Nick, to accept Nick and me as a couple."

"Don't worry about Ma. She's going to do what I'm going to do," *Nanna* said with a small smile. "She's your mother and she will always love you, no matter what you do. That's a mother's job."

We looked at each other for a while, accepting each other, flaws and all, yet again. Some relationships you can't sever.

"I am glad though that you didn't marry him in the dark, like Anand married Neelima," *Nanna* said quietly. "I am glad you had the courage to tell us. I would have preferred to hear about it earlier but at least you told us, so many others just wouldn't have. This colleague of mine, his son lives in Europe, married a British girl and called them after the wedding . . . broke his heart."

"I thought I broke yours."

Nanna laughed. "Cracked it a little, but it is not broken. I am proud that you are who you are. I am happy that I raised you . . . because I raised you well."

"I thought you were angry, felt that I stabbed you in the back, cheated you," I told him.

"Well, last night I felt that way," *Nanna* admitted. "But now . . . after drinking all night, I can see the light."

"The clarity of the drunk?" I joked, and he laughed again. Yesterday night I had thought that he would never laugh again, at least never with me.

"We're thinking of getting married this fall. Will you come?" I asked impulsively.

"Are *you* inviting me to your wedding?" *Nanna* asked, incredulous.

"Times have changed," I said, realizing how ridiculous the situation was. My father had forever planned to marry me off and now when the time was here I was marrying myself off, while he was being invited as a guest.

"We will see," he said, and I understood that he couldn't commit himself.

"I should go to *Thatha's* and tell them that I'm not going to be the next Mrs. Sarma," I said, standing up.

"I'll drive you," *Nanna* said. "The liquor has worn off. . . . Your daughter marrying a *firangi* is bad for the buzz."

"What about him?" I asked, pointing to the sleeping Nate whose mouth was just a little open and drool was pooling, slowly trickling down his chin.

"He'll be fine," *Nanna* said. "Probably not the first time he is drunk and hung over. Now, on our way to *Thatha's*, I want you to tell me all about Nate's girlfriend. Is she at least Telugu?"

I hugged *Nanna* tightly then, let the floodgates open and sobbed in relief. He rubbed his cheek against my hair and I wasn't sure if the wetness I felt was sweat or *Nanna's* tears.

✳ ✳ ✳

Sowmya was making buttermilk instead of coffee for the early-evening *tiffin* along with some almond biscuits. "Too hot for coffee," she told me, as she poured water into the earthen pot in which she made yogurt every day.

"Where did *Thatha* go?" I asked, annoyed that he wasn't there when I was ready to explain to him why I couldn't marry Adarsh and why I had to tell him the truth.

"Something happened at the house construction. . . . Some wall was put up that shouldn't have been put up or something like that," Sowmya said as she added powdered cumin and coriander along with a teaspoon of chili powder and salt to the earthen pot.

She churned the yogurt with a wooden mixer, tasting as she churned. "Will you drink this," she asked, "or should I make some separate with sugar?"

"This is fine," I said, smiling at the fact that she remembered I always drank buttermilk with sugar in it.

Lata strolled into the kitchen then, a slight waddle creeping into her walk as she massaged her back. "None of my previous pregnancies gave me this much trouble," she muttered and then sighed when she saw me. "Why did you have to tell Adarsh everything? Your mother is waiting to kill you."

It annoyed me that Adarsh had gone home and been a good boy, telling his parents the truth about my personal life, something I thought I had revealed to him to ease his hurt. I had believed there was a tacit understanding between us not to reveal our conversation to any of the elders. I felt cheated out of the money I paid for his *chaat* and *ganna* juice.

"Well, he told me that he had a Chinese girlfriend," I countered, deliberately keeping the ex-girlfriend part out.

"Chinese?" Lata's eyes widened, and she came and leaned against the wall beside me. "What, are there no Indians in the States for you all to meet?"

Neelima came into the kitchen right then, her eyes slightly puffed up and lethargy swirling around her like an irritating mosquito. "Can you make me some coffee, Sowmya?" she asked as soon as she was in. She sat down on the floor next to the large stone grinder. "I am so sleepy," she complained.

"Happens in the first trimester," Lata told her caustically. "And why are you and Anand so late? I thought you would be here in the morning. Sowmya and I had to mix the dried mango for the *maggai* all by ourselves."

The scolding didn't faze Neelima who wanted nothing more out of life at that instant than coffee. "My parents wanted us to have lunch with them," she said.

"Here no one has eaten lunch," Sowmya muttered. "*Nanna* came and just took some of the morning's curd rice and *Amma* is still having a headache. Radha *Akka* and I unnecessarily cooked so much rice and *pappu*."

"We'll have it tonight," Lata said, and then focused on me. "How is your father doing?"

I smiled. "He's going to be just fine."

Lata put her hand on my shoulder and squeezed. "I think you are very brave," she said. "It would have been easy for you to not have said anything . . . like Anand. But you did and that was very brave."

I was surprised by her assessment. I didn't feel very brave, just helpless in a situation that I couldn't alter.

"I wish more women would stand up for what they want," Lata finished with a smile.

"Maybe it's time you did," I suggested to her.

Sowmya finished churning the buttermilk and started pouring it in tall steel glasses that stood shakily on the not-so-smooth stone kitchen counter.

"Can you take this to your father and mother?" Sowmya pointed to two glasses.

"They are in the veranda-bedroom," Lata told me. "Your mother is very angry. Good luck."

I took the two glasses and went to find my parents. I knew my father was probably telling Ma that he was not going to raise any objections to who I wanted to marry. That was not going to be a pretty sight but I wasn't going to back out after I had come this far. Even though Adarsh had annoyed the hell out of me he had shown me that hiding Nick from my family was detrimental to my relationship with Nick.

"Nothing doing," Ma was yelling at *Nanna*. "She told Mallika . . . she told Mallika about this Nicku person. Mallika phoned everyone and told them. Sarita just called me here to tell me. What is she doing to us? Dragging our name in the dirt?"

I almost didn't enter the bedroom, but took that heavy step across the threshold, pushing the slightly closed door. "*Lassi*," I said, holding the glasses high.

Ma glared at me. "What, Priya, what are you doing to us?"

There were tears in her eyes and I wondered if they were there because she was sad or because she was angry. I never really got close to Ma the way daughters were supposed to get close to their mothers. I had managed to develop a very close relationship with my father but with Ma, things were better left unsaid. I think I never respected her or credited her with too much intelligence— that was for *Nanna*. Ma was the nuisance parent in my life, and even though Nate bitched about Ma, I knew that he always bought her a gift for her birthday, remembered my parents' wedding anniversary, and sometimes just for the hell of it would bring home *jalebis*, Ma's favorite sweet.

Why was it that we had divided our affections like this? It was a subconscious thing because when I looked inside myself I could feel that *Nanna* loved me more than Ma did. Sometimes I actually felt that Ma disliked me because I was so different from her and because I was so close to *Nanna*.

When I was a little girl, and Nate had yet to be born, I used to imagine that Ma was actually my stepmother. *Nanna* was my real father but my real mother had died and no one was telling me the truth. Ma's curtness and her lack of overt affection or physical affection of any sort always bothered me, left me empty. Whenever I told her that I loved her she would shoo it away, saying that love had to be shown in actions and not in words. Maybe she was right. I couldn't show what I didn't truly feel. I was ambivalent about my feelings for my mother; there was love, I was sure, it was just sometimes submerged under dislike.

"I'm really sorry," I said sincerely. "I thought Adarsh would be discreet since he told me about his Chinese girlfriend. I really didn't think he'd put out an ad in the newspaper."

Ma seemed to be surprised by my apology but she recovered from that fast. "So if he tells something you have to counter it? Don't you have any shame?"

"What has shame got to do with this?" Politeness be damned. The woman was as usual getting on my nerves.

"And why would you tell Murthy Auntie about this? Don't you have anything better to do?"

"She asked about Adarsh and I told her the truth," I said, now regretting my rash decision of telling Murthy Auntie about Nick. I had done it because I was angry with the family, irritated with Murthy Auntie's interrogation. It was juvenile and I was now embarrassed.

"But I'm sorry I told her," I said, my eyes downcast. "It was a stupid thing to do."

"She told everyone," Ma said, and then added sarcastically, "No need for Adarsh to put it in the papers, you did a fine job yourself. Why don't you yell it off the rooftops?"

"Radha," *Nanna* intervened. "She made a mistake and she is sorry."

"Sorry?" Ma looked at my father in bewilderment. "Sorry does not make this right, Ashwin. She is insulting us and"—she turned to look at me—"get out of here and I don't ever want to see your face again. If you marry this American, that is it, you are never welcome in my house anymore."

My mouth dried up because she was imparting the small

knives with great precision and they were striking me the way she wanted them to. I may not love her as much as I loved my father but she was my mother. How can a mother turn away from her daughter?

"Radha." *Nanna* put his hand on Ma's shoulder just as her chest heaved. She jerked the *pallu* of her sari that was falling off of her shoulder and tucked the edge at her waist.

"What, Ashwin, I had such great dreams . . . such hopes, all shattered." Ma started to weep, the words pouring out of her through hiccups and tears. *Nanna* put his arms around her and rocked her gently.

"Everything will be okay," he murmured into her hair, and smiled sadly at me.

The lump in my throat burst and I set the glasses of *lassi* down on the bedside table. *Nanna* held out an arm for me and I ran into it. We all held each other through the torment of acceptance.

Ma was the first to push us both away. She wiped her face with her *pallu* and looked at me with eyes that glistened with the aftermath of tears and rage. "Are you really marrying this American boy?"

I held on to my father as I turned to face her. "Yes."

Ma nodded. "When?"

"This fall. Maybe October."

Ma nodded again and walked out of the bedroom.

I leaned into *Nanna* some more and whispered an apology. I didn't know what I was sorry about anymore, just that I wanted it to end, I wanted things to go back to normal.

* * *

By the time a tired *Thatha* came home, dinner was ready. We all sat down quietly to eat. Anand and Jayant, who were in a heated discussion about the riots that were raging in Gujarat, also fell silent when they reached the dinner table. There was an ominous flavor to the air around us.

Everyone was waiting for me to reveal my defection yet again and to tell *Thatha* about my meeting with Adarsh, my improper conversation, and my impending marriage to a man they would all refer to as the *firangi*.

Sowmya was serving leftovers from lunch but no one, not even Anand who always had a problem with leftover food, complained.

"Lata's ultrasound and amnio test is tomorrow," Jayant said, I think to stop everyone from thinking about my American fiancé.

Thatha looked up at Lata and smiled. "It will be a boy," he said confidently.

Lata, the first to finish dinner, washed her hand in the plate with the remaining water in her glass and rose, plate in hand. "No," she said looking at me, her eyes triumphant. "There will be no ultrasound and no amnio test."

Jayant stood up, pushing his chair away sharply, its four legs squeaking against the floor's polished stone, a look of total panic on his face. "What do you mean you won't do it? Sixteen weeks, they can tell the sex in sixteen weeks these days."

Lata moved and the curd rice mixed with water sloshed on her plate. "I don't want to know the sex of this baby."

"But you said that if it is a girl you would . . ." Jayant stopped himself from revealing too much but it was already too late, everyone was privy to what they had decided would be the fate of a baby girl.

"I want to have this child and I want it to be a surprise like it was when Shalini and Apoorva were born," Lata said and left for the back yard to put the plate in the tub for the maid to clean the next day.

While she was gone, *Thatha* demanded an explanation from Jayant. "What is going on, Jayant? If it is a girl . . . You know we want a boy."

Jayant threw his hands up in exasperation. "I don't know what to do. I . . . will try and talk to her."

"Why?" Sowmya asked and surprised everyone with her voice. "If she doesn't want to know, we should not force her. We are not that kind of a family."

Everyone in the room became very still. *Ammamma*, who had been fanning herself with the day's *Deccan Chronicle* with one hand while eating with the other, stopped in midair and looked at her husband, seeking out a reaction.

Sowmya had put it out there, told everyone, especially *Thatha*, that if he complained or insisted too much about knowing the gender of the baby he would be slotted away with all those other despicable middle-class men who participated in female infanticide. She had managed to corner the great old man himself with a few words.

"Okay," *Thatha* said, looking at Sowmya as if he had never seen her before. "Whatever Lata wants."

Lata, who was waiting by the back yard to hear the outcome of her announcement, smiled. "We will leave for the night," she said, coming into the kitchen. "We want to go to my parents' house so that we can drop Apoorva and Shalini off at school tomorrow morning."

Jayant washed his hands in the plate but unlike his wife did not bother to put his plate away.

"*Thatha*," I started, and fell silent when he raised his hand.

"I will not accept it, Priya. If you marry this man, then you are not my family," *Thatha* said.

I had expected it all along but I had not been prepared for the pain that followed his announcement. My heart felt heavy and I clenched my teeth in an effort not to cry. I didn't want to give the old man the satisfaction. He had hurt me just as deeply as I imagine I had hurt him. Were we even now?

"Then that is your choice, I have no problems with who Priya marries," *Nanna* said clearly and rose from the table with his plate. Jayant and Lata who were about to leave stood still by the doorway between the dining area and the hall to see the drama through to its end.

Sowmya took *Nanna's* plate and he walked up to the sink by the doorway to the back yard. No one said anything while the water from the tap splashed on his hand and cleaned it.

"And you think that marrying this American is going to make her happy?" *Thatha* demanded while *Nanna* dried his hands on the towel hanging on a rusty nail over the sink. In all the years we had all been together, I had never seen or even heard of *Thatha* and *Nanna* having a confrontation.

"I think that how she lives her life is her choice and yes, I believe that she will be and actually she is happy with Nicholas," *Nanna* said, still standing, keeping his advantage by looking down at *Thatha*.

Thatha washed his hands in his plate and looked at Ma. "Radha? Is this okay with you?"

Ma sat still for a very long moment and then nodded.

"It is going to only end badly," *Thatha* told *Nanna*. "And when it does," he pointed a finger at him, "I want you to know that *you* will be the person with the most blame. You can stop her. Do it now."

Nanna shook his head. "She is my daughter and this is my choice to make, just like you are making yours. I trust her. I believe her to be a smart and intelligent woman. I think that if she says she is happy with Nicholas, she is telling the truth. Priya is no fool."

"But you are for letting her do this," *Thatha* said agitated, his chest heaving with the rage he was trying to control. This was his family, he was supreme here. How dare anyone go against him.

"In that case, my family and I will take leave of you," *Nanna* said politely, so politely that it was insulting in its weight.

Ammamma cried out then. "No, no. Why do you talk like

this?" She looked at her husband of fifty-one years with admonishment. "He didn't mean it, Ashwin." She tried to assuage my father.

"Then he shouldn't have said it," Ma said angrily. In all the years that we had all been together, *Thatha* had never called *Nanna* names. This was quite an event and I was solely to blame, or so I felt. Guilt that I had banished just a little while ago came back in big waves rolling me into them and throwing me on the shore of repercussions.

"I shouldn't have said it," *Thatha* said slowly, realizing that he was breaking up his family.

"It is not right but ... she is a daughter's daughter," *Ammamma* said, patting *Thatha's* shoulder. "And if Radha and Ashwin feel it is okay, who are we to say anything?"

Thatha nodded grudgingly but didn't look at *Nanna* or Ma or me. This was the end, I realized. There would be no sneaking away to the pomegranate tree or taking walks with him. There wouldn't be phone calls on the weekend where he would complain about the Indian politicians and how the corporation he had leased the mango orchards to was treating him.

"I hope that you will one day feel better about this," I told *Thatha*. "I'm happy with this man. I thought that would be important to you."

Thatha shook his head, defeated. He didn't say anything. He was coming to terms with the fact that he was not master of my father's house, that when push came to shove, Ma would always stand by her husband and they both would stand by me, regardless of my decision and their consequences.

"And at least," *Ammamma* said with a broad shrug, "he is white, not some *kallu*."

I froze.

Damn it!

Had I forgotten to mention Nick was black?

❋ ❋ ❋

To: Priya Rao <Priya_Rao@yyyy.com>
From: Nicholas Collins <Nick_Collins@xxxx.com>
Subject: Sorry!

I am so sorry for being out of touch all day yesterday but things have been a total mess. I went to lunch with Steven and Susan to this pub in the city and someone got away with my leather bag and my leather jacket. My cell phone was in the jacket and my Palm along with my computer was in my bag . . . I am completely fucked!

I think I have some old stuff on your laptop so once you're back you can have a look and let me know. For now, I have lost all my contacts but at least I have some CDs that I used to backup my hard drive two months ago.

I spoke with Frances and she told me you were worried. I'm right here . . . a little light on hi-tech toys but right here.

How was everything? Are your grandfather and father feeling any better?

I can't wait for you to come back home. And Frances told me that you agreed to get married this fall in Memphis? Are you sure about that? I thought your heart was set on Monterey or Carmel, somewhere by the ocean. And she said that you want to get pregnant by the end of the year? I'm assuming that a lot of this is wishful thinking

ON HER PART, IN ANY CASE, WE'LL TALK ABOUT IT WHEN
YOU GET HOME.

OH AND I HOPE YOU HATED THAT GUY THEY TRIED TO
HOOK YOU UP WITH.

I LOVE YOU AND I MISS YOU, SO COME HOME SOON
NICK

✴ ✴ ✴

Epilogue
Ready to Eat

The *avakai* arrived with an Indian who was coming to the Bay Area and whose parents Ma and *Nanna* knew. Raghunath Reddy didn't seem to mind carrying the midsized glass jar. "One amongst the many," he told me when he dropped the mango pickle off at my office, which was right next to his. "I have two more jars and one sari to deliver," he added.

Nick thought the pickle was too spicy but continued to eat it without *ghee* or rice, which was as close to killing yourself as you could come with the hot-hot pickle.

My experience with India in the summer had left me with a better understanding of Nick and my relationship with him and my family. Nick was pleased that I didn't end up marrying a nice Indian boy and assured me that he had never thought about leaving me because I couldn't tell my family about him.

"We come from different cultures, I understand that," he said. "I was frustrated at times but never enough to not want to be with you. This is who you are; you'd not be you if you didn't care about your family."

It was a relief to be back in the U.S. This was familiar territory and I didn't feel like a cross between a delinquent teenager and a bad daughter anymore. That feeling had passed when Ma, at the Hyderabad International Airport, had waved good-bye with tears in her eyes.

I got an email from Nate with all the family gossip. *Thatha* was not speaking with *Nanna* anymore as the last time they talked, which was just a week ago, they ended up talking about me and almost came to blows. Ma was back to normal, bitching and moaning that I didn't call enough and when I did, she bitched and moaned that I talked too long with *Nanna* and wasted my money.

"Write long letters, tell everything there, don't waste money on phone calls," she said. "Send email, send us a picture of Nick. We still haven't seen him."

Lata had ballooned up with her advancing pregnancy and couldn't wait for the baby to get out. Despite Jayant's insistence she refused to have an ultrasound done. When I called her, she told me that she thought it was another girl and that she was just fine with that. She even had a name picked out, Nithila, which meant "pearl" in Telugu. If it was a boy, she said, she would go with Abhay, "the one without fear."

Sowmya was getting married on September 21 and was very sorry that Nick and I couldn't make it to the wedding. She understood our predicament as our wedding date was set for October 3.

Nanna and Ma were coming and even Nate had decided to make an appearance.

"Your wedding and I won't be there?" Nate had written in his email. "Are you trying to be funny or something? So, are you going to introduce me to some hot chicks?"

Apparently, Tara, the girl from Delhi Ma would have hated, proved to be unsuitable as she had kissed another boy at a cousin's wedding in Madras.

"It was *just* a kiss, she said," Nate wrote in yet another email where he told me the entire sob story and how much her betrayal had hurt him. "I go for lots of weddings, don't catch me kissing anyone, *just*." But at Nate's age, relationships come and go with little pain and Tara had already faded into a forgotten yesterday.

Frances was planning our wedding with great pleasure. Nick and I'd caved in and had agreed to a Memphis wedding (a Hindu ceremony followed by a Baptist one) and a San Francisco reception.

It was going to be a small wedding, Frances told me, just three hundred of her closest family and friends and *then* we could add to that with our close friends and my family.

The invitations were to go out in a few days and I wanted to make sure I sent my parents a personal letter along with the invitation.

The envelope with the wedding invitation, a note from me, and a picture of Nick had been ready for days but I kept forgetting about it. It wasn't deliberate. Finally, with just a month left to our wedding I dropped the letter off at my company mailroom. The mailroom guy assured me that the letter would reach its destination in five to seven days. . . .